GIRL
(in real life)

If I ever got abducted by aliens, my parents would make a YouTube video about it before they called the police. I know they love me. I mean, they tell practically the entire world on a twice-weekly basis. Along with sharing everything else about me too. It's not easy when the two people who love you the most are also the ones ruining your life...

For Felix

First published in the UK in 2021 by Usborne Publishing Ltd., Usborne House, 83-85 Saffron Hill, London EC1N 8RT, England. www.usborne.com

Usborne Verlag, Usborne Publishing Ltd., Prüfeninger Str. 20, 93049 Regensburg, Deutschland, VK Nr. 17560

Text copyright © Tamsin Winter, 2021

Author photo © Andrew Winter, 2017

Cover illustration by Charly Clements © Usborne Publishing, 2021

A CIP catalogue record for this book is available from the British Library.

J MAMJJASOND/22 ISBN 9781474978484 05787/3

Printed and bound in Great Britain by CPI Group (UK) Ltd, Croydon, CR0 4YY.

USBORNE

TAMSIN WINTER

GIRL
(in real life)

1

WELCOME TO OUR CHANNEL

The first thing you should know about me is that I'm not extraordinary. Not even in the slightest. When people find out I'm *that* Eva – Eva Andersen, the one with the YouTube channel – they expect someone special. Only, I'm not. Sorry if you find that disappointing. But I've got kind of used to disappointing people lately.

I know there are probably a lot of people out there who would like to swap places with me. My life looks pretty good – from the outside anyway. And I get a lot of free stuff. Like, way more than I can ever use. There are boxes of new products in the garage that we haven't even opened yet. Last November, we got free tickets to the Alton Towers Ultimate Fireworks display, and all the big rides were open. The vertical drop on Oblivion in the dark was pretty amazing, even if I did feel kind of sick afterwards. Last summer, we got to stay in this luxury treehouse in Portugal that had parts of the tree growing inside. I have my own iPhone, tablet, Xbox, laptop and even a custom-made charging station with my name on it. I have stacks of wellness journals, bullet journals and monogram journals (I don't even know what they are). And every kind of fairy light you can imagine, from panda bears to pineapples. Last week, I was sent lollipops with real edible gold inside them. Sometimes, all that stuff can be exciting.

But sometimes it can feel like it's crushing me. Maybe that sounds weird, and maybe if there wasn't a camera pointed at me the whole time it would feel more fun. But the camera is always there. Staring, like a giant eye that never blinks, recording everything that I do. And then there are all the other eyes – hundreds of thousands of them. Every single one of them watching me.

It would be so much easier if I was an outgoing person. That's what my friend Hallie says and she knows everything (apart from when she ties her braids in an extra-high bun and claims she's taller than me). But she's right about that – everything is easier if you're an outgoing person. When I was younger, I would sing and make up dumb dance routines and show off in front of the camera.

Being the star of a YouTube channel was a lot easier when I didn't care about what people thought. Or maybe before I *realized* what they thought. But now, I feel like a snail who wants to curl back inside its shell, only someone's smashed it off.

I should be used to it. My parents started posting stuff about my life before I even existed, on this blog called *Everything But the Baby*. They had ten thousand subscribers by the time I showed up. They'd shared everything they did in the five years it took to have me – even the gross stuff. That's longer than I waited for my hair to grow all the way down my back. Mum keeps the scan photo next to her bed in a picture frame that says *Our Miracle*. Only, to me, it looks more like a floating alien. Showing everyone that picture was their first ever YouTube video. Nine minutes of my parents crying and hugging each other, along with millions of love-heart-eyes emojis popping up. I can't watch it without cringing. I doubt anyone can. Dad always says, "Eva went viral before she even came out of the womb!" Like that's an accolade anyone would want.

Anyway, the video where I star as a floating alien was only the beginning. My parents called their new channel *All About Eva*, and I guess the name is pretty accurate. There's something from almost every day of my life. Only somehow, the Eva in their videos doesn't feel that much like me any more.

It's probably because recently, I've spent most of my time wishing it *wasn't* me. Like the first day back at school after the summer, when Alfie Stevens in my class found the clip of me going down the X-Treme Blaster slide at Tropical Islands Water Park. As I drop six metres into the plunge pool, my swimsuit wedgie is visible for exactly 1.8 seconds. My friend Spud told me not to worry about it. He said, *swimsuit + high velocity = wedgie*. Apparently it's simple physics. Although physics has never felt very simple to me. I'm still not sure which was harder to survive: the X-Treme Blaster or the first day of Year Eight.

When I got home that day, I begged Dad to edit my wedgie out of the water park video, but he said it was the only footage they had of me going down that famous slide. "And besides," he said, "no one in their right mind would even notice the wedgie with your gawky belly flop!" Which was not exactly reassuring. So, my swimsuit-wedgied belly flop is still on YouTube, along with ten thousand other embarrassing moments of my life. But all the stuff that *my parents* don't want anyone to see? That never goes on the channel. Like the flapping chicken-arms thing Mum does to get her deodorant to dry, or Dad using his electric nose-hair trimmer.

In case you've never watched an *All About Eva* video, let me give you the highlights reel:

Age 0 – *Introducing Eva.* 325k likes.

A stump of umbilical cord is still attached to my stomach. It's blackish-yellow, like a too-ripe banana, and that's not even the most disgusting thing. The video includes Mum doing my first nappy change.

Age 1 – *Eva's First Steps!* 293k likes.

This is supposed to be a secret, but these weren't even my first steps. Mum had been filming me non-stop for days because she was certain I was about to walk. Then the one time she put the camera down, I tottered across the living room. Accidentally doing important milestones off-camera really annoys my parents. My first steps happened twelve years ago and Mum still goes on about it.

Age 4 – *Eva's Cutest Tantrums!* 441k likes.

A compilation video of me crying that's over fifteen minutes long. The first comment says, *Spoiler Alert: she's spoiled.* In the last section, I'm at the dinner table pushing my plate away and shouting, *"I DON'T WANT A PEA!"* Alfie Stevens had that as his message tone for the whole of Year Seven.

Age 6 – *Christmas Day – Eva Complaining to Santa!*

2.8m likes.

No one ever hears my side of this story, so here goes. The Ultimate Hamster Grooming Salon was literally the only Christmas present I wanted. It was for grooming my hamster, Coco, after Mum had banned me from giving him baths in the sink. When I met Santa in his grotto, that was the only thing I asked for. Anyway, I got the entire collection of Rebel Dolls instead. The video of me shouting my complaint to Santa up the chimney has been shared over a million times. The camera's shaking because Dad was laughing so much. They call it *All About Eva*'s first big success. I mean, technically Dad refers to it as the moment "*Vi skød papegøjen!*" which means *We shot the parrot!* But like anyone can understand Danish sayings apart from him and my grandmother. It was the most views their channel ever had and they got thousands of new subscribers. It's kind of depressing when your likes peaked at six years old.

A few weeks after *Eva Complaining to Santa!* went viral, the company that made the Ultimate Hamster Grooming Salon sent me one for free. There were five different kinds of fur brushes and this special powder to sprinkle inside the cage that hamsters like to roll in. It was too late for Coco though. He died a few days after Christmas. Dad said he died of old age. I said he died from a lack of grooming. His funeral is probably still on YouTube.

Mum said Coco wasn't very popular anyway, so they got me a kitten instead. I was allowed to keep the grooming salon though. And Miss Fizzy got used to the hair combing eventually. I was six when I chose her name, by the way. Now it's kind of embarrassing. But still, her unboxing video is the only one I like watching. Mum tries to tie a pink bow around her neck and she hisses at her. Thinking about it, I guess me and Miss Fizzy were destined to get along.

Age 9 – *The Letter on Instagram*. 36k likes.

I guess this was what started to change everything. It was just this dumb letter I wrote one night before I went to bed. I'd been sent this stationery kit from some company my parents were promoting on Instagram, and I decided to write a letter to myself. I'd got this really low score in a spelling test and Mr Eliot had announced the results in front of the whole class. I wanted to make myself feel better. I used some of these motivational phrases I'd read in one of Mum's magazines. I didn't even understand what half of them meant: *Impossible is just an opinion. The journey is the destination. You are the CEO of your life!* I stupidly left the letter out on my desk. After school the next day Mum said it was the sweetest thing she'd ever seen. And told me it already had ten thousand likes on Instagram. It was like Mr Eliot reading out my test results all over again. Only in front of the whole world.

The entire thirteen-and-a-quarter years of my life is all there online if you want to take a look. Every moment preserved, like the jars of pickled red cabbage my Danish grandmother, Farmor, kept in her larder for years. Everything from my first breath to the patch of pimples that appeared on my chin yesterday. You can read comments from over a decade ago if you really want to. But I don't recommend doing that. Maybe there's something up with my brain, because it seems to delete all the nice comments I read and save all the bad ones. Farmor says *All About Eva* is "just one tiny stitch in the intricate tapestry" of who I am. And that I shouldn't take it too seriously. She also says it's a pineapple in its own juice. But I've never been able to figure out what that means.

Mum wouldn't delete the *You are the CEO of your life!* letter, no matter how upset I got. She said I was overreacting and that I'd get over it. It's what she says about everything. Even Dad agreed. He said #selfcare was trending and they were getting a spike in new followers. That's the kind of thing that's important in my family: Views and Shares and Likes and Dislikes and Subscriber Growth and Engagement Stats. Not feelings or visible swimsuit wedgies. That's why sometimes it feels like *that* Eva – the one on the channel – is more important than the real me. If I ever got abducted by aliens, my parents would make a YouTube video about it before they called the police.

I know my parents love me. I mean, they tell practically the entire world on a twice-weekly basis. Along with sharing everything else about me too. It's not easy when the two people who love you the most are also the ones ruining your life.

2

TAGGED

I'd been thinking about quitting the channel for a while. Probably because of all the filming I'd had to do over Christmas. Being told to "Give a bit more emotion, Eva!" kind of sucks the joy out of opening your presents. The matching "Let's take an elfie!" pyjamas didn't exactly help matters. And there are only so many times you can pretend to enjoy eating gluten-free roulade with "skinny" custard before you want to spew. Then there was the vlog they'd posted a few days before I had to go back to school: *Surviving Eva's Puberty! Do Not Mention Pubic Hair?!!!?* My life may as well have been over. By the next morning, Alfie Stevens and his friends had already reposted bits of it on TikTok.

People from school were still commenting on it the

next day. Dad was taking Farmor to the airport, but I wasn't allowed to go because I hadn't done my homework. So, I sat in the kitchen, scrolling through comments on Alfie's TikTok and sucked yogurt through a straw. It had pieces of coconut in it that kept getting stuck, so it wasn't exactly an easy way to eat it. I don't even like coconut that much. But the yogurt company were sponsoring us to post a photo and I didn't want to. I was still in a mood about the pubic hair post and I knew it would annoy Mum if I ate all the yogurt before the shoot. Hopefully I'd get out of doing it entirely. It was a bonus the slurping noises I made annoyed her too.

"EVA! Honey, can you *please* stop making that noise?" Mum called for the fourth time, in the voice she does when she's annoyed but she doesn't want to shout because she needs me to do a sponsored post later. I waited a few seconds then slurped again even louder. I don't know precisely when annoying my parents became a major part of my life. But, without wanting to sound too big-headed, over the last few weeks I'd got really good at it.

Mum eventually came out of her office and shouted, "EVA! That's enough!" Then she saw what I was eating and her jaw dropped. "THAT'S THE YOGURT FOR THE SHOOT!"

"Oh, is it? Sorry," I said innocently. "It is super

delicious though! So they're right about that." I scooped up the final blob on the end of my straw and held it up. "I still have this bit." But then it splatted on the kitchen table. "Whoops."

Mum smiled through gritted teeth. "I'm sure I told you we needed that, honey! I don't think you've been listening to a word I say recently!" It wasn't true. I had been listening. It's just that I'd done the exact opposite. "We'll have to fill it up with regular yogurt," Mum said, then scraped her finger around the inside of the pot and popped it in her mouth. "Ooh, it is good though, right?"

I flashed the tiniest smile I could do.

Mum started looking in the fridge for some replacement yogurt. I sighed and refreshed my screen. Below the pubic hair video, a girl from school had commented:

Not to be dramatic but I'd die.

Someone else had put:

Imagine if that was your mum tho. 💀💀💀

And Tyler Davidson had tagged me and put about a million crying-with-laughter emojis.

Just then, Dad staggered in carrying a giant cactus. I could just see his head poking over the top. My dad is 198 cm tall. He used to play basketball for Denmark. Not as an actual job – Uncle Gareth says it was more like charity work. Every time we go anywhere, a stranger will say,

"You're tall!" Adults like stating the obvious when it comes to stuff like that. Dad always replies with the exact same thing, "No, I'm Lars!" It gets annoying. I inherited Dad's blue eyes and white-blond hair. The height thing I'm not sure about yet. So far I'm pretty average. If I get white armpit hair the same as his I will die.

"I'm back!" Dad said. "Farmor is on the plane back to Copenhagen and I have collected Prickles here as requested." He grinned, trying to avoid its spikes.

"It's perfect!" Mum said, laughing. She put a pack of yogurts on the worktop then walked over to Dad and tried to sweep the hair out of his face. Only Dad's hair isn't obedient like mine. It's extremely curly. It looks like his head's stuck in a cloud.

"Eva," Dad called from behind the plant, "that doesn't look like homework to me." Dad must be the only person on the planet who thinks about homework while he's getting impaled by a giant cactus.

Now I'm in Year Eight, I'm supposed to be trying harder at school. It's not like I wasn't trying last year exactly, it's just that most of the time there were more interesting things happening outside the classroom window. Like starlings pecking at the grass on the football field. Wonky icicles along the guttering of the old science lab. Leaves being blown into patterns by the wind. Miss

17

Wilson says noticing those little details is a gift, but she's an art teacher. My other teachers call it a distraction. Dad doesn't understand why I'm not a high achiever at school. Since he and Mum went to university and everything, I guess he figured having their genes combined would make me doubly smart. But it didn't. It's annoying because what I *did* get was his practically-invisible eyebrows and Mum's outie belly button.

Mum smiled. "Oh, leave her, Lars. Eva's been working this whole time. Farmor said she did brilliantly with her Danish over Christmas. She's almost better than me." Mum winked at me from across the room.

Dad laughed. It's a running joke in my family that Mum's Danish is so bad no one can understand what she's saying. When we're at Farmor's, it's a good excuse to ignore her.

Dad carefully placed the cactus next to the window and looked out at the frosty garden. "So," he said, clapping his hands, "the light's great! Are we ready to go?"

Mum looked at him like he'd made a bad joke. She took down the picture by the window that said, *All you need is Love and Prosecco* and replaced it with one saying, *There is always a reason to smile!* I thought about the pubic hair post being shared all over TikTok and thought, *There is always a reason to face-plant a giant cactus!* might be more accurate.

"There!" Mum said, carefully placing a couple of magazines on the coffee table. "Eva, can you go get changed, sweetie? You've got yogurt down your T-shirt." I looked at the yogurt spatters on my chest, then closed the school books I'd barely looked at and headed towards the stairs. "Nothing grey!" Mum called. "You wore grey in the nail stickers ad last week."

"Sure." I picked at what now looked like a beheaded cat on my fingernail. Then another notification flashed up on my phone.

Alfie had tagged me in a photo of a gigantic white candyfloss:

@EvaA2007 pubes!!!!

My skin felt like it was being punctured with cactus prickles. So I came out with it. Right there. At the bottom of the stairs, with headless cats on my nails and blobs of coconut yogurt soaking into my T-shirt. "I don't want to."

"Sorry, what, honey?" Mum said, not even glancing up from her phone. "That yellow T-shirt with the love hearts might look nice. I'll be up in a sec."

"No," I said. "I don't want to do the photo."

Mum looked up at me then, confused. "You not feeling well, sweetie? I can't say I'm surprised after eating all that yogurt."

"It's not the yogurt," I said. "The whole of TikTok is laughing at me for that vlog you did the other day, you know, about…" My cheeks burned. I couldn't say the words "pubic hair" out loud.

"Oh, you mean the puberty thing?" Mum gave me a sympathetic smile then poked her bottom lip out. I hated it when she did that. "It's nothing to be embarrassed about, honey. And it was meant to be funny!"

"It's not funny," I said. "It's totally embarrassing. Look!"

I was about to show her the candyfloss picture, but Dad suddenly chimed in. "Eva, do you think we're embarrassed about our pubic hair? It's totally natural – nothing to get uptight about!" Which made me wonder if my parents even went to secondary school.

"They'll have forgotten about it by Monday," Mum said. "Anyway, you've got nothing to worry about with a photo shoot about yogurt. Now go on, sweetie, before we lose this beautiful light." And she turned back to her phone.

I looked pleadingly at Dad, but he jogged up to me and kissed my cheek with his stubbly mouth. "We're so proud of you, Eva. But we are losing this morning light, so hurry up. You can talk to us about anything you like later, okay. Pubic hair or whatever!"

Only that wasn't true. I couldn't talk to them about anything. Because they always made it impossible to tell them how I really felt about the channel.

On the Sunday before I had to go back to school, I was supposed to be watching Hallie in a gymnastics competition. We've been best friends since Year Four. We used to do everything together. Her mum, Rose, even braided our hair together once. Only my mum kind of ruined it by putting the photo on the *All About Eva* Instagram without permission, and Rose made her take it down. Then in Year Six, I had to give up gymnastics because practice started clashing with the filming schedule. I didn't mind that much. I used to get nervous in competitions and mess up anyway. But I miss doing them with Hallie. She was the first person in our age group to do a back handspring. I never even mastered the front one. So now she shares lifts to gymnastics with Gabi Galloney, and I watch from the sidelines.

On Sunday morning, Hallie had messaged saying to arrive at the competition early, so I could get a seat on the front row. But Mum had arranged a last-minute photo shoot at Clevedon Hall, about half an hour out of town. She promised we'd be back in time to watch "at least the second half". But it was already late when we arrived for the shoot so I knew it would be impossible.

Me and Mum had to wear matching T-shirts saying *PRETTY AND PROUD*. And it was freezing inside Clevedon Hall. You'd think with all that money they'd be able to afford decent heating. My skin felt goose-pimply as the make-up lady pinned a gigantic bow in my hair and stuck little pink gems around my eyes. It wasn't bad. I mean, I was being treated like a film star. Only the kind of film star who wears the exact same clothes as their mum.

We had to pretend to have afternoon tea in this room called the Morris Suite that had a domed ceiling and low-hanging chandeliers. Tiny cakes and triangular sandwiches were laid out on four-tier stands in front of us. They were real, but we just had to pretend to eat them. Mum said I could have some sandwiches at the end of the shoot. Only by then the corners had curled up, my face was aching from smiling and I wasn't sure how many people had touched them. As the photographer showed Mum the pictures, I wiped off my make-up. All I could think about was Hallie searching the crowd. And seeing an empty seat where I was supposed to be.

On Monday at school, Hallie said it was fine I didn't

make it, but I could tell she was annoyed with me. Because when Kahlil called, "PRETTY AND PROUD!" and Alfie shouted, "BIG HEEEEEEEAD!!!" as I walked into form, Hallie didn't say anything.

I sat down and scrolled through the *All About Eva* Instagram. There were loads of nice comments. But there's only so many times HappyMelon3000 can post the love-heart-eyes emoji without it feeling kind of creepy. Then I read one that said, UGLY AND STUPID you mean, and I put my phone back in my pocket. I don't know why I read the comments. Mum and Dad told me I wasn't supposed to. But it was like trying not to scratch an itch. I wanted to know what people were saying about me, even if it did make me feel worse.

Alfie shouted, "BIG HEEEEEEEAD!" at me about a hundred times that day. It was almost as bad as when Mum and Dad made me wear a giant avocado costume on World Vegetarian Day in Year Seven. There's still an avocado scraped into the paint on my locker – a permanent reminder of the most embarrassing day of my life. If I printed out all the avocado emojis I'd had posted on my personal social media that week, I could probably wallpaper my entire bedroom.

I'd told Mum about Alfie so many times. But she always said, "Ignore him, sweetie. He's just jealous of all the attention you get!" and would go back to tapping out replies on her phone. Most of the time, *All About Eva* takes priority over my actual real-life problems.

No matter what I said, my parents didn't seem to notice the disaster *All About Eva* was turning into for me. They have this habit of forgetting that I also have to live in the real world. I'd figured out ages ago that I was *not* the CEO of my life. But now it felt like my life didn't even belong to me. And I really needed to figure out a way to get it back.

3

THE CREEP CABIN

The weekend after the Pretty and Proud shoot, I spent most of Saturday lying on the sofa in the snug with Miss Fizzy. It was raining and I had the worst stomach ache ever, so I was watching old episodes of *The Vampire Diaries* and doodling raindrops on my notepad instead of revising for the physics test Mr Jacobs was giving us on Monday. I'd googled Isaac Newton, but so many pages came up I couldn't face reading any of them. If Mr Jacobs liked Newton's theories that much, they were probably kind of boring.

I sent a message to Hallie asking her if she'd started revising for the physics test yet. Stupid question.

Hallie: You mean you haven't even started??

EVA!! Test is MONDAY!!

She sent a link to a revision site called *Bright Sparks*.

Thanks x, I typed back, but I still had pains in my stomach and Mum had put new scented diffusers around the house and they were giving me a headache.

Another message from Hallie popped up:

Want to get a milkshake?? I've just finished my homework. I can help you revise? 😄

I wondered if Gabi would be with her. She'd been stuck to Hallie like a wart ever since Kaja left at the end of Year Seven. Gabi had even asked Miss Wilson to put her name on the student council waiting list – which wasn't even a real thing – just because Hallie was on the council too. I knew Gabi was trying to push me out. But Hallie couldn't see it. She thought we could hang around together as a three. Which maybe would have worked if Gabi wasn't so annoying.

I checked the time on my phone. Dad would be back from his bike ride soon.

"Mum?" I said. "Can I meet Hallie for a milkshake? I need her notes on…" I scanned my brain for something scientific-sounding, "…the pH scale."

Mum frowned at the rain outside. "Mmm, it's a bit wet to be walking into town, sweetie."

"I'll take an umbrella!"

"Can't Hallie email her notes? I wanted us to sort out

our wardrobes using those organizers I showed you last week. For the Sunday vlog?"

"But my test is on Monday," I said.

Mum sighed through her nose. "Hallie could always come over and film it with us! And you could revise afterwards."

I put my head on one side. "You know her mum won't let her be on the channel."

Mum shrugged and removed an invisible piece of fluff from her sleeve. "I thought Rose might have changed her mind by now."

"I doubt it," I said, mostly to myself. Hallie's mum is a child psychologist. She thinks the channel is damaging me psychologically. Last summer, she said if I ever wanted to talk to her about it I could. She gave me a card with her email and phone number on it in fancy writing and her initials *RW* in a gold circle at the top. Mum got kind of annoyed about that. And Hallie stopped coming over so much, because her mum didn't want her to be "exposed to public scrutiny" like I was. While I was stuck doing dumb stuff for the channel, Hallie started hanging out with Gabi more outside of school. It got even worse when Mum and Dad got a bunch of new sponsors. I had to do even more photos and even more filming – and I started missing out on everything real.

"Please, Mum?" I begged. I really didn't want to miss this milkshake with Hallie, especially if there was a chance Gabi wouldn't be tagging along.

"Mr Jacobs will put me in detention if I fail another test." That didn't get a reaction. "I could go to that new crêpe place that's opened. Didn't you want me to take some photos there?"

"Oh, the Crêpe Cabin!" Mum said, suddenly interested. "Actually, that's not a bad idea. I'll let them know you're on the way. But take the big umbrella. Your hair always goes flat in the rain."

I silently sighed. I was sick of Mum obsessing over my hair. I'd asked if I could get it cut short before Christmas, but she'd said no. They'd just agreed some sponsored posts with a new hair-mask company to *Refresh and rejuvenate dull and lifeless hair!* Which I was trying not to take as a personal insult.

I messaged Hallie telling her to meet me at the Creep Cabin – which is what everyone at school had been calling it – and put on my trainers.

"Eva!" Mum called. "Wait a sec. You can't go like that."

I rolled my eyes. Even meeting my best friend for a milkshake required a costume change. I followed Mum upstairs and waited while she picked out a new jumper and restyled my hair. As she dotted concealer on my chin

I looked down at the jumper she'd chosen. It said *SRSLY?* in massive letters.

I looked at Mum in the mirror. "Seriously?"

"Very funny." Mum kissed my forehead then pouted and repinned a strand of hair so it dangled in front of my eye. "Get that jumper in the pics, okay?"

I nodded, and swept the hair behind my ear when she wasn't looking.

My stomach was still aching when I reached the Creep Cabin, and my trainers were soaked from the rain. Inside, about a hundred light bulbs dangled from the ceiling. I could just make out Hallie through the steamed-up window. She was sitting on a stool by herself and waved when she saw me. I felt instantly relieved Gabi wasn't there.

"Oh my God, you have to see this!" Hallie said, spinning on the stool and holding out a menu. She had her gymnastics leotard on under her hoodie and her brown cheeks had a warm glow. The hoodie has her name in capital letters on the back. Mine's in a drawer somewhere at home. I thought maybe I'd be allowed to go back to training one day, but it's been so long I doubt it would even fit me any more. Maybe it would have been different if I was any good at gymnastics, like Hallie. But the general rule of my life is that I'm rubbish at just about everything. Mum says that's what makes me so relatable. So now me failing at stuff is part of their brand.

"They do flavoured popcorn!" Hallie said. "I'm so getting jalapeño pepper flavour."

I wrinkled my nose. "That sounds gross!"

"Eva!" said a man standing behind me. He had pens tucked behind both ears and his apron said *The Crêpe Cabin*. "I'm John. Thanks so much for coming!" He didn't look that creepy to me. But then he smiled and one of his canine teeth poked out over his bottom lip, like a fang. "Order *whatever* you want. It's on the house!"

Hallie let out a small *whoop* and I accidentally snorted.

"I'd appreciate it if you could photograph our signature crêpes. We can do…vanilla bean with peaches and ice cream?"

"Amazing!" Hallie said.

"And maybe the Strawberry and Chocolate Extreme for you, Eva?"

"Thanks," I said. "And can my friend try the jalapeño popcorn?"

"Sure! But I'm warning you – it's pretty spicy!" He did a double eyebrow raise as he took our menus then headed through a door that said *Crêpe Cabin Crew Only*.

Hallie stretched out her arms until her back clicked. "This is so awesome," she said. "And *all* for free." I smiled. Sometimes it felt like there was a different kind of price to pay for all the free stuff though. "Honestly," Hallie said, giving me a sideways glance as though she could read my mind, "if you complain about *All About Eva* right now, I'm going to slap you in the face with my crêpe."

I laughed, which made my stomach ache even worse. Hallie once said that other people have to work really hard to get a life like mine. I get everything handed to me, and I never did anything to earn it, except get born. So that dread in my stomach I'd been getting about the channel – thick and murky, like Dad's potato soup – I hadn't told Hallie about that. It had joined the other stuff that no one ever sees about me. Like the little patch of eczema behind my left knee and the spots Mum hides under concealer.

Anyway, I thought as Creepy John brought our food over, *Hallie is right – the channel does have its upsides.* I tried to take a photo with both the crêpe and my *SRSLY* top in the shot. Which wasn't exactly easy, particularly when Hallie was trying to smear chocolate sauce on my face. I chucked a piece of jalapeño popcorn at her then sent the photos to my mum. Hallie twirled round on

31

the stool and pulled a gigantic smile. I took a video and uploaded it to my TikTok. Then I scrolled down and accepted follower requests from names I recognized, and deleted the ones from total strangers. I kept all my own accounts private. I didn't want any of my parents' followers seeing my actual life.

"So, are these your physics notes?" Hallie asked, picking up my notebook.

"Oh, they were meant to be," I said, sucking chocolate sauce off my fingers. "But I ended up doodling instead."

"Good job I brought mine, huh?" She pulled out a wad of coloured cards. "They're ordered by topic. Don't mess up the order because it took me ages and Mum's testing me on them later."

I nodded, and noticed a comment from Gabi flash up on my phone:

hey where are u at with Hals???

I turned my phone over so Hallie didn't see. It had been ages since just me and Hallie had hung out together. I did not want Gabi turning up.

Hallie put a spoon of ice cream in her mouth and flicked through my notebook. "Your doodles are seriously good, Eva. You should show Miss Wilson." She tossed a handful of popcorn in her mouth.

"Maybe." I was looking out of the window at people

trying to avoid the rain. *Maybe,* because art is the only subject I'm any good at. And *maybe,* because I didn't want everyone knowing. It would probably be another thing for the channel to ruin. Like water parks and gymnastics and avocados (although I was never that keen on avocados).

"Oh my God," Hallie said, grabbing another handful of popcorn. "You have to try this."

I took a piece and tossed it into my mouth. It was like chewing fire. I coughed and gulped down my milkshake while Hallie laughed and patted my back. It did not help my stomach-ache situation.

"Hallie!" I said, after I'd gulped down half my milkshake. "I now have third-degree burns on my tongue!"

"Sorry, I forgot your lameness about spice! Oh my God, remember that time at my house you thought hot pepper sauce was tomato ketchup."

"Remember?" I said. "I think the inside of my mouth is still scarred. I'm going to the toilet. Don't eat all that ice cream, okay? I need it to cool my throat down."

I could still hear Hallie chuckling as I went through the door to the bathroom and into a cubicle.

Then I saw my underwear. I wasn't one hundred per cent sure what it was at first. I'd expected it to look like regular blood. But this was a brownish-red, like the colour of the Birkenstocks Farmor wore in the summer. So it took a few seconds to sink in. I'd started my period.

I sat there for a minute, not really sure what to do. I had this weird feeling, a mixture of relief and fear. It meant I wasn't the last girl in my class to start, because Jenna Bextor and Dinah Jackson had told me a couple of weeks ago that they still hadn't started either. During PSHE, Miss Wilson had said, "Puberty isn't a race!" But, like most things adults tell you, that's not true. I felt so glad I didn't start at school. Susie Greenwood started hers the first week of Year Seven in a German lesson. By lunchtime she was crying because everyone had found out about it. I still don't think I'll ever forget the German word for period, I heard it so many times. And Susie's not even in my class. She always changes into a sports bra for PE apparently. I wondered if my boobs would magically spring into action now I'd finally started my period. I peered down my top at my flat chest. Nothing seemed to be happening.

I texted Hallie:

Emergency! Need you in toilets xx

I made a wedge of loo roll, put it in my underwear then pulled my jeans back up. It felt a bit bulky. I prayed no one would notice.

The door swung open and Hallie called, "Eva? You

okay? Are you sick?"

I opened the cubicle door and checked no one else was in there. "I got my period."

"Oh my God! Finally!" Hallie said, and hugged me so hard my feet practically lifted off the floor. She'd started hers in Year Six, and I'd been waiting for mine ever since. I'd been with her when she started, in Mr Eliot's class, and now she was with me. Just us two. Like when we used to make dens in her back garden out of branches and bed sheets. No one else from school. No camera watching me. No followers. It felt kind of nice.

Suddenly, Hallie let me go and said, "OH NO, EVA!"

"What?" I said, looking around, thinking someone must have walked in without me noticing.

"I just realized." Hallie looked me dead in the eyes. "You started your period in the CREEP CABIN!"

And I'm pretty sure the entire cafe heard our laughter.

4

HAPPY FIRST PERIOD

"Mum!" I called as soon as I got home. I ran upstairs and searched through the bathroom cupboard. Reusable make-up wipes, chemical-free shampoo, clay face masks, organic cotton flannels. But nothing whatsoever to deal with the period emergency that was happening right now. "Mum!" I called again, then I heard Dad coming upstairs.

"Everything okay, Eva?" he asked. "Jen's on the phone." He always called Mum "Jen". I know it's her name and everything, but it was one of those things that they did for the channel, and I found it kind of annoying. "Can I get you something?"

I could feel my cheeks flushing red even though I was behind a locked door. The words "period" and "Dad" do not belong in the same sentence. "I need Mum, okay?

It's kind of an emergency." Dad muttered something under his breath, then he went back downstairs.

A few minutes later, Mum's voice drifted through the door. "Everything all right, sweetie? Has something happened?"

I undid the lock and slowly opened the door, making sure Dad wasn't hiding behind the laundry basket with a camera. You never know with my parents. "I got my period," I whispered.

"OH MY GOD!" Mum hugged me so tight I almost suffocated. "EVA! THIS IS AMAZING!"

"Shh!" I said. "Dad will hear!" When she finally let me go there were tears in her eyes. "Mum…are you actually crying?"

"Oh, it's silly, I know!" She sniffed then wiped her eyes with a reusable facial wipe.

"Everything okay?" Dad called.

"Don't say anything," I said, deadly serious.

"Oh, Eva, don't be silly. He's your dad! He'll want to celebrate too!"

"Celebrate?" I said. "I don't want to tell anyone. I just need some, you know, erm, products."

Mum squeezed my hand. "Wait right here." She disappeared for a minute then came back holding a large red box in one hand and a camera in the other. "So, I've had this for a while and I just want to say, I am so proud of you."

"Mum, can you stop filming?" Mum lowered the camera, but didn't put it away. "I mean it, Mum. Don't film this!"

"Eva!" she said in a jokey voice. "This is a major milestone! I know you'll want to give our subscribers a little peek… "

"No way." I pushed the box away and folded my arms.

"Okay," Mum sighed. She put the camera down and pushed the box back towards me. "Please open it."

Inside the box were sanitary pads, tampons, a hot water bottle, an eye mask, a massive bar of chocolate, underwear with sparkly unicorns on, tissues, a teddy. And even a book called *Don't Ovary Act! How to Survive your First Period.* "Mum," I said, "this is—"

"I know! You think it's totally embarrassing! But this is a big deal to me, Eva. I never thought I'd be able to have a baby. And now look." She dabbed her eyes with the facial wipe again. "You're growing up."

I reached over and hugged her. "It's really nice, Mum. Thanks." Then I must have leaned on something because suddenly a confetti bomb exploded, sending millions of tiny silver tampons hurtling into the air.

We both jumped. "I'd forgotten about that! I got it

specially made," Mum said, laughing, as she picked bits of tampon confetti out of my hair. "And tomorrow we'll have a proper celebration!"

"I thought this was the celebration."

"Eva! I think we can do better than a confetti bomb in the bathroom." She kissed me on the head then pulled off a bit of confetti stuck to her lip. "Something special."

I woke up late the next morning. The house was weirdly quiet. I sat up in bed and looked at my phone. I already had three messages from Hallie. She always got up early on Sundays to go to church. It's the exact reason I'm glad my parents aren't religious.

Hope you're okay?

Making my gran's Guyanese lime cookies to celebrate your P Day at school tomo!

Told Mum it's for a bake sale in the library

😊 she said leave out the rum lol.

A photo popped up of Hallie with a wooden spoon in her hand and a gigantic smile on her face.

I messaged back:

OMG you're amazing, THANK YOU ♥ ♥ ♥

There was a tap on my bedroom door and Mum's face appeared. "How are you feeling, sweetie pie? Want me to run you a bath?" I yawned and rubbed my eyes. "Oh, don't rub your skin like that, sweetie, it blotches." Mum opened the curtains and I squinted at the light. "I've sent your dad on an all-day bike ride, so we can have a girlie day!" I tried so hard not to roll my eyes it was physically painful. "Wait until you see downstairs!"

"What's downstairs?" I asked suspiciously.

"Get washed and dressed first!" Mum opened my wardrobe and examined the contents, then pulled out a T-shirt and dungaree dress. She placed them on my bed then hugged me until there was no oxygen left in my lungs. "I'm so excited!"

"Mum," I said, wriggling free, "it's just my period."

"Oh, come on! I only get to throw a period party for you once."

"A period party? Mum, I hope you haven't invited half the—"

"Don't be silly! I haven't invited anyone."

"Good," I said. "And especially do not say anything about this to Spud."

Spud has been my next-door neighbour since for ever. There's a gap in the hedge between our back gardens that you can climb through. His real name's Euan, but he's always been Spud to me and everyone who knows him. He's the closest thing I have to a brother. Mum says when we were little, we used to say we'd get married and have a hundred babies. Now, I can think of a hundred reasons why that will never happen. Number one being that he once got his head stuck in our cat flap.

"Don't worry," Mum said. "It's just us. And Netflix. I mean, what period party would be complete without a movie marathon?"

I noticed a sticky note on my desk in Dad's handwriting:

REVISE PHYSICS TODAY!

I groaned. "I'm supposed to be revising."

Mum read the note, sighed and dropped it in the bin. "Eva, there will be other physics tests. You only start your period once. Besides, you revised yesterday with Hallie. You don't want to over-prepare for these things."

"Oh yeah." I didn't mention that I'd barely even glanced at Hallie's revision cards.

"Now get ready. There are more important things in life than physics," Mum said, and closed the door.

I wondered if she'd write that in a note for Mr Jacobs tomorrow.

I put the clothes Mum had selected back in my wardrobe and pulled on leggings and a hoodie. Wearing a sanitary pad felt kind of strange. I wondered how I would get through three to eight days of this without someone noticing.

Downstairs, music was playing and Mum had written on the chalkboard in the kitchen:

HAPPY FIRST PERIOD, EVA!

A bunch of red helium balloons floated above the table, and red pompoms and fairy lights dangled from the walls. It took me about three seconds to figure out what she was doing. I stood at the bottom of the stairs with my arms folded.

"Don't mention it." Mum beamed from behind the camera. "You're worth it!" And she exploded a confetti bomb, showering me in shiny bits of red paper.

I shook the confetti out of my hair. "You can't film this."

"Oh, Eva, don't start this now," Mum said. "Not after I've gone to all this effort."

"I'm serious, Mum," I said. "If you're putting this on *All About Eva* then I'm going back to my room and revising physics."

I don't even know why I was disappointed. They'd invited some of their "most loyal" subscribers – the For-Evas – to my tenth birthday party. The "Ten Years of *All*

About Eva" party, I mean. Farmor was upset when she found out they'd invited subscribers, so she didn't come. She said it wasn't safe to invite "internet people" to our house. Maybe she thought one of them would kidnap me or something. But actually, most of them were pretty nice. Although one of them had knitted her own "Eva doll", and read out a bunch of poems she'd written about me. She didn't try to kidnap me or anything. But my parents didn't invite any For-Evas to stuff after that.

"I'm sorry you don't like it," Mum said, putting down the camera and fiddling with a set of red fairy lights. "I honestly just want today to be special for you."

I glanced around the room, taking everything in. It must have taken her hours. I had no idea where she got the inflatable womb at such short notice.

"I do like it, Mum," I said. "It looks amazing. I just don't want it to be on the channel, okay?"

Mum smiled. "Fine. Understood."

"You promise?" Mum nodded as she hugged me. I noticed a giant cardboard box in the corner. "Dad's not hiding in there, is he?"

"Ha!" she said. "Don't be silly. I ordered some special balloons and stuff ready for us hitting half a million subscribers. I know it's probably a bit early. I mean, we've technically only just passed 400,000, but it's best to be

43

prepared for these things. Subs are creeping up every day! Exciting, huh!"

My heart deflated like a balloon. Thousands *more* people watching me every day did not feel like something to celebrate.

An hour later, we were drinking red berry smoothies and watching a film on the projector screen when Mum started fiddling with my hair. "I was listening to this podcast a while ago," she said. "And they were saying that periods shouldn't be this big secret thing, you know? Period parties are becoming a massive trend because, actually, girls should—"

"Nope," I said, not taking my eyes off the screen. "I'm not making a vlog about my period."

Mum was quiet for a minute, then she said, "I'm just saying, it's nothing to be embarrassed about."

"Mum, I already told you. Don't put anything on the channel about my period, okay. If people at school find out I will literally die."

Mum looked at me. "It's just...I think we have an opportunity to change the narrative surrounding girls' and women's bodies. You know, considering we have such a big platform."

"Mum!" I shouted, sitting up. "I don't want my period on a platform!" I slammed my smoothie down and a blob of red gloop landed on the coffee table.

"Okay, okay," Mum said. "I'll just take some pictures to show Lars later then. He was a little upset he wasn't invited."

"So, you told Dad?"

"It's a natural part of growing up, Eva," Mum said. "It's nothing to be embarrassed about." I wished I could have normal parents who *were* embarrassed about stuff like this. "I've been having periods for over thirty years now," Mum continued despite me squirming, "Lars is more than used to them."

"Gross."

"Eva, the whole point I'm making is that it's not gross. We could use the channel to show people that periods are—"

"I know what they are, Mum! I don't want your subscribers commenting on mine." I crossed my arms, and shook my head when Mum tried to hand me my drink.

"I'm sorry," she said, putting her arm around me. "Forget about the channel. Let's just eat cake and enjoy celebrating." Mum held up her glass to do "cheers". I reluctantly took my glass and clinked it against hers. "Welcome to womanhood, sweetie. And I promise – all of this is for *you*." She took a sip then straightened out

45

my hair at the front. "Unless I can get a sponsorship deal with one of those period tracking apps, or a big tampon brand, now that would be cool." I glared at her. "Relax, I'm joking!" She hugged me and I felt her warm breath through my hair. "My little Eva's growing up."

Even after all of that, I didn't think Mum would break her promise. I blew out the red candles and ate cake and unwrapped the presents she'd bought me. I even stuck womb-shaped stickers on my face. Happy First Period, Eva. Get ready for the worst day of your life.

5

SPUD

The next morning, I was wearing special period pants and a sanitary towel just in case. I still felt totally self-conscious. I checked my reflection about a million times in my room, and again in the patio doors downstairs. For the first time ever I was grateful our school made us wear pleated skirts. I quietly pulled my homework diary out of my bag, but Dad must have super-sensitive hearing because he looked over straight away. Maybe being tall means you get extra sound waves.

"Eva!" Dad wiped his hands and picked up his camera. "Isn't Monday morning a little late to be checking if you have homework?" He spoke in the jokey voice he always uses when he asks me stuff on camera. They only post a "family vlog" twice a week, but they film content pretty much all the time. And if something's trending, they'll post about that too. Then there's the sponsored posts and special updates and the lives they do sometimes. Put it this way – I've lost count of how many times people have watched me eat breakfast. "You've had the whole weekend to get your homework done!" Dad said as I sat down.

"Weekends are supposed to be a break from school," I replied and smiled for exactly half a second.

Dad turned the camera on himself and frowned. "Did you hear that? Eva thinks weekends should be a break!" Then he launched into a monologue about how hard he worked at school.

I pretended I wasn't listening and flicked through the pages of my homework diary. I'd completely forgotten about the history homework. "In that case, Dad, could you explain the multiple causes of the English Civil War? Like, briefly?" I flashed another fake smile.

Dad let out an exaggerated sigh to the camera and handed me his iPad. "Anyone else have kids like this? Let us know in the comments!" He turned the camera back onto me and said, "Google King Charles the First."

"Thanks," I said. "Mrs Peters will appreciate it."

Dad rolled his eyes behind the camera. "Good to know at least your teachers take your schoolwork seriously!"

"I guess it's like Mum told me yesterday," I said. "There

are more important things in life than schoolwork." And Dad almost choked on his smoothie.

King Charles I's Wikipedia page is the longest entry ever. It was typical of Mrs Peters to make us find out about someone this famous. I scrolled down for a few minutes, trying to find some good bits to copy-paste. I zoomed in on a picture of King Charles I. I liked his cape, but his pointy beard was kind of disturbing. There was a familiar knock and the front door swung open.

"Hey, Spud," I called. I didn't even need to look up. "You know this Civil War thing – was Charles I the baddie?"

"It certainly didn't end well for him," Spud said, waiting by the door. "You're doing the history homework *now*?"

"Kind of." I air-dropped the Wikipedia link to my phone.

"Have a good day, you two," Dad said, handing me my lunch bag.

"I'm considering cutting my hair like a Roundhead," Spud said as I pulled on my school shoes. "What do you think? Mum's against the idea."

"What's a Roundhead?" I asked.

He grinned. "You really haven't done the history homework, have you? They were the supporters of parliament. Look." He held up a picture on his phone.

"Erm, didn't we talk about this when we were learning about the Romans?" I said.

He thought for a moment. "That was a balaclava with a mohawk attached."

"Spud, I'm just saying, your life would be a lot easier if you didn't make fashion statements based on stuff you learn from Mrs Peters."

"Hey, Spud!" Mum called as she opened the office door. "Did Lars get you some breakfast?"

"It's okay, Mrs Andersen," Spud replied. "I had four Weetabixes at home."

"Four!" Mum said, eyes widening. "Gosh! I can barely manage one!" I went cross-eyed at Spud, who tried not to laugh. Mum liked only eating half of things. It was this weird kind of diet she always seemed to be on. "You got everything you need, sweetie?" she said, kissing me on the side of the head. My cheeks burned. She may as well have handed me a jumbo-sized pack of sanitary pads right there.

"Let's go," I said quickly. "We don't want to be late."

"Good to hear!" Dad called as we left.

"And don't be late home, Eva," Mum said. "We're shooting that ad straight after school, okay? No loitering." The front door closed before I could answer.

"I thought you didn't want to do those ads any more," Spud said as we walked up the hill.

Spud was one of the real-life witnesses of the avocado costume. He'd even offered to wear it instead of me. He figured that people at school make fun of him already, so what difference could a giant avocado costume make? Mum didn't go for it, but still, it proves he's probably the best next-door neighbour on the planet.

"You know what they're like," I replied, pulling on my gloves. "They don't listen to me, do they? Anyway, they promised no more vegetable costumes, so…"

"Avocado's a fruit," Spud said, grinning.

"Whatever." I hit his arm with my lunch bag. "It's not like I have a choice."

I spotted Hallie waiting for me on the corner. Spud's friends were outside the shop on the other side of the road. Me and Spud have this unwritten rule that we don't hang around together at school. I don't know when it started exactly. We've never really talked about it. But as soon as we get to the top of the hill, we separate.

"Listen," I said, "don't let any of your friends talk you into getting a Roundhead haircut, okay?"

"Sure," he said, fanning his bushy hair in the cold breeze. "See you later."

Spud crossed the road to join his group of friends, collectively known in our year as Nerdophobia. They are actually pretty nice, but they say quotes from *Star Wars* way too much. Spud says the name "Nerdophobia" is incorrect, since it technically means a person who *fears* nerds. I told him saying stuff like that is the reason they're called Nerdophobia in the first place.

"Maybe I'll try out the Roundhead haircut on Fizzy!" Spud shouted from the other side of the road. "It would suit her aggressive personality!"

"Like you'd dare, Spud," I shouted back. "And that's *Miss* Fizzy to you." I tried to look serious, but I couldn't help laughing. Because it's true – she hisses at Spud any time he goes near her. Spud's laugh drifted over the traffic and made me laugh again. Then I saw Gabi crossing the road the opposite way. I tried to keep the smile on my face.

"Freshly made cookies!" Hallie said, opening the tin she was holding.

"Oh my God, Hals," I said. "They look amazing, thank you."

"What did Spud just say?" Gabi said. "I can't believe you still walk to school with him. He's so weird."

I opened my mouth to say something, but Hallie looked at me. I'd promised her before Christmas that I'd try harder to get along with Gabi. Some days it was more difficult than others.

"Hey, did you bake?" Gabi said, practically shoulder-barging me out of the conversation.

"Yep! They're to celebrate Eva's…er…" Hallie smiled awkwardly at me. "Sorry, I told Gabi last night."

"That's okay," I said, but inside I felt a stab of anger. I'd asked her not to tell anyone, and she'd told Gabi "Dead Eyes" Galloney. *And* they'd been messaging without including me.

"Oh yeah, your period," Gabi said. "I got mine in, like, Year Six." She stuck her nose in the air, like she was the Queen of Periods or something. "They're so annoying when you do gymnastics."

"Right," I said, avoiding eye contact with Hallie. "Well, maybe I can get out of PE this afternoon."

"I doubt it," said Gabi. "Mrs Marshall didn't let Lucie Simms sit out of that netball match when she'd dislocated her shoulder."

"I think she just had cramp," I said.

"Whatever," Gabi said. "She cried for the whole second half. You wouldn't really get it because you're not sporty like us."

I bit my lip to keep from saying anything back. It was physically impossible to not find Gabi annoying. She gave me a sarcastic smile and linked arms with Hallie, so I had to walk on the kerb. Me and Hallie were still officially best friends. But whenever Gabi was around, it felt as though I'd been demoted. Like whatever glue had been holding me and Hallie together had dried up.

In form, Miss Wilson reminded us it was our turn to host the Year Eight assembly next month. "And *some* of you still need to bring something in for the Cool Wall!" she said, smiling directly at me.

The "Cool Wall" was this noticeboard thing she'd started at the beginning of term. We were supposed to bring in pictures of our achievements and stick them underneath our names. Hallie already had teacher commendations, pictures of her gymnastic medals, the Student Councillor badge. Under Gabi's there was a picture of her and Hallie at gymnastics, and some of the commendations that actually she got ages ago in Year Seven, but maybe Miss Wilson hadn't noticed. Rami had a Principal's Award for science. Anjuli had a picture of her hockey team sitting behind a trophy. Everyone had something good up there. Apart from me. And Spud, who had a Photoshopped picture of his guinea pig holding a lightsaber. Every time I'd tried to find a piece of work to put up, nothing looked good enough. Hallie had suggested one of my doodles, but they felt kind of personal for the Cool Wall. I kept hoping Miss Wilson would give me an art commendation. But she never gave them out because she said art wasn't meant to be competitive. Which was typical. Unless a miracle happened and I suddenly became better at something else, my Cool Wall spot would probably be blank for ever.

"I'm expecting something from you *this week*, Eva," Miss Wilson said as she staple-gunned the corners of Nadira's gold reading certificate. "You're the only one now who hasn't put anything up. I'm sure you've got lots of cool things you can share with us!"

"She shares everything on her YouTube channel, miss," said Gabi, smirking at me. "Just print out some screenshots, Eva."

"It's my parents' channel, not mine," I said and Hallie gave me a look, like *I* was in the wrong.

"Okay, so our assembly!" Miss Wilson said, clapping her hands. She had rings on every finger, even her thumbs, and her feathery earrings almost reached her shoulders. "I hope you all came up with some ideas for it over the weekend, like I asked."

Gabi's hand shot up. "Hallie could do her gymnastics routine, miss. She got through to the county finals!"

I looked at Hallie as if to say, *How come you didn't tell me?* But she gave me a look back that said, *How come you didn't ask?* then fiddled with the Black Girl Magic badge on her pencil case to avoid my eyes. I thought back to doing the Pretty and Proud shoot at Clevedon Hall while my seat at her gymnastics competition stayed empty.

I swallowed, and my insides felt kind of cold.

"That's a lovely idea, Gabi, and I'd love to see your routine, Hallie," Miss Wilson said, "but the idea is that we involve everyone."

Spud put his hand up. "We could do some ju-jitsu."

"Thank you, Euan," Miss Wilson said. "But I don't think that would quite fit with the school's anti-violence policy."

"Ju-jitsu is a non-violent martial art!" he said.

But Miss Wilson ignored him and tapped on her keyboard. "I wonder if there's some kind of special day next month...National *Toast* Day? Oh dear!"

Spud sprang up from his seat. "I could bring in my guinea pig, miss! His name's Toast!"

Miss Wilson laughed. "I would love that, Euan, but I'm not sure Mr Andrews allows pets in the assembly hall."

Gabi said quietly, "It cannot be safe for Spud to keep a pet." And Hallie gently elbowed her.

"What about a live painting again, miss?" Dinah said. "Like last year! That was so fun."

Miss Wilson smiled. "That was amazing! But Mr Andrews wasn't very pleased about all the paint on the hall floor." She tapped her computer. "Oh, now this sounds interesting. The International Day of Unplugging. *A day that invites people to unplug from technology from sunrise to sundown.* It's a few weeks after we have to do our assembly, but I don't see why we couldn't do our own day of unplugging. In fact, this is perfect. A whole twenty-four hours without screens!"

Alfie put his hand up. "How are we supposed to talk to anyone?"

"You could try opening your mouth," Miss Wilson said, laughing. "When I was at school, we didn't rely on screens to communicate. Our FaceTime was talking to people face-to-face." She folded her arms. "You know, the more I think about it, the more I am convinced this 'unplugging' will do you the world of good. We'll all take part and write up our experiences for the assembly. Are we all agreed?"

Not a single person put their hand up.

"Good," Miss Wilson said. "All the more reason to do it. Get your homework diaries out everyone and write in the date to unplug please. I think the last day in January would be good as it's a Sunday." She wrote the *8W Day of Unplugging* date on the board in her swirly handwriting. Suddenly she turned to look at me. "Oh, Eva! I didn't think about you. Will unplugging be a problem?"

"It's fine," I said quickly.

"Are you sure, Eva?" Gabi said, a look of fake concern plastered on her face. "You don't want to lose any subscribers."

I didn't say anything, but Hallie saw me pull a face behind her back.

At lunchtime, I sat in the canteen with Hallie, Gabi and some of the other girls from our class. I wasn't exactly in the mood for celebrating, considering I was pretty certain I'd just failed the physics test. I'd only been able to answer about four questions, and one of those was my name. But I smiled as Hallie passed around the cookies and tried not to mind that Gabi had taken the seat next to her.

"So, what did your mum say?" Jenna asked, squashing up next to me. "I bet you'll get sent loads of free period stuff now!"

"I hope not," I said, biting my cookie. "She agreed not to post about it so…"

"Oh my God," Gabi said, spraying cookie crumbs everywhere. "Can you imagine? I would literally die if my mum even wrote the word *period* on Facebook."

For once I agreed with Gabi. I honestly didn't think my mum would do it. I mean, she promised. It seems so dumb now that I actually believed her.

It was after lunch when it happened. Or should I say, when Alfie Stevens happened. I was used to him playing stuff from the channel. He'd find old videos of me doing stupid dance routines, or saying something embarrassing. When Mum made a video about spot creams, Alfie called me "All About Acne" for a month. But it's not like he needed the channel for his material. He'd been making jokes about my non-existent boobs ever since we did sex education. During the end-of-year quiz in geography, Mr Khatri had asked, "Where is the flattest place on earth?" and Alfie had shouted out, "Eva's chest!" Followed by a laugh that sounded like a machine gun. Alfie spent the whole of lunchtime in detention. I spent the rest of term wanting to chuck Spud's oversized eraser at his head.

But that was different. Because I *knew* Alfie would say stuff about it. I was expecting it. Maybe there's something less bad about being humiliated when you know for sure it's going to happen.

After lunch, we walked into German. Mr Scott wasn't there yet and Alfie was sitting on a table with his feet resting on a chair. His friends were gathered round watching something on his phone. They nudged Alfie when I walked in and his face lit up like a flamethrower. He tapped his phone and whatever they were watching started replaying. I recognized Mum's voice right away. Squealing words that made my heart stop: "MY LITTLE GIRL IS A WOMAN!"

6

THANKS FOR WATCHING

Everyone in the classroom was staring at me. And I had this weird feeling, like maybe it wasn't real. Maybe I was trapped inside a bad dream. But Mum's voice carried on, and my heart beat so hard everyone in the classroom must have been able to hear it.

"*My little baby passed a very important milestone this weekend. Yep, our tiny Eva isn't our baby girl any more! She started her period!*"

Alfie held up his phone so everyone could see. "Eva, did you have a *period* party?" He said "period" like it was something disgusting, then showed his phone to Buddy, Kahlil and Lucas. "How fit is her mum though?"

My face burned a fiery red and tears stung the backs of my eyes. I wanted to grab Alfie's phone and chuck it out of the window. Ideally while he was still holding onto it. But my feet were glued to the spot. Anyway, our German classroom's only on the ground floor.

"Alfie, grow up," Hallie said, striding over and trying to grab his phone.

Alfie stood up on his chair and the video carried on playing. I caught the words, *products* and *period kits* and the title of that book Mum had given me. If Farmor was right, and the channel was *just a tiny stitch in the tapestry of my life*, then why did it feel like my heart was unravelling? With every word Mum said, and every sniff and every sigh, she was trampling a tiny piece of me into the carpet. I blinked away tears that felt like vinegar.

"Alfie!" Hallie shouted. "Turn it off!"

I still couldn't move. So I stood there, staring at a poster about German grammar, listening to Mum's voice announcing my period to the world.

"*We had a quiet little celebration, just us two. No offence to Lars, but Eva said no dads allowed! Let me know what you think about that in the comments. Should dads be more involved? I already had a special gift box prepared, because of course you never know when it will happen! It was reassuring for Eva knowing that I had all this stuff ready. We can make this such an empowering moment for our daughters! We can show them we're not embarrassed. We're not icky about it. We're period warriors! As usual I'll drop links to where you can get all the products in the description. I mean, just look at these super cute period pants with unicorns on! Aren't they just so great? They're made by a company called Don't Cramp My Style. They look awesome, they're comfy and, most importantly, they prevent leaks."*

"Ewwww!" Alfie said, screwing up his face. His friends laughed as Hallie tried to grab his phone again.

"Period warriors!?" Lucas said, and everyone laughed. I tried to hold in my tears as Jenna linked my arm.

And that was the moment. Feeling like my shoes were glued to the brown carpet of my German classroom, waves of humiliation and anger surging through my body, and my entire class gawping at my new leak-proof underwear. I wiped a tear from the edge of my eye and realized my hands were shaking. I had so many things I wanted to say, but I knew if I opened my mouth the only thing to come out would be a scream. I *hated* my mum.

Hallie told Alfie to turn the video off again, then I heard Mr Scott's voice asking what on earth was going on. Alfie climbed down from the chair and everyone else quickly found their seats.

Jenna squeezed my arm and said, "Alfie's an idiot. Your mum is so amazing!" then she went to sit down.

"You okay?" Hallie asked as we headed to our table and sat down. "Alfie is so immature."

My German book was full of little doodles, but I didn't do any new ones that lesson. I listened to Mr Scott speaking to us in German, as usual with no idea what he meant. My heart thumped in my ears and I blinked away tears that kept on coming back.

"Don't worry about it," Hallie whispered to me as she flicked through the textbook to the right page. "No one thinks it's a big deal apart from Alfie. And he's such an idiot. Everyone will have forgotten about it by tomorrow." I looked at her. "Okay, well, maybe by the end of the week." She smiled. "It's just a period, Eva. Every girl gets them."

"Yeah," I whispered back, "but not everyone's mum puts it on YouTube."

Mr Scott glanced at us and Hallie quickly started copying down German phrases from the board. "But," Hallie said as soon as he turned his back, "my mum went live on Instagram telling me off for not coming straight home after gymnastics that time, remember?"

"That was by accident."

"It was still really embarrassing!" Hallie nudged me to start writing. "Loads of people saw it."

"It's not the same," I said. "About ten people saw that

video. *Hundreds of thousands* of people will see my mum's."
I peered into the little mirror on the inside of my pencil case. The skin around my eyes had turned red, which made my eyebrows look even more invisible than usual. A blotchy rash was creeping up my neck.

"Eva, things aren't worse just because they happen to *you*," Hallie said quietly. "I feel embarrassed about things too."

"I know, I didn't mean—" I started, but Gabi leaned over and said, "Remember, it is 'all about Eva'."

Her words felt sour. They smiled at each other, and I could tell from Hallie's face it wasn't the first time Gabi had said that about me.

Before I could say anything, Mr Scott called, "Eva!" and told me to read out the first phrase he'd written on the board. I looked at it. He may as well have asked me to read Ancient Greek. Hallie put up her hand and said it perfectly.

"*Danke*, Hallie," Mr Scott said. "It's nice to know someone's been paying attention." He gave me a look then picked on someone else.

"Thanks," I muttered then leaned my elbow on the desk and started colouring in the corners of my page. I looked over at Alfie. He had probably shared Mum's video with everyone at lunchtime. It was probably going around school already. I waited until Mr Scott was facing the board, then slipped my phone out of my pocket. *Eva's Started her Period!!!* was in the *All About Eva* "Story Specials". In the thumbnail Mum was holding the red balloons from the party. 14,493 views. 3.5k thumbs up. 36 thumbs down. 102 comments. I felt sick.

Hallie kicked me under the table.

"Eva, are you with us?" Mr Scott asked.

I dropped my phone on my lap and looked at him.

"*Was hast du am Wochenende gemacht?* What did you do at the weekend?"

Everyone laughed. I wondered if Mr Scott was making some kind of sick joke.

Alfie turned around. He had a stupid grin plastered on his face. "Come on, Eva!" he said. "What happened at the weekend?"

Mr Scott put his hands on his hips. "Well?"

"Erm," I started, but the sound of giggling put me off. I heard Spud say, "I'll answer it, sir."

"Thank you, Euan," Mr Scott said firmly. "But I've asked Eva."

"*Möge die Macht mit dir sein.*" No one had any idea what Spud had said, not even Hallie. I would normally mouth "Thanks" across the classroom, but I was too embarrassed about Spud finding out I'd started my period to even look at him.

"Euan, we've spoken about the *Star Wars* references outside of Games Club, right?" Mr Scott said, then he turned back to me. My cheeks went burning hot again. "Eva, *was hast du am Wochenende gemacht?*"

"I went for a milkshake," I said quickly.

Mr Scott sighed. "*Auf Deutsch!* In German!"

"Oh, yeah." I groaned. How on earth was I supposed to know the German for "milkshake"? I desperately tried to think of phrases I knew, which didn't exactly give me many options. I was pretty sure "*getrunken*" meant to drink. And did "*Kuh*" mean milk? I sighed. It was close enough. "*Ich habe eine Kuh getrunken.*"

Hallie shook with silent laughter beside me.

"Well done, Eva," Mr Scott said. "You just told me you drank a cow."

Which actually did make me laugh too.

On the way home, Spud told me he'd said, "May the force be with you" in German. He'd thought it would distract Mr Scott from asking me about the weekend.

"Thanks, Spud," I said when I got to the bottom of my drive, "but you really don't need to stick up for me."

"I know," Spud said, taking a run-up so he could

hurdle over his garden wall. "I guess you can stick up for yourself – now you're a woman!" I heard his shoes scrape on the gravel as he landed, and even though I still felt upset, a snort-laugh escaped from my nose.

But when I turned to my house, stabs of anger went through my skin. Yesterday Mum and I were laughing and eating cake and pointing out the funny cartoons in the *Don't Ovary Act!* book. And now everything – all that private stuff – had been seen by thousands of strangers. And half of my school. I'd spent the afternoon planning what to say. But now, I didn't even want to go inside. I tapped my phone. *135k views?* I felt like I was falling. And I couldn't stop myself from scrolling through the comments.

Bless you, Jen!

Thank you so much for sharing this moment!!!!

OMG made me cry

I gave my daughter an emergency period kit for her locker!

Happy first period, Eva!!! Enjoy your presents!!

Thought she started already

Sad we didn't get to see the party 😥

Like if you've been here since Eva was a baby and this is blowing your mind. [1.4k likes]

The doorstep was out of the wind, but it was still

freezing cold. Some of the street lights had come on already, creating little halos of orange. My hands shook as I read comments and replies, refreshing the views counter until my thumbs felt numb. Almost five hundred thousand people knew I'd started my period. I hadn't even wanted Dad to know. I wondered what those people would say if they could see me right now. The Eva standing outside the front door, a murky feeling of dread spreading from my stomach to my brain, then pouring down into my heart like rain. But no one ever sees this Eva. This Eva would get edited out, deleted, thumbs down. Unsubscribe. This is the Eva no one wants to see. Standing on the doorstep by myself, watching my life exploding on the screen without me. Trying my best not to cry.

7

DON'T READ THE COMMENTS

Mum was coming downstairs when I opened the front door. My heart dropped. Her face was covered in green gunge. It was so typical of my mum. She'd probably put on some weird face mask to make me laugh. Well, it wouldn't work. If I had to talk to her while she looked like an extra from *Doctor Who*, fine. I stared, unsmiling, into the camera she pointed at me.

"Oh, Eva, you're freezing!" she said; the green crust on her skin cracked slightly around her mouth as she spoke. "Are you all right?"

"I'm not speaking to you with the camera going," I said, my chest thumping with anger.

"Eva, please. It's just some filler stuff for Wednesday's vlog. How was school? Want to try out one of these face masks? You've heard of pink clay, right? Well, this is green mud! It's infused with eucalyptus, purifying charcoal and four different minerals. And doesn't it smell incredible, Eva?"

I glared into the lens. "You look like a witch."

Mum put the camera down and tipped her head to one side. "Eva. That's not exactly the reaction footage I was after."

"You vlogged about my period!" I shouted. "You promised you wouldn't!" It wasn't the big speech I had planned. But they were the only words I managed to say before my voice cracked, and they slammed down between us like a falling tree.

"Oh, you've already seen it," Mum tried to say, but she couldn't move her mouth properly because of the mask. "I'm so sorry, sweetie! I was going to talk to you about it tonight. I didn't think you'd see it at school. I know you said you didn't want me to film the party, and I respected that, but I needed to share the stuff I put in your gift box." She tried to put her hand on my shoulder but I shook it off. "Oh, please don't be upset with me!"

"Of course I'm upset!" I said, tears burning my cheeks. "Everyone at school has seen it! It's totally embarrassing. Even Mr Scott knows! You *promised* you wouldn't!"

Mum flinched. "I'm so sorry, sweetie. I didn't want to

upset you, honestly. I wanted to talk to you about it first. But this sponsor has been putting pressure on me and…"

Her words stung, like when Farmor used to dab tea tree oil on my grazes. I felt like my chest was about to explode. "I can't believe you!" I shouted.

"Oh, Eva, honey." She tried to hug me, but I stepped backwards. Then she said she loved me a bunch of times. Like that means anything. "I do understand you're embarrassed," Mum said, or at least I think that's what she said. Her fask mask had completely set and she had to stretch her mouth into weird shapes to get her lips to crack. "I hate seeing you so upset. But listen, periods happen to every girl. And it's already one of our most popular 'Specials'. The attitude to periods is changing, sweetie. It's no longer this big embarrassing thing."

"Mum, you don't get it," I said, my voice shaking with anger. "You have to take it down right now. Before anyone else sees it."

"Listen, Eva. Once you've calmed down, you'll see—"

"I'm not going to calm down! I don't even want to do the stupid channel any more. It's ruining my life!"

Suddenly, an alarm started ringing. I felt so angry I didn't even jump.

"Oh, goodness!" Mum said, tapping her phone. "I'm so sorry, honey, but I have to take this face mask off."

She tapped her cheeks. "I'd leave it, but it's actually stinging a little bit. Then we'll talk about this properly, okay?" She ran upstairs and called over the bannister, "That nice man from the Crêpe Cabin called round earlier to say thank you. He gave us a tub of their marshmallow ice cream! Help yourself while I take this off, okay? I'll have half a scoop." The mask cracked further as she smiled. Her face look like a dried-up pond.

I dropped my coat on the floor, grabbed my sketchbook out of my school bag and headed into the snug. I wanted to go to my bedroom, but Mum was upstairs and I didn't want to be anywhere near her.

I wiped my eyes with my sleeve and sat down on the sofa next to Miss Fizzy. She yawned and stretched her paws onto my lap. I drew the outline of a huge butterfly and kept adding spirals until its wings looked like they were covered in gigantic black holes. I began adding tiny eyes around the edges, when I heard Mum coming downstairs. I quickly closed my sketchbook and covered it with a cushion. I never show Mum or Dad my drawings. I keep all my sketchbooks in my locker at school, or hidden at the back of my wardrobe. I'd thought about showing them a few times, especially when Miss Wilson gave me an *Excellent* on my art report last year. As dumb as it probably sounds, doodling is the only private thing

I have. My sketchbook felt a bit like a diary. I could put stuff in there – in my pictures – that I couldn't share with anyone. So there was no way I wanted to share it with the world.

"There you are!" Mum said. She couldn't sit down because Miss Fizzy was stretched out and neither of my parents ever dared move her. She looks cute and cuddly, but it would be safer to rattle a wasp's nest than to disturb Miss Fizzy when she's asleep. Dad calls her *Den Onde*. It means The Evil One. I glanced at Mum standing by the door. *That name would suit her a lot better right now*, I thought. She came over and crouched in front of me, so I kind of had to look at her. Tears started in my eyes again.

"Can we talk about it, sweetie?" she said softly. "I honestly didn't think the video would upset you this much."

I took a deep breath and said, "You betrayed my trust." It was one of the things I'd planned to say earlier. Only out loud it sounded stupid, like something a character would say in one of the eighteenth-century novels Miss West read to us in English last year. But it was too late to take it back. So I looked her dead in the eyes, like I'd meant to sound like I was about to challenge her to a duel.

"I know it probably feels like that, sweetie," she said, taking my hands in hers. Up close, her skin had a green tinge, the colour of an artichoke. Maybe the mask had permanently stained her skin. I hoped so. "I'm sorry I broke my promise. And that you've been teased at school. I'll email Miss Wilson about it right now if you like." I looked down. Miss Fizzy's fur twitched as my tears fell on it. "But honestly, Eva, you shouldn't feel ashamed. You've got so many people out there supporting you, cheering you on. Hundreds of thousands! It may seem awkward and embarrassing right now, but—"

"It's not my period that's embarrassing, Mum. It's you." She looked like I'd thrown a dart at her head. But I didn't care. Maybe I wanted to hurt her. Maybe I wanted her to feel how I did when Alfie played her video to my class. How I felt every time I read a nasty comment. Or watched one of their stupid videos.

"Okay, well, maybe I deserved that," she said, and a wave of guilt went over me. I swallowed. It should be *her* feeling bad, not me. "I know you're angry with me right now, Eva, but let's try to keep this in perspective—"

"You're not going to change my mind," I said. "I don't want to be on the channel any more. So you and Dad will have to figure out something without me." I chewed on a strand of my hair and waited for her to say something.

Mum sighed and bit the inside of her cheek. Then she said, "I'm sorry, Eva. Maybe I got this one wrong. I should have waited and got the okay from you before I uploaded the video. It was really silly of me." I rolled my eyes at the word *silly*. Like that could even describe any of it. "I should have thought about your classmates seeing it before you. But I was excited! We had such a great time yesterday. I wanted to share that with everyone. Most of our subscribers are other parents, and they want to hear about this stuff, you know. I think you sometimes forget what a positive influence the channel has on people's lives." She stroked my face and gently pulled the hair I was chewing out of my mouth. A tiny blob of spit went on her finger. "Do you think maybe you're overreacting just a tiny bit?"

"No," I said firmly. "I want you to delete the period video and I'm not being in any more videos ever again. You and Dad said ages ago that if I didn't want to do the channel any more, then you'd stop. Well, I want to stop. I want a normal life where private stuff about me doesn't get shared with the entire world! A life where people don't talk about my body on YouTube! If you want to carry on the channel, then change it to *All About Jen and Lars*. Share stuff about your own bodies and keep me out of it."

I felt kind of stupid saying that last bit about their bodies. So I squirmed out from underneath Miss Fizzy, grabbed my sketchbook, and ran upstairs. As I reached my bedroom door, Mum called my name. I turned and peered over the bannister. Her skin still looked slightly green from up here. But there was something else I could see in her face too. She knew I was serious.

8

GOOD MORNING

Upstairs, I lay on my bed and messaged Hallie, telling her what had happened. But she didn't reply. I heard Dad's car pull up and I held my breath, trying to listen to what Mum was telling him. But they must have been talking really quietly, and anyway he didn't come upstairs. I opened my sketchbook and carried on drawing the butterfly wings, adding swirly clouds and raindrops around them. A reply from Hallie flashed up on my phone:

Don't worry about it, Eva. Everyone feels weird about starting their period. I had to tell Mr Eliot about mine remember! 😵 It's only Alfie who thinks its funny. At least it's just your mum in the video. Personally I think the avocado costume one was way worse. xx

I sank further into my bed and watched the views counter go up and up. 500k. 550k. 600k. I wished I could stay in my bedroom for the rest of my life. The idea of getting abducted by aliens was weirdly appealing.

Later, Dad called, "Eva, can you come down and talk to us, please? I've made *æbleskiver*!" They were definitely taking what I'd said about ending the channel seriously if Dad had made *æbleskiver*. They're these Danish pancake balls, a bit like spherical doughnuts. Farmor made them whenever we went to stay at hers in Dragør. Dad only usually made them on special occasions, like Christmas and birthdays. And this one time when Denmark beat Sweden in the World Cup qualifiers. I guess they're good for when you've totally humiliated your daughter too.

I hid my sketchbook in the back of my wardrobe, then I slowly walked downstairs. My mouth watered as I smelled the warm, doughnut-y smell. Farmor's were nicer than Dad's because she put way more sugar in. We'd eat them on her patio looking out to the harbour. She'd tell me these Danish folk tales that always had some moral message in them that she'd make me guess. I'd always get it wrong. As I got older, I'd get it wrong on purpose, just to hear her laugh.

Dad smiled as I sat down at the table. "I'm sure there's a way we can sort this out." His voice sounded gentle and calm. It was like landing softly on the grass after sitting in the swing seat for too long. I had to block out what it was doing to my heart, because I didn't want to disappoint him, but I didn't want private stuff about me on YouTube either. Dad dipped an *æbleskive* into maple syrup and held it out to me, but I shook my head. No matter how good that little pancake ball looked, it was a bribe and I wasn't going to eat it. "We know you're upset right now, Eva," Dad said, putting the *æbleskive* on a plate and pushing it towards me. "But let me just read you some of the comments: *Love this video! So inspiring! Thank you for all the lovely recommendations! My daughter will love this! Thank you! Amazing mum!*" I felt his eyes on me, but I couldn't look up from the tablecloth. "*Love Eva so much! Love you, Jen.*"

I rubbed the tears caught in my eyelashes. "That's Alice_Sparkle1000," I said. "She puts the exact same comment every time. So, when are you taking it down?"

Dad took a deep breath. "Listen, Eva, I agree with you that Jen's period post was personal."

My cheeks flushed when Dad said the word "period". He was speaking in his serious-business voice. Like he did whenever he talked about the channel. My dad used

79

to be a commercial architect. He designed buildings and renovations for businesses and stuff. I loved going to his office because he let me draw at his gigantic desk, and there were old scale models of buildings I could play with. But a few years ago, the channel got too big for Mum to manage on her own. So, he quit his job and started working on the channel full-time. He stopped drawing buildings and started talking about things like "metadata" and "monetized content" and "optimizing revenue". Mum calls the channel a community; Dad calls it a business. Which I guess means I'm an employee. Only, employees are allowed to quit, so it technically makes me a hostage.

Since Dad quit his job, everything's felt more pressured. Like this experiment Mr Jacobs showed us once in science. He put an alarm clock inside a bell jar then used this machine called a vacuum pump to suck all the air out of it. I was afraid to watch in case the glass imploded. But it didn't. I guess that's how I feel sometimes. Like there's all this pressure on me but no one can see it because it's invisible. And no one on the outside can hear me either.

"So," I repeated, "when are you taking it down?"

Dad put an *æbleskive* in his mouth and gave Mum a look. She nodded at him. Clearly, they had rehearsed who was saying what.

"Eva, listen," Mum said. "We know you're unhappy about the period video. I messed up, okay. I'm sorry. I should have told you about it."

"You shouldn't have done it! Like you promised!"

Dad leaned forward and put his hand on my arm. "Hey, we appreciate you're growing up and from time to time we share things you find embarrassing. We get it. But this is all part of building the brand." The Brand was like the fourth member of our family. Most of the time, The Brand felt like the most important member of our family.

"I want you to stop the channel," I said, and pushed the *æbleskive* away from me.

"Okay, well…" Dad shifted his feet under the table and accidentally kicked me. I sighed and moved my feet under my chair. "The thing is," he carried on, "we had a pretty important phone call earlier." A smile flashed on his face for a split second then he went back to looking serious. "There's no easy way to say this. But, as I'm sure you know, Jen's period vlog has gone viral and we've been asked to go on television on Wednesday to talk about it."

It felt like he'd dropped a boulder on my chest. I couldn't breathe.

"You know the breakfast show, *Good Morning*?" Mum said. "They've invited us on! And we know this is the worst timing because you're still upset, sweetie. But this is an amazing opportunity. They have literally *millions* of viewers. It's what we've been waiting for!"

She clutched my hand as she carried on speaking. I listened, but it was like the room was plugged into Mr Jacobs's vacuum pump machine and it was sucking out all the air. I couldn't hear what she was saying. I couldn't even breathe.

"And naturally, they've invited you on too!" Mum said, unable to disguise the excitement in her voice. "It's totally up to you, Eva. We'd love you to come on with us. It would mean missing a day of school, but Lars and I can go on by ourselves. No pressure, okay. We want it to be a really positive interview. So…Eva? Say something, sweetie."

I squeezed my eyes shut to try and stop this from happening. Like, if I wished hard enough I could make all this disappear.

"Eva, please say something," Mum said. "It's *Good Morning*! We know you're not exactly going to be happy about it right now, but can you at least understand why we can't say no?"

I wanted to scream, but it felt like I was detached from my body. Their voices sounded far away. As though all this was happening to someone else. "No," was all I could think to say, then, "no," again. I'm not even sure if I said it out loud.

"It's unfortunate that this has come at a time when you're upset about Jen's vlog," Dad said. "We've talked about it and both agreed not to cross this kind of boundary again. It's your body, you get to have a say. But we hope you can see, this isn't about just this one vlog. This is about the whole channel. It wouldn't make financial sense to turn down this publicity. Our lifestyle costs a lot of money, Eva. The holidays, the visits to Farmor, the cars, saving for the future…"

I closed my eyes. I'd already heard it a million times. This speech was the reason I put on that stupid avocado costume. But it wasn't going to work. Not this time.

I stood up, scraping my chair against the floor. "If you talk about my period on TV, I will never speak to you again."

"Oh, Eva! Please don't say that," Mum said.

"Eva," Dad said. "You are sounding a little ridiculous."

"I don't care," I said. "I'm serious. If you speak about my period on that show, I will never speak to you again."

"Okay, well, that's up to you," Dad said. "But you know, the period vlog is the reason they want us on the show. Will you please sit down so we can talk about this?"

"What's the point? You're not even listening to me." I walked over to the stairs, deliberately knocking over a pile of washing on the bottom step.

"Eva, please don't be like this," Dad called after me. "There are millions of kids who dream of the kind of life you have."

"Well, adopt one of them and leave me off your stupid channel!"

I heard Mum start crying, but I was too angry to care. They were going to talk about my period in front of the entire country? My life was sinking into quicksand. And there was nothing I could grab hold of.

"Eva, please try to understand, sweetheart," Mum called. "We love you. We don't want you to be upset with us!"

"You're going to do it anyway, aren't you? No matter what I say." But I already knew the answer.

I ran upstairs, slammed my bedroom door and threw myself onto my bed. Then I let out a scream into my pillow. I turned over and hot tears slid down my face. They were never going to stop *All About Eva*. Everything I did would be captured by their cameras, and streamed for their subscribers. Now they were going on TV, the channel would grow faster than ever. They'd gain even more views, more subscribers. I was never going to escape. Not unless I did something drastic.

Only, it wasn't until a few days later I figured out what that could be.

9

CARYS

My first period lasted a total of three and a half days. But even when it was over there was no way I could forget about it. Because by Wednesday morning, Mum's video had been viewed over a million times. And today, it was going to be played on TV. The most humiliating video they'd ever made about me was the one to go viral. I'd even have preferred it to be the one with the swimsuit wedgie.

I slammed the front door behind me as I left for school, even though Mum and Dad had left for London ages ago. It was only half an hour to Paddington, but they had to be at the TV studio really early for some reason, so they'd taken the first train. I had thought about staying at home, but they'd said they'd be back by lunchtime. School would probably call them if I didn't show up anyway. Their interview would be around 9.30 a.m., when I was supposed to be doing PE. They'd said I should watch it on the *Good Morning* website at break or lunch. Only there was no way I was going to miss watching it live.

My phone beeped with a message from Mum. It was a selfie of her and Dad at the TV studio. There was a giant sign saying *Good Morning* behind them. They were both grinning into the camera, like they didn't even care how much pain I was in.

We love you ♥, it said. I tapped the message so she'd know I'd read it, then locked my phone without replying.

My nose was blocked up and my eyes stung in the wind. I don't know exactly how many times I'd begged them not to go. It was a lot. But it didn't make any difference. *This is a once-in-a-lifetime opportunity for* All About Eva*! It could put us up there with* The Carter-Youngs *and* TwoAgainstFour*. It's our chance to put The Brand out there! You've got to look at the bigger picture, Eva. How could we say no? You'll understand one day.*

Only, I didn't care about one day. I cared about today. When I had to share a classroom with Alfie Stevens.

Spud was sitting on the low wall at the bottom of his garden, waiting for me. He usually came bounding into the house. Maybe he'd heard me slam the front door. I hoped not. "You okay?" he asked.

"Can't get any worse, right?" I smiled, which for some reason made me want to cry again.

"Did you know," Spud said, jumping up next to me, "the average woman will have her period for thirty-eight years! By then, you'll probably feel better about this."

"I doubt it," I said.

"But someone like Alfie Stevens in thirty-eight years?" Spud carried on. "He'll still be a grade-A idiot. Even if Alfie was immortal, he'd still be an idiot! He'd just carry on being an idiot for ever." I don't know what it is about Spud, but sometimes all the dumb stuff he says is exactly the kind of stuff you need to hear. Not very often. But sometimes. He told me pointless facts, like an octopus has its mouth in its armpit and wombats have cube-shaped poo, all the way up the hill until I laughed. I'm not sure if they were even true, but Spud made me feel slightly better about being human that day. It's probably one of the nicest things he's done. And once he built a catapult in his garden that could – if you stood in exactly the right spot – fire marshmallows right into your mouth.

When I walked into form with Hallie and Gabi, Alfie and his friends immediately burst out laughing. I'd got used to the sound of people laughing at me over the past two days. In corridors, in the canteen, in lessons. Even when it was silent, I could still hear it inside my head. I was about to sit down when Hallie nudged me.

"Look."

There was something stuck on the Cool Wall underneath my name. A sanitary pad with red felt-tip scribbled on it. My stomach flipped. As I walked over to the Cool Wall I heard Gabi laugh. I looked at her and she turned it into a cough.

"Oh, very mature whoever did that!" Hallie said as I pulled down the sanitary pad. Little bits of pad got stuck underneath the staples. Whoever it was must have gone overboard with Miss Wilson's staple gun.

"I know it was you, Alfie." I said it like I didn't care. But if anyone looked closely, they'd have seen my hands were kind of trembling.

"It wasn't!" Alfie said, laughing. "Anyway, what you going to do, dust it for prints?"

"Alfie," Hallie said, "just because you *are* an idiot, doesn't mean you have to act like one every day."

A slow "Oooooh!" erupted from Alfie and his friends.

"Come on, Eva," Hallie said. "Let's get Miss Wilson."

"Really, Hals?" Gabi said, sitting down. "Can't we just ignore them?"

I didn't exactly want to show Miss Wilson the sanitary pad, but I expected Hallie to march out of the classroom anyway. I mean, she was on the student council. But she sat down.

Hallie's eyes went from mine to Gabi's then she said, "Yeah, probably best to ignore them." She smiled at me, then gave Alfie and his friends evils.

Just then, Miss Wilson walked in chirping, "Morning, everyone!" Her hair was tied up in a bandana the colour of a sunset.

I crumpled the sanitary pad into my blazer pocket. A girl with short, dark hair and black-rimmed glasses hovered by the classroom door, chewing her bottom lip.

"Come in, Carys!" Miss Wilson beckoned her inside. Her fingernails were bitten down really far. My mum would never let me do that. "Everyone, this is Carys Belfield. She's just moved to Hope Park Academy and Mr Andrews has chosen to put her in our form because he knows we're such a friendly bunch!" (I do not know where Mr Andrews got this information.) "Now, Carys, meet Hallie, our fantastic form captain."

Hallie stood up and beamed.

"Carys," Miss Wilson said, "grab a seat on Hallie's table and she'll show you around the school properly at lunchtime."

"Oh," Hallie said, "sorry, I can't, miss. I've got gym

practice. I have the finals coming up and Mrs Marshall said I could use the sports hall…"

"Okay," Miss Wilson said, smiling around the room, "who else would like to volunteer?"

There was an awkward silence. I looked around the classroom. Was no one going to put their hand up? Carys chewed her nails, like she wanted the paint-stained floor to swallow her up. I knew that feeling pretty well.

"I'll do it," I said, putting my arm in the air.

Everyone burst out laughing. That's when I realized the sanitary pad was attached to the bottom of my sleeve. I shoved it back in my pocket, feeling my cheeks blaze red. Carys's eyes flicked sympathetically to me.

"Great! Thank you, Eva," Miss Wilson said. "Take a seat, Carys. I'm sure Eva will do a wonderful job of showing you around and *everyone* in 8W will make you feel very welcome."

"Thanks," Carys whispered as I swapped seats with Gabi, so she was next to Hallie and Carys could sit next to me. "Nothing like a completely embarrassing experience to start a new school."

"Don't worry," I whispered. "I know everything there is to know about embarrassing experiences."

* * *

90

Later that morning, I was supposed to be in PE like everyone else in my class. But when your parents are about to go on TV, hitting shuttlecocks over a badminton net seems even more pointless than usual. So while everyone else got changed, I sat with my feet up in one of the toilet cubicles. I didn't expect anyone to notice, it's not like I'm good at sports or anything, and Mrs Marshall never takes a register when we play inside. Still, my heart was pounding as I heard everyone leave. I waited a full five minutes before I dared move. The cubicle door creaked as I opened it. The changing rooms were weirdly silent. I crept into the corner, moved a few coats and bags so I could sit down, then leaned against the wall and took out my phone. Mum had put the selfie she'd sent me on her Instagram stories.

Sooooooo excited!!! Getting ready for
@GoodMorning!!! Who's watching??!!
#GoodMorning #OMG #AllAboutEva
#periodwarrior #excited

I groaned, and heard it echo back at me around the room. My parents being on TV would make the channel ten times more popular. And my life at school would get ten times worse.

Suddenly, I heard, "Eva? You okay?" I jumped, and wiped away the tear that had just slid down my face.

"Carys?" She was still in her uniform. Was she skipping

PE on her first day? I'd been here since the start of Year Seven and I'd never dared do it before. Even when they made us do cross-country in practically a blizzard.

"I don't have any kit yet," Carys said. "Miss thingy told me to sit on the bench and watch. But I saw you weren't there and thought I'd check if you're okay." She walked past the rows of bags and coats and sat on the bench opposite me. "Have you been crying?"

I wiped my eyes again. "I'm okay." Only as soon as I said that another tear escaped.

"Hey, what's the matter?" Carys moved to sit beside me. "If it's that sanitary pad thing in form, honestly don't worry about it. Once, at my old school, I chewed a fountain pen and it exploded in my mouth." I let out a laugh. "It wouldn't wash off properly, so literally the whole day I looked like an ink-sucking vampire."

"Is that why you moved here?"

"Ha!" Carys smiled. "I wish! So, what's up?"

A message from Mum appeared on my phone:

Please don't be upset with us, Eva. It's exciting!!! We love you sweetie 😘 😘 😘

I swiped it away and swallowed the lump in my throat. "Any minute now, my parents will be on *Good Morning*."

"Oh, wow!" Carys said. "That is definitely a reason to skip badminton."

"To talk about me starting my period."

Carys's eyes widened and her glasses slipped down her nose. "What?"

"Yeah," I said. "They have a YouTube channel and my mum posted this video about it, and it's gone viral. Now my mum and dad are getting interviewed on TV and talking about it in front of the entire world. I don't normally skip PE. It's just, I want to see it before anyone else at school does."

Carys pushed her glasses back up and scraped her fringe sideways. "Sorry, Eva. I don't mean to be rude but I would be so mad if my parents were doing that! I mean, don't you mind?"

"Yeah, I do," I said. "I kind of begged them not to go on TV actually, but..." I let my words slide away into silence.

Carys licked her fingers and flattened down the bits of fringe that were sticking up. "That's really bad, Eva," she said. "Shall we just stay in here for ever?" Then she wrinkled her nose. "The only problem is the slight smell of armpits."

I smiled. I'd only known Carys for a couple of hours, but she seemed to just get it. She was the first person in forever to ask me if I minded this stuff. And the whole story of *All About Eva* came tumbling out. The non-stop filming, their "For-Eva" subscribers, the summer of "challenge videos", that stupid avocado costume. The never-ending scroll of comments and replies, the fake smiles, the teasing from Alfie, the comments in corridors, the dread any time a notification came up on my phone. The feeling I was sinking into quicksand.

"Woah," Carys said quietly after I'd finished. "I can understand why you're upset."

I blew my nose on some loo roll. "I think they're on after this ad break."

"In that case," Carys said, pulling an iPad out of her bag, "I think we need a bigger screen."

"Erm, Carys," I said, "you're not meant to bring those to school."

"Oh," she said, smiling. "Do the teachers check your bags here?"

"I don't think so."

Carys swiped the screen; its reflection glowed in her glasses. "Exactly." She fished around in her pockets then handed me an AirPod. "Now, do you know the code for the Wi-Fi or should I guess it?"

And that was it. The moment me and Carys became friends. Sitting next to each other in an echoey changing room, sharing AirPods and half a packet of pineapple Chewits she'd found in her pocket. Together, we watched my parents smile and laugh and talk about being part of the "period warrior movement" on TV. Throughout the entire interview, Carys held one hand over her mouth in shock, and squeezed my hand with the other. And for the first time in ages, I felt like someone was on my side of the screen.

10

"WE VLOGGED OUR DAUGHTER'S FIRST PERIOD"

I'd watched Mum and Dad's interview on *Good Morning* so many times over lunch, that by the end of school, I could practically quote it word for word. Mum's make-up was way heavier than usual, and they must have blow-dried Dad's hair or something because it was about thirty centimetres higher than it normally was. Spud was at Games Club, so I sat on the wall at the end of my drive and tapped the *play* icon. I didn't want to watch it again, but I couldn't help it. Like I had to keep checking it definitely happened.

"Welcome back!" Lisa the presenter says to the camera with a bleached-teeth smile. "Now, starting your period can be a tricky time in any girl's life, but imagine sharing it with millions of people online. That's exactly what our guests this morning have done. They are parent vloggers Jen and Lars Andersen and their video about their daughter Eva starting her period has gone viral. They are here to tell us all about it. Jen, Lars, welcome to *Good Morning!*"

Mum and Dad smile at exactly the same time and say, "Good morning!" They probably rehearsed it on the train.

Jeremy, the co-host, leans towards them and says, "Your channel is called *All About Eva* and you've shared everything about your daughter from toddler tantrums to birthday parties to spot outbreaks. So far your video about Eva's first period has had over a million views and the hashtag 'period warrior' is trending. In case you haven't seen it yet – here's a clip."

I sniffed, and felt cold air go up my nose, as they played the first bit of Mum's video. Thankfully, it stops before Mum holds up my unicorn pants.

"So," Lisa says, "you're established family vloggers and you've shared many things about Eva over the years." Mum and Dad smile and nod together, like synchronized swimmers. Lisa glances down at a card she's holding. "Eva's thirteen now. Quite a tricky age. What made you decide to share her first period with your subscribers?"

Dad squeezes Mum's hand. I only noticed it the third or fourth time I watched.

Mum smiles and says, "Lars and I always think very carefully before we post anything about Eva." I couldn't help snorting at that. "And, you know, Eva's a bit of a late starter, so I'd had this period gift box for a while! We had the most wonderful period party to celebrate this important milestone in Eva's life…"

"Yes," says Lisa, looking at the camera, her caramel-coloured hair glistening in the studio lights. "I think we have some photographs of the period party."

Photos of our living room covered in period-themed decorations come up on the screen and you can hear Mum's voice saying, "It was a really important moment in Eva's life, and in mine as her mother, and I wanted her to feel supported, and that I…*we*, sorry, Lars!" The camera cuts to her smiling at Dad. "We wanted to give Eva the message that periods aren't embarrassing, they're nothing shameful, and share that message with our subscribers."

Just then, Dad stretches out his leg and accidentally kicks the coffee table. He laughs and says, "Jen and I wanted to make reaching this milestone a positive and empowering experience, and use our platform to help empower other parents."

"And was it a positive experience?" Jeremy asks. "I mean, for Eva? Because we have had some comments that are quite critical on our Facebook page this morning.

No parent has the right to share this kind of thing online – that's from Audrey in Milton Keynes, and John in West Lothian says, *What a cruel thing to do to your daughter.* What do you say to those people, who think some things about our children should remain private?"

"Well," Dad says, "I would say that we're an open family. We talk frankly about these things at home, on and off camera. Our channel is an extension of that openness. Jen and I don't believe Eva should feel embarrassed about it."

I press *pause*, because I know what's coming up. This is the bit that hurts the most. I take a deep breath and get ready, like when you're about to rip a plaster off.

"It's important to say that we're careful about what we put on the channel. We make sure Eva is okay with it!" Mum's fake eyelashes flutter, like she knows what she just said is a total lie. But no one seems to notice. "We wouldn't film anything she was uncomfortable with. *All About Eva* is a really special channel. We have this enormous bank of amazing memories that we get to keep and share. And Eva's grateful she gets to live this fabulous life. If she was ever uncomfortable, then we'd stop filming." Every time I watched that, it felt like getting punched in the stomach.

"Yes," Lisa says, "Eva was invited to be here with us today, but she's at school, is that right?"

Dad smiles and nods. "School has to come first."

"Very sensible!" Jeremy says, and they all laugh. "So, Eva is thirteen. Isn't she just a little bit embarrassed that millions of people know she's started her period?"

"Everything is a little bit embarrassing when you're thirteen!" Dad says. "But she's used to it. Eva went viral before she even came out of the womb!" And all of them laugh again.

"Jen and Lars, thank you so much for talking to us..."

I stopped the video and flicked through the messages from Hallie and Jenna. Then I dropped my phone in my blazer pocket without replying. Inside my chest, a rain cloud was gathering, getting darker and heavier as I walked towards the house. By the time I reached the front door, it was ready to explode. I stormed through the door and ran upstairs without taking my shoes off. I could hear Farmor on speakerphone and Mum calling, "Eva!" as I shouted, "Leave me alone!" and slammed my bedroom door. I curled up on my bed with my shoes still on, staring up at the strings of fairy lights criss-crossing my ceiling, and waited.

A few minutes later, Mum's head poked around the door. "Hey, sweetie. Are you okay?" I glanced at her then looked back up at the ceiling. The smoky black eyes that looked nice on TV now made her resemble a badger.

She slowly walked over, like she was expecting a bomb to go off. I felt her sit down next to me on the bed. "So, you watched it?" I folded my arms and twisted my hands in so she couldn't take them.

"I know it's difficult for you to see right now, sweetie." I felt her hand rub my shoulder and I squirmed away. "You will be really proud of us one day. And proud of yourself."

"You lied about me," I said quietly.

"Sorry, what did you say, sweetie?"

"You lied," I repeated. "On TV. You said I was okay with it and you would stop filming if I was uncomfortable. Those were your exact words." Mum rubbed my shoulder again and I pushed her hand off, willing my eyes not to let out any more tears.

"Eva, as your parents, sometimes we have to make decisions about what's the best thing to say in certain situations. Dealing with the media is like juggling fire. Say one wrong word and that's it, total disaster. I'm sorry you're upset. I feel awful. But what could I say? We were on live TV." She squeezed my arm, then got up. "I am sorry. I hope you know we do all of this for you."

"Yeah, right," I whispered. I blinked and a tear rolled down my face. I looked over to see if Mum had noticed, but she'd already turned around by then.

My phone vibrated for the millionth time, and Carys's name flashed up.

You okay? What did they say??

I'd ignored everyone else. Messages, tags, screenshots, all the clips being shared. I don't know, maybe I thought if I ignored them I could pretend this wasn't really happening. The only one I'd replied to so far was the picture Spud sent me of his head Photoshopped onto King Charles I's body. I wiped my eyes and replied to Carys.

The usual stuff they always say. Like it's not a big deal.

Carys replied: Talking about you on TV is a big deal. ♥ Hope you're okay.

My phone buzzed with another message from her:

So glad you volunteered as my class buddy btw ☺

I replied: Me too ☺

Dad's voice came up the stairs. "EVA! Farmor wants to speak to you!"

I threw my feet over the side of my bed and went out to the landing. Dad was at the bottom of the stairs, holding out his phone. I ran down, grabbed it out of his hand then went back up to my room and closed the door.

Hearing Farmor's voice say hello was enough to make my eyes watery again. I tried my best to sound like I was okay. But holding tears back made my nose sting, and Farmor asked if I had a cold.

"Did you watch their interview on TV?" I asked.

Farmor was quiet for a moment. "Yes, your dad sent it to me. Did you know it's only four weeks now until you're coming over! I'm hoping it won't be blowing a gale by then."

"So what did you think? About the interview?" The line went quiet so I said, "Farmor?" to check she was still there.

"I think your mum and dad are very busy with the channel. It must be getting very popular. And I think *you* are wonderful. You know what else I watched today? A porpoise!" I smiled, leaned back against my pillows and listened to my grandma's voice. I could hear gulls in the background. It was like being carried all the way across the ocean and swaddled in her arms. I could feel the prickly softness of her woollen cardigan, her breath on my hair, the smell of *grønkål* soup on the stove. And I was that other Eva again. Not the one everyone was laughing at. Or the one Mum and Dad lied about on TV. The real one.

11

NOPE

The next day after school, Hallie and Gabi went straight to the sports hall for gymnastics practice, so Carys and I walked to the lockers together. On the way, practically everyone I walked past said, "Happy first period, Eva!" I wondered how long it would take to save up for a face transplant.

"I still cannot believe how many people watch this stuff," Carys said, scrolling through the *All About Eva* videos. "Eighty thousand people watched you get a filling!"

"I know." I sighed. "The good old days."

Carys laughed. "So, how many views has the period one had now?"

I refreshed the page. "Two point eight million."

Carys whistled. "Periods are a lot more popular than I realized."

"It's got comments from people in Malaysia, the Philippines, Uruguay!" I said, scrolling. "I mean, where even is that?" I shoved my phone in my pocket and sighed. "I wish I could just delete it."

"You know, you could…" Carys said, then she stopped, like she'd changed her mind. Or maybe she'd clocked Jenna running towards us.

"Eva!" Jenna called. "Did you see my TikTok?"

I shook my head and she handed me her phone. I tapped *play* and immediately the words Period Positivity!!! Jenna A!!! flashed up on the screen. It cut to a jar stuffed full of tampons and then to Jenna doing a headstand. 3 reasons I love my period!!! Number 1!!! You can finally join in with girl talk!!! The video cut to Jenna throwing tampons around her bedroom. The words: Number 2!!! It's natural!!! Number 3!! You can still work out!!! popped up as Jenna did a headstand.

"So, what do you think?" she asked, gazing at me.

"It's really, erm, good," I said.

Then she skipped off shouting, "Anyway, Eva likes it!" to her friends.

Carys smiled. "My friends at St Aug's were into doing stuff like that."

"St Augustine's is your old school?" I could hardly believe she hadn't mentioned it before. St Augustine's is a private school outside town that looks exactly like Hogwarts. People at school sometimes ask why I don't go there because they assume my parents are millionaires. They're not. Anyway, I doubt I would pass the exam to get in.

Carys cleaned her glasses on her sleeve. "You're wondering why I left St Augustine's, right?"

"Kind of," I said, closing my locker and trying to ignore the gigantic avocado engraving. "I mean, don't get me wrong. This school is pretty nice…" As I said that a Year Ten boy walked past and spat into a bin.

We both laughed and Carys didn't say anything else about St Aug's.

I pulled my gloves on as we walked outside and started heading down the hill. Carys kept her eyes on the pavement.

"Sorry, I didn't mean to be nosy," I said. "You don't have to tell me why you left."

She bit her fingernails then said, "There were some people bullying me. My parents wanted me to have a fresh start here, so…don't tell anyone, okay?"

"Sure," I said. "I won't say anything."

Carys linked her arm through mine and I felt this tiny fizz of excitement that she was my friend, like when school announces a snow day. "If anyone asks, say I was homeschooled but my parents got sick of me." We reached the bottom of the hill and Carys stopped. "Want to hang out for a bit? I don't feel like going home yet."

"Me neither." I smiled. "Want to walk into town and get a milkshake or something?"

"Hmm," Carys said. "I was thinking of somewhere more peaceful."

We'd been walking across fields and down little country lanes for about fifteen minutes when we arrived at a brook. It was surrounded by beech trees. Little clusters of brown leaves were skating across the water in the breeze. On our side of the brook, the edges were frozen, and little twigs and stones were encased in ice. I poked it with a stick and watched the ice break into shards, like spindles.

"Come on!" Carys said, jetéing like a ballerina onto a large stepping stone. She flung her school bag onto the bank on the other side, then carefully placed her feet on protruding stones until she had crossed the stream.

"Is it slippy?" I asked, carefully placing my foot on the first stone.

"Nope," Carys said, stretching her arms up towards the clouds and pirouetting. "It's glorious!"

I tried to place my feet in the exact spots Carys had trodden on, but my shoes were completely soaked by the time I got to the grassy bank.

"So, the water is kind of freezing," I said, feeling my teeth start to chatter.

"Here." Carys handed me her scarf then lay on the grass, gazing up at the sky. "It's been ages since I watched the clouds."

I checked to see if the grass was dry, then sat down and wrapped Carys's scarf around me.

"My mum's going to kill me for not going straight home," I said, as my phone glowed with a missed call from her. I was supposed to be helping make dinner. They were being sponsored by this new recipe box called Box of Yum. I thought about Dad setting up the camera, ready to record as soon as I walked through the door. I followed Carys's gaze up to the wispy clouds forming whirlpools of grey and white. Patterns you could lose yourself in.

"Want to head back?" Carys said, leaning up on her elbow.

I dropped my phone into my bag, pulled out my sketchbook and fished around in my pocket for a pencil. Then I lay back on the grass, gazed up at the clouds and said, "Nope."

12

LUCKY

It was dark by the time I got home, but my parents hadn't called out a search party. Or even recorded a vlog appealing for information, which was more like them. I had about a thousand missed calls from them though.

"Finally!" Dad said as I opened the door. "Where have you been? We've been worried sick." He didn't have the camera on, so he might have been telling the truth.

"I was at the brook," I said, casually taking off my coat.

"At the brook?" Dad said. "What's that supposed to mean?"

"It's like a small river," I said, pulling off my muddy shoes.

"I know what it means, thank you," Dad said. "Why were you at the brook when you're supposed to come straight home? It's almost five-thirty! It's dark! We had no idea where you were."

I shrugged. "Guess I needed some fresh air." I walked past Mum, whose face looked even more gobsmacked than Dad's, and headed upstairs. I had this prickly fear on my skin, like they were both about to shout at me. But I had this other feeling too. I mean, I know it was a small thing. Going to the brook after school isn't exactly the Roundhead rebellion or whatever it was Mrs Peters was going on about today in history. But it was the first time I'd ever done what I wanted, not gone straight home to record content or whatever. And it felt kind of good.

I left my door open a tiny bit so I could hear what Mum and Dad were saying. I'd messed up their plan of filming us making the Box of Yum live. Dad wanted to show me a new homework app, but they weren't sure I was in the right mood. Mum said she'd try to get me to play a Virtual Escape Room game after dinner, so at least they'd have some "fun" content for Sunday's vlog.

I leaned against my bedroom wall and flicked through the missed calls and messages on my phone.

There was one from Hallie:

You okay? Where are you? Your mum just called me!!

I had the same kind of message from Spud, only his said:

Jen's blowing a gasket.

They'd phoned my friends? Was it in their Daily Goals to completely humiliate me or something? I sent a message to Hallie explaining what happened, and a thumbs up to Spud. Then I heard footsteps on the stairs.

"Hey, sweetie," Mum said as she opened the door. "Lars was just worried about you. You weren't answering your phone." She perched on the edge of my bed. I flicked my eyes up to make sure she wasn't filming. "So…were you with some friends? Hallie didn't seem to know where you were."

I shrugged. "Just a new friend from school."

"A boy?"

"No!" I felt my cheeks redden and I pulled my knees up closer to my body. I didn't want to tell her about Carys, but I didn't want her filming a vlog called *Has Eva Got a Crush??!!* or something either. I sighed. "Her name's Carys. She's just moved to our school. I'm her buddy for the week. I'm supposed to be showing her around."

"And Carys wanted to see the brook?"

I sighed again, even louder. "I wanted some time to myself, and to avoid getting a camera shoved in my face, okay?"

Mum moved back, like she'd been blasted with cold air. "Okay, sweetie, that's fine. But you need to let us know, okay. What were you doing at the brook?"

"You don't need to interrogate me," I said. "You're not in *Justice Force* any more."

Justice Force was this TV show Mum was in when she was younger. It was about this detective called Justice Force, who solves impossible-seeming crimes from the past. Mum played the part of Stephanie Knowles, the lawyer in season two. But she was killed by a gunman after only four episodes. All these years later, Mum's still annoyed about it. They only showed her face in that episode for a total of eight seconds – she timed it. She didn't get another TV show after that and she hates anyone bringing it up. The same way she hates anyone knowing her real name is Rainbow. She changed it when she was eighteen – she has a special certificate from the government. All those years ago, years before they started the blog, Mum rebranded herself. It wasn't even Mum who told me, it was Dad. And he said Uncle Gareth's real name is Garfunkel, but I've never been sure if he was joking about that or not.

"Okay, Eva," Mum said, standing up. "You don't need to be hurtful. We were worried about you, that's all."

"Worried about the channel," I said.

Mum pursed her lips. "You know that's not true. We care about you, Eva. You're our world! It's just, the channel is getting a lot of attention at the moment. Your dad and

I have to maximize it. And yes, that means new content. We work hard to give you this life, Eva. It's taken us years to build the channel to this level. You can have anything you want, you know that, don't you? All we need is a little cooperation."

"A little humiliation, you mean," I mumbled.

"What, sweetheart?" Mum said, but I'm pretty sure she heard me.

"Nothing," I said, and I did the smile she knows is my fake one.

Mum looked really upset as she closed the door.

And if I said I didn't feel good at that exact moment, I'd probably be lying.

When I came downstairs the next morning, Mum and Dad were celebrating. They'd had a call from a national newspaper asking them to write a weekly parenting column. It would start the next weekend. I fake-smiled in between gulps of vitamin-enriched orange juice, and listened to Mum's squeals of excitement as she spoke into the camera about it. I took a bite of toast and pretended to have a coughing fit, so Mum kept having to re-record her monologue. Eventually, Dad told me to go to school early if I couldn't stop ruining the video. I grabbed my things and headed out without saying goodbye.

It would have been a more dramatic exit if I hadn't left my books for Languages Club on the kitchen table. Dad ran barefoot down the drive to hand them to me.

"Hey, have a good day, kiddo," he said, or at least I think that's what he said. I can never be one hundred per cent sure when he speaks in Danish. I have Languages Club every Friday lunchtime. None of the teachers at my school speak Danish, so me and a few other people who are supposed to be bilingual have to go to Madame Chapelle's classroom. It's the one with loads of computers at the back. We play games and watch videos in whatever language we're supposed to be learning until the bell goes. Madame Chapelle speaks loads of languages, but not Danish and not Arabic either. Spud's friend Rami has to learn that. It looks way harder than Danish. Madame Chapelle sits at her desk reading French magazines and sometimes speaks to Clarissa in Mandarin. It means I have to take extra books on Fridays, but it's not too bad. Madame Chapelle always gives us biscuits at the end. The worst bit is Dad asking me about the new vocabulary I've learned, which I've usually forgotten by the time I get home.

There was no sign of Spud, so I sat on the wall at the bottom of his drive and put my headphones on. I clicked on *All About Eva*. A new Update Vlog appeared called *Letting Go*. It had been posted late last night. I tapped *play*.

"*Hi guys! Welcome back to our channel!*" Mum said. "*So, I had a little fight with Eva.*" She bit her bottom lip. "*And I'm sharing because I'm seeing so many people in the vlogging community right now making out their lives are perfect, and I don't want us to be like that, you know?*"

I jumped as Spud sprang out from behind the wall. "Spud!" I shouted, almost dropping my phone.

"First rule of ju-jitsu, Eva," he said, grinning. "Always be prepared for attack."

I pulled my headphones off. "You don't do ju-jitsu."

"You're wrong," Spud said. "I'm a ju-jitsu master."

"Spud, we both know you're only the master of those weird insect-plant things you keep in your bedroom."

Spud rolled his eyes. "You mean *Dionaea muscipula*. Venus flytraps to the novice."

"Yeah, and Venus flytraps are probably better at ju-jitsu than you. In fact, *I'm* probably better at ju-jitsu than you." I stood up and knocked his water bottle out of his hands then ran up the hill. By the time we'd reached the top, Spud had stood on the back of my shoe about six times and I'd hit him with my lunch bag about the same. We hadn't played a dumb game like this for ages. I stood by the postbox watching him, a little out of breath from laughing, unsure if reaching this spot meant we were quits or if he was about to whack me around the head with his pencil case. He flared his nostrils.

"Eva!" Hallie called.

Spud smiled. "Lucky escape, Andersen." And he headed across the road.

As I caught up with Hallie and Gabi, I spotted Carys heading up the hill. "Hey, let's wait for Carys." Hallie had her braids tied up in two buns, but as I said it looked nice, she and Gabi exchanged a look.

"Listen, Eva. We're not sure about Carys hanging around with us," Hallie said.

I stared at her. "What? Why not?"

They looked at each other again and it was obvious they had already decided this without me. Gabi said, "My cousin goes to her old school and she said Carys is trouble."

"What?" I looked at Hallie. "And you just believe that?"

Hallie shrugged. "Gabi's cousin was in her class, and...I don't really know Carys."

"Exactly," I replied. "So what about giving her a chance? Miss Wilson assigned me as her buddy. I can't just ditch her."

"She's already got you into trouble," Gabi said, her words forming little clouds in the cold air. "You know. With your mum. I'm sure Miss Wilson would understand."

I tried to meet Hallie's eye, but she looked at the pavement. "I told Gabi about your mum calling me."

I didn't plan to say anything mean, but my eyes started stinging. I felt stupid. And maybe I was a bit sick of Gabi too. "Well, I've been getting to know Carys and I like her," I said. "Maybe Gabi's cousin is the one who isn't very nice."

"Eva!" Hallie said, as though I'd dumped a bucket of cold water over her head.

"I'm just saying, you don't even know Carys yet. Why are you siding with Gabi all the time! What about what I think? I'm supposed to be your best friend, not Gabi Galloney." I don't know why I said Gabi's surname like that. Maybe because I knew she didn't like it.

Gabi looked at Hallie and raised her eyebrows. "See?"

"Eva," Hallie said. "Gabi thinks you don't like her."

It wasn't a question, which is one of the reasons I didn't answer her. The other reason is that it was basically true. And Hallie could always tell when I was lying. Anyway, Gabi was giving me her trademark dead-eye look, which made me want to hit her in the face with my lunch bag. Flask-side up.

"I'm going," Gabi said. "You wait with her if you want."

Hallie looked at me for a second. "I'll see you in form, okay?" And she followed Gabi towards school, leaving me standing there on the pavement.

A lump formed in my throat as I watched them walk off together. I'd known Hallie since primary school. Her mum used to make us fried plantain on a special plate that we could share. We'd mix our squash together at break times and call it magic potion. We used to write our names like a crossword puzzle. I probably should have run after them and said sorry. But, at that exact moment, I would rather have gouged out my own eyeballs than apologize to Gabi Galloney.

"Hey," Carys said, out of breath. "Thanks for waiting. Shall we catch Hallie and Gabi up?"

"No, they have some student council thing to do," I said. I didn't want to tell her about what Gabi had said. Knowing Gabi, she was probably making it up. Or maybe it was Gabi's cousin who had been bullying Carys.

"Are you okay?" Carys asked, watching me swipe my phone. "Did your parents post something else?"

"You want to see?" I asked, and she nodded.

I tapped *play* and handed Carys my phone. "*So, I had a little fight with Eva…*" Mum's voice started. I rolled my

118

eyes and tried not to listen. But it was kind of impossible.

"...*I don't want us to be like that, you know? I think it's important to share the stuff that goes wrong too. Those days you feel kind of rubbish. I've never claimed to be the perfect mum, but as you guys know, Eva and I are really, really close. But lately, we haven't truly been connecting as well as we usually do. Maybe it's her hormones going crazy, but... I'm going to be honest, guys, tonight she slammed her bedroom door. As you know, that doesn't sound like our Eva. She's usually so...chill! Lars says she needs us to back away sometimes. You know Lars, he is the voice of reason! But I don't know...*" Mum fans her hands in front of her face then wipes her eyes.

I almost felt sorry for her at this point. Almost.

"*So, if you guys have any tips for connecting better during the teenager years, do drop them in the comments. We have a big announcement tomorrow morning, so don't miss it! You can subscribe to our family updates by clicking on the link right here...*"

"Well, that was kind of weird," Carys said. "What's the big announcement?"

I sighed. "They're getting a newspaper column. About me, I guess."

"Oh God, I would literally die if my parents did that about me." She looked at me and added, "Sorry."

"It's okay."

I stopped the video before another one automatically started playing, and shoved my phone in my pocket. Once we watched a video in geography about coastal erosion, where this person's entire house slid off a cliff. I kind of felt like that. Like my life was slowly sliding into the sea and there was nothing I could do about it.

13

TROLLS

In form, Hallie barely looked at me. I wanted to talk to her, but Miss Wilson made us do silent reading, and even though I willed Hallie to look over, her eyes didn't budge from her book. I tried to speak to her when the bell went, but Miss Wilson asked me to stay behind. Her hands were covered in dry paint splotches that she picked at while she was talking to me.

"So, Eva!" she said. "Your Cool Wall spot is still blank." I bit my lip. "You know, I could choose one of the many beautiful drawings you've done for me. But the whole idea, Eva, is you display something that *you* are proud of." Miss Wilson smiled at me. "I know you have a busy schedule, Eva. You can talk to me, you know. If things are getting a bit too much."

"I'm okay," I said, trying to avoid her eyes.

Teachers have a way of telling when you're lying. They must get special training. Miss Wilson looked at me for a moment. "All right. Promise me you'll try to find something for the wall."

I nodded and she let me go.

In science, Mr Jacobs put on a video about electromagnetism. I moved my stool next to Hallie's, but Gabi deliberately moved in between us, so I couldn't speak to her. Anyway, it seemed like she was really into the electromagnetism video.

I tried to speak to her again at the start of lunch, but she said, "Sorry, I've got to go. Mrs Marshall said she'd watch my routine. Anyway, you've got Languages Club, haven't you?" And she left without looking back even once. Carys went for lunch with Jenna and Nadira, and I headed to the languages lab.

"Saved you a seat," Rami said when I got there, taking his pencil case off the chair next to his.

"Thanks." I sat down and logged on to *Hej Danmark!* – this Danish website with pronunciation videos, tourism information and a pretend chat room where you have conversations with computer characters. I doubted it got many hits.

I'd selected a video about Copenhagen when Rami

started tapping me on the arm. I pulled one side of my headphones off.

"Saw you've been hanging around with the new girl." He glanced over at Madame Chapelle, who was reading a magazine at her desk, then he whispered, "Did you hear she lied about being homeschooled? And that she really moved here from St Augustine's?"

Carys had told me not to say anything about her getting bullied. I guess people had found out anyway. I shrugged one shoulder. "She told me, but…"

"Pretty bad, hey?" Rami raised his eyebrows. "Apparently one of her friends told the head teacher. Soooo bad!"

"Told? About what?" I had no idea what he was talking about.

"Cutting out the school Wi-Fi!" He looked over at Madame Chapelle again to make sure she wasn't listening. "Carys hacked into it somehow and shut the whole thing down! She told you though, right? And that's not even the worst thing!" Rami blew out his breath.

"I don't think that's what happened, Rami," I said and turned back to my computer screen. "Someone's making stuff up."

"Okay," Rami said, putting his headphones back on. "But Gabi said her cousin goes to St Augustine's and she was in Carys's class."

"I wouldn't believe everything Gabi Galloney says."

"I don't," he said. "But Becca Matthews's friend goes there and she said the same thing. She's deputy head of the student council." Rami went back to watching *The Simpsons* with Arabic subtitles.

I stared at my screen. Becca Matthews said it? Why would she make something up about Carys?

And, she wasn't the only one. By the end of lunchtime, when Madame Chapelle was handing out Oreos, I'd already seen three group chats, all talking about the same thing. According to Amber, this girl in our year, Carys set up a new signature on her science teacher's email that said, *To infinity and beyond!* and changed his profile picture to Buzz Lightyear. Luca said Carys had cut out the school Wi-Fi during an ICT lesson, and everyone had lost their work. Callum said she'd hacked into the St Augustine's website and changed photos of teachers on their *Meet the Team* page to ogres from the *Trolls* movie.

I messaged: Someone must have made that up.

But then this boy in 8T called Charley Rhodes sent an old screenshot his brother had been sent. And there it was. The St Augustine's *Meet the Team* page. *Mr Denham, Head Teacher*, it said, and underneath was a picture of Prince Gristle. And underneath that about a million laughing emojis from Charley Rhodes. I couldn't believe Carys had done it. And I couldn't think about anything else.

Carys was waiting for me in the corridor outside English, playing a game on her phone. I tapped her arm and she took out her AirPods.

"Hey, how was Languages Club?"

"*Fint, tak!*" I said, which means "Good, thanks!" Or at least I think it does. I waited until the corridor was empty. "Hey, can I talk to you about something?"

"Sure," Carys said. "I think I know what this is about."

"It's just…I heard a few things—"

"About the hacking, right?" She twisted a little transparent stake in her earlobe.

"You don't have to tell me, it's just…we're friends, right?"

Carys sighed and leaned her head back against the wall, narrowly missing a 3D picture of Jane Austen. "Do you still want to be friends if it's true?"

"Yes!" I said. "So, is it true?"

"Not all of it." Carys shrugged. "I'm sorry I didn't tell you. I don't know what you've heard, but some things have been exaggerated. I disabled the Wi-Fi a few times. I changed a few photos on the school website, made a few videos."

"I didn't realize you could do that stuff. It's amazing!"

Carys smiled. "It was supposed to be a joke. It just got

kind of out of hand. I was figuring out what I could do with the advanced coding I'd been learning, see what I could get away with, but…the school didn't find it very funny. Neither did my parents. I got kicked out when they found out it was me. If I mess up again, my dad's sending me to live with my Aunt Edna. She's a hundred years old and lives on this freezing cold Scottish island in the middle of nowhere. With no broadband."

"I'm sorry they kicked you out," I said, checking the corridor for Miss West. "They should have given you a second chance."

Carys bit her lip. "I'd already had a few chances. Stupidly I trusted one of my friends not to tell anyone."

"One of your friends told?"

"Her older sister lost some of her A-level work so…" Carys glanced behind her. We both spotted Miss West at exactly the same time. "Maybe we should talk about this later."

I walked into the classroom with Carys, and Hallie shot me a look that said, *I told you so.* She must have heard the rumours. I smiled, but she looked away. I wondered if I should just apologize to Gabi, even if I didn't mean it. Gabi looked over and I smiled at her, but she squinted sarcastically at me. So, I decided that actually, I'd rather watch Mr Jacobs's electromagnetism film every day for the rest of my life than say another word to Gabi Galloney. I just hoped I wouldn't lose Hallie over it.

That night, Mum and Dad were looking at takeaway menus on the iPad, trying to decide between aubergine burgers or black-bean noodles. I was on the sofa with my knees up scrolling through the group chats about Carys. She'd said she'd made videos too, but no one had mentioned those. I wondered if it was rude to ask her.

I jumped as Dad nudged my leg with his foot. He had the camera pointing at me. "So, what'll it be, Eva? You want to go for the noodles?"

I dropped my phone face down on the sofa. "Sure," I said, fake-smiling. If I couldn't stop them filming me, maybe I could sabotage it. "I mean, they can't give me diarrhoea every time, right?"

"Eva!" Mum said. "They did not give you diarrhoea!"

I really wanted to laugh but I held it in. "Okay, noodles then. Just tell them not to put any of those weird yellow things in mine. They do not taste nice!" I added my own sick noise sound effect.

"I don't even know what you're talking about, Eva!" Mum looked shocked, like I'd sworn or something.

Dad tutted. "Eva's been in this mood all week. And it's

127

getting noticeably worse." He nudged me again. "Maybe I should make *brunkål* instead of getting takeaway, huh?"

Brunkål is Danish for "brown cabbage". That gave me an idea. "*Yes, brunkål would be great!*" I said, in my best Danish.

Dad smiled for a second, then he realized what I was doing. "Eva, speak in English when we're filming, please."

"*But, Dad!*" I said in Danish. "*You said yourself I need more practice!*" I told them all about my day and the beautiful city of Copenhagen in the best Danish I could manage, which probably wasn't very good. But it was definitely working – Mum looked horrified.

"Eva, you don't have to ruin the vlog!" she said. "How are we supposed to…"

"Don't worry," Dad said. "Carry on! I can add English subtitles. It might get us some new Danish subscribers!"

It was enough to make me stop.

"Whatever. I don't care." I grabbed my phone and went up to my room, my face feeling hot with embarrassment. I heard them giggling as I slammed my door, just lightly enough to not get into trouble.

I lay on my bed and scrolled through the stuff about Carys again. Then I went onto the *All About Eva* page. Any time I read a bad comment, I took a screenshot. Mum always said negative comments were from rival family vloggers, jealous of us or something. I honestly used to believe her. I tapped on the screenshots I'd taken and sent them to Carys.

Michaela188: This is a disgusting thing to do.

Kelly_Sandra: Feel sorry for your daughter.

Hennessey: Disgraceful. Why would you share something like that?

SparkleyAlice: OMG is nothing private any more?

UFCC: Fame hungry.

OnlyBuzzin: i hope you get tape worm.

Carys replied: What is that?

I sent her the link, then wrote: Fan mail 😮

It was a few minutes before Carys messaged back.

Sorry. Watched the period vlog again. REAL bad the second time.

I replied: IKR. I asked them to delete it, but it's on 3.5m views. No way they'll take it down.

Carys wrote: OMG they should take it down. It sucks! Your period, your rules! I feel so bad for you, Eva ♥ ♥ ♥

I sent her the smiling emoji, and put my phone down. The fairy lights that Mum had strung up all over my ceiling twinkled above me like fake stars. Carys was right. It was *my* period. And it was *my* life. But my parents didn't seem to care about that.

* * *

The next day, I was lying on my bed, doodling, thinking about what Carys had done at St Augustine's, when I heard a tap on my bedroom door.

"Eva, you HAVE to see this!" Mum came in without waiting for me to say she could. Dad was behind her, filming. I quickly closed my sketchbook. "Look what I just found!" She held up a book that said:

The Top Secret Diary of
Rainbow Jennifer Jones
1987
READ THIS AND DIE GARFACE!!!!!

I wanted to laugh, only because of what she'd called Uncle Gareth. But I said, "Great!" sarcastically, and hoped they'd get the hint to leave me alone. They didn't.

"Lars has been screaming with laughter," Mum said, a huge smile on her face.

"I didn't hear anything," I said. "Anyway, I don't want you filming in my bedroom."

Dad kept the camera pointing at me. "Oh, Eva, come on. This is Jen's diary from when she was your age! It's funny! Want to hear some of it?"

"Not if you're filming," I said, although Mum was already clearing her throat. I rolled over so I was facing the window. "I hope there's nothing gross about you and Dad in there!"

Mum laughed. "Eva! I was thirteen. I hadn't even met Lars then!"

"Thank God for that."

"So, this is from 8th June 1987," Mum read. "*Mum ALWAYS has a go at me for EVERYTHING! She's confiscated my cassette player for TWENTY-FOUR HOURS!!! because I accidentally played it too loud a COUPLE of times. She must be the only person on the planet unable to appreciate the music of Kim Wilde. Anyway, she forgot about my Walkman so I can still listen to my tapes! HA HA! I've told her to call me Jennifer a million times, but she STILL calls me Rainbow!!! She knows I hate it. Why can't she respect my wishes and call me JENNIFER!!!? I can't wait until I'm a famous actress called JENNIFER JONES and then she will have to stop calling me Rainbow. I practised my autograph loads of times today. Who knows when I'll get discovered! In other news, Garface has started wearing Dad's aftershave!! He's eleven! He doesn't even have stubble and it STINKS.*"

Mum collapsed onto my bed giggling. I curled up my legs so she didn't touch me.

"Oh my goodness!" she said, wiping tears of laughter from her eyes. "Your poor granny. What a brat I was!"

"Yeah, poor Granny," I said seriously, and Mum howled with laughter again.

"Oh, Eva!" Mum said, hugging me. I kept my body rigid, like a plank, and eventually she got the message and stopped. "It's so tough being thirteen, isn't it?"

I knew she was trying to make friends, but if she wanted to make friends that badly, Dad wouldn't be in here filming it. And she wouldn't be crying with laughter.

"So," Mum said, scraping my hair back. "What do you think of your mum at thirteen?"

"Annoying."

Mum laughed, and kissed me on the head. I wiped it off straight away. She laughed again but I didn't join in, and it was awkward for a moment.

"I found growing up tough, you know," she said. "I didn't always agree with what your granny did. But now, I can see that actually, she always had my best interests at heart."

I sat up. "Did Granny announce your first period to a worldwide audience?"

"No," Mum said. "But she did make me share a bathroom with your Uncle Gareth."

I rolled my eyes. "Like that's even the same. If you're

trying to say I'm a brat because I don't want my life broadcast to the entire planet then fine, I'm a brat."

Mum looked at Dad, confused, like an actor who'd forgotten their lines. Dad put the camera down. "Eva, you do understand we can't stop making new content right now?" he said. "Especially with our newspaper column going live next weekend. It wouldn't make sense."

"Right," I said. "It wouldn't make sense." Because what was the point in saying anything else?

"Want to play a Virtual Escape Room later?" Mum asked, like we hadn't even had this conversation.

I shook my head and waited for the door to close before I got my sketchbook out again.

So what if Granny confiscated Mum's "cassette player" a million years ago? Like that proved anything. I didn't feel sorry for her, if that's what she'd wanted. If Mum knew what it felt like to not be understood by Granny, why couldn't she at least *try* to see what she was doing to me?

I unlocked my phone and looked again at the screenshot Charley had sent of the St Augustine's *Meet the Team* page. It was hard to believe Carys had done this. My *friend* had done this! And she'd almost got away with it. If she hadn't told her friend, no one would have found out it was her. If only she'd kept it a secret. A proper secret, from everyone. She would have got away with it.

I knew what I was thinking was bad. I had this cold feeling in my stomach, like when I'd forgotten to do my science homework. But I was excited too. Like, maybe I'd figured out a way to finally get my life back.

I picked up my phone and clicked on Carys's name.

Feel like helping me with something big? I wrote, and tapped *send* before I could change my mind.

Carys: Sure. What?

I hesitated for a few moments before I replied:

Hacking All About Eva.

14

DON'T LEAVE A TRAIL

The next morning, I woke up to Mum's voice shouting, "Lars! Can you check this article? I want to send it today."

Followed by, "Just a sec!" and Dad's footsteps going down the stairs. I opened my door and listened carefully as Dad read Mum's article aloud:

"Introducing our new columnists, Lars and Jen Andersen, founders of the popular parenting vlog All About Eva. *They produce twice-weekly YouTube videos sharing their parenting highs and lows featuring their thirteen-year-old daughter, Eva. In this brand-new column, they bring us both sides of the parenting puzzle."*

"It sounds great!" he said. "Perfect! And I love that headline: *When your little girl grows up...and goes rogue!*" His laughter travelled up the stairs. "It sounds just like Eva!"

I don't know why I was surprised they were making me out to be some kind of major idiot.

"And what about this for an opening?" Mum said. "*Parenting a teen is always revealing to us new skills. Like, how to talk your daughter through the traumatic experience of her first spot, learning to accept a shrug as a meaningful conversation, and how to remain calm when the mobile phone becomes your new dinner guest.*"

Dad laughed, then suggested some changes and I could hear Mum's fingers tapping the keys on her laptop. I crept back into my room. The article was going online next weekend. I wondered if I could anonymously post sick emojis.

Later that day, Hallie posted TikToks of her and Gabi practising gymnastics on some mats in Hallie's living room, like we always used to do. Hallie did a perfect back extension roll and I could hear Gabi cheering into her phone. There was one of them doing headstands opposite each other so their feet touched in an arch above their heads. Watching them together was like being dragged across gravel. But I tapped to like the videos anyway.

By Sunday night, Carys still hadn't replied to the message I'd sent her about hacking *All About Eva*. I'd seen the little grey bubbles appear and disappear under my message a few times. And now I felt really bad for sending it. But she'd liked the sketch of Miss Fizzy I'd done for art homework that I posted on my Instagram, so I guess she wasn't too annoyed with me.

On Monday morning, Spud talked about Minecraft the entire way up the hill, and I barely said a word. I wasn't even listening. I was going through what to say to Carys in my head. I'd only just made friends with her and already I'd messed it up. She'd been excluded from St Aug's for hacking, why would she want to risk doing the same thing for me? I was waiting on the corner, feeling completely stupid and selfish, when I spotted her walking towards me. She had a giant grin on her face.

"Hey!" she said. Her hair was tied in a tiny ponytail. The front bits were pinned up, but most had fallen out. I wished I could get mine cut short like that. But there was no way Mum would ever let me. "Thanks for waiting."

"I'm so sorry about that message," I blurted out. "I feel like an idiot for asking you that."

"It's okay. I was going to reply, but—"

"Just forget I even sent it. I was annoyed with my parents and…it was a *really* bad idea. I know you've just got in a load of trouble at your old school and…I'm sorry."

Carys squinted at me in the morning sunshine. "Who said it was a bad idea?" A tiny smile flickered on her lips.

"Just don't send me any messages about it. And delete that one you sent on Saturday. If you're serious about doing this, we can't leave footprints anywhere." I looked down at my shoes and Carys laughed. "I mean *digital* footprints."

"Right!" I said, my stomach churning with excitement. "I knew that."

"I mean it," Carys said. "We can't leave a trail. So don't tell anyone." She looked me dead in the eyes. "I mean literally not a single person. Even if you trust them, okay?" I nodded, wishing I could write all this down so I wouldn't forget. "It's the only way to avoid detection."

Detection? That sounded serious. The pavement suddenly felt uneven, like when you first step off an escalator.

Carys turned and started walking towards school. "Are you coming?"

"You'll do it?" I said. "I mean, you'll help me?"

A wide smile spread across her face. "I can't believe you didn't ask me sooner."

It was weirdly easy after that. Hallie and Gabi still didn't want to hang around with us. I felt a stab of jealousy when they walked off together at the start of lunchtime. But me and Carys needed to speak somewhere in private, so we went to the big oak tree on the far side of the football field, where no one could hear us. We sat on its low branches, eating our lunch and making plans.

Carys munched on a cheese sandwich while I picked weird yellow bits out of leftover black-bean noodles. Dad must have given me extra yellow bits deliberately. "The computer where your parents edit and upload stuff. Reckon you could get the password to log into that?"

"I already know it," I said. "It's 1990_TambourineMan, same as their Netflix password." Carys gawped at me. "What?"

"Eva!" she said, laughing. "You can't just share passwords like that!"

"Oh, sorry. It's just easy to remember because it's the year they met and the name of the song that was playing."

Carys raised her eyebrows. "Sounds like they're about as security-conscious as you are."

"I don't know the one for their channel, though."

"It's okay, as long as you have the main computer password, you should be able to access the rest. I'll tell you how." I fished around in my blazer pocket, looking for a pen. "Hey, you didn't tell your parents about my hacking at St Aug's, did you? I don't want them to get suspicious."

"Course not," I said, pulling my pencil case out of my bag.

"What about Spud?" Carys said. "You think he might

suspect anything?"

"Don't worry about Spud," I said. "He lives on another planet most of the time." I pulled out my notebook. "Okay, I'm ready."

Carys frowned. "Eva, you can't write any of this down. You'll have to remember it. We can't leave any kind of trail. Hacking your parents' channel could get us into serious trouble."

"Oh right. Sorry, I know." I stuffed the notebook back into my bag. "I just don't want anything to go wrong."

"It won't." Carys smiled. "At least not for us."

When I got home from school, Mum was being extra nice to me. Mainly because they had a new sponsor – this recycled stationery company called Salvage – and she still hadn't got a photo of me using their stuff.

"Please, Eva. It will only take ten minutes. We're a week late with it now. *Please*."

"I have homework to do." Carys and I had agreed for me to act as normal as possible, so my parents wouldn't get suspicious. We had it all planned out – every last detail. Only maybe me wanting to do my homework wasn't strictly normal, because Dad laughed for about ten minutes.

"Did I hear that right?" he said. "Eva actually thinking about her homework? That's a good one!"

"But this is stationery," Mum said. "You can do your homework while we take the photos!"

"I doubt it," I said. But they wouldn't leave me alone until I'd agreed to do the shoot. "Fine!" I said eventually, letting out a long sigh. "But don't complain when I fail my GCSEs."

Half an hour later I was sitting on the swing seat in the garden with a giant feather headdress on, pretending to write with a pencil made out of recycled newspaper. The sunlight was fading and the sky was striped pink.

"Eva, tilt your head up slightly," Mum called. "And hold the notebook a little higher?"

I held it up as far as my arm would stretch.

"Very funny," Mum said. "And smile, or do a neutral face. Anything other than that scowl would be great!"

I could tell she was getting annoyed. I stretched my mouth into a stupid smile.

Mum sighed. "Lars, will you try?" She handed the camera to my dad. They talked quietly for a moment then Dad smiled at me.

"Eva, indulge us, please, or we'll be here for ever trying to get this shot. It's one photo. Surely you are a tiny bit happy that this stationery is saving the planet?"

I wrote the words *THIS IS SO STUPID* on the notepad and smiled.

"Perfect!" said Dad. "Oh, of course, the F-Bomb!" Miss Fizzy jumped onto my lap and rubbed her face against the corner of the notebook, purring.

"Photobombed me again, did you?" I whispered into her fur. She sniffed at the headdress, then started chewing on the feathers.

"Don't let her eat that!" Mum shouted. She rushed over to retrieve the headdress and wiped off cat saliva. I picked up Miss Fizzy and headed inside. "Hey," Mum called. "Do you want to see the shot? You look amazing!"

I was about to say no, because I was getting cold, and I probably looked like an idiot with that feather thing on my head. But it was the first time Mum had asked if I wanted to see a photo before she uploaded it. Maybe she was starting to listen?

"Okay." I put Miss Fizzy down, and Mum's face lit up. I walked over and shielded my eyes so I could see the photo on the screen.

"See? Amazing girl," Mum said, kissing my head and pulling a couple of tiny feathers out of my hair. She let them go and I watched them float towards the hedge. That's when I noticed Spud's face in the bushes. I watched Mum as she typed replies to comments on the photo that were instantly popping up. So she hadn't waited for me to say the photo was okay. She'd already uploaded it.

"It looks like I have a peacock growing out of my head," I said, and walked over to Spud.

As I got closer, I realized his guinea pig's face was sticking through the bushes too. And they were both wearing army helmets. Spud's parents don't let him appear in any of our videos, but that doesn't stop him spying whenever we're filming outside. Dad got this octopus hosepipe sprinkler a few summers ago, and Spud ended up on the video. They blurred out his face, but you could still see his *Star Wars* swimming shorts and when his mum realized she made them cut him out totally.

"Spud, you can't put helmets on animals," I said through the bushes, and gently pulled the helmet off Toast's head. "Where did you even get this? Is it from a Barbie?"

"Reconnaissance mission. Stand by," Spud said in an American accent. "Is feline in close proximity? I repeat, is feline in close proximity?"

"Relax, Spud," I said, laughing. "Miss Fizzy's gone inside. But actually, I have some homework to do so…"

"Roger that," Spud said. "It's a negative. I repeat, negative. Retreat!" And both of them disappeared back into the bushes. A moment later, Spud's hand protruded

143

from the leaves and grabbed the doll's helmet I was still holding.

I heard Dad take a deep breath. "That boy gets weirder every day."

I headed inside and went up to my room. Suddenly the reality of hacking into my parents' computer later hit me. I went through the plan in my head: log on, open their channel, see if the password is saved, find it in security settings and memorize it, then delete stuff. Like Carys said, it was simple. Only, now it was all planned, it didn't exactly feel simple.

Maybe that's why I tried my best on my maths homework that night. As though figuring out the hypotenuse of right-angled triangles would somehow make up for what I planned to do to their channel. I checked the time on my phone. Mum and Dad usually went to bed around midnight, so I set my alarm for two a.m. and stuck my phone under my pillow. I let out a deep breath. Part of me felt terrified, the other part could not wait.

15

LOGGING IN

When my alarm went off at two a.m., I was so confused I accidentally hit *snooze*. I'd almost gone back to sleep when I remembered what I was supposed to be doing. A slow, cold fear spread over my skin. I sat up, then silently crept across my room. Holding my breath, I carefully opened my bedroom door. Miss Fizzy came bounding in and almost gave me a heart attack. I put her on the warm spot on my bed, then barely dared breathe until I was all the way downstairs. I stopped and listened for a few seconds. The house was dark, apart from the tiny red lights of the dishwasher and the dull orange glow from the street lights outside.

Once I got in their office, I took a few deep breaths. But that just made me feel dizzy. I quietly clicked the door closed, sat down and wiggled the mouse. Mum and Dad always left the computer in *Sleep* mode. The light from the screen felt blinding. I listened by the door for a moment then typed in their password with trembling fingers, half-expecting some kind of intruder alarm to go off. But it was just like Carys had said. I silently repeated her words to myself: *Log in, open their channel, see if the password is saved. Log in, open their channel, see if the password is saved.* My hands were still shaking as I clicked on the icon on their desktop. Suddenly, the music from the MEET THE ANDERSENS reel came on full blast. My heart jumped out of my chest. I quickly tapped mute and froze. No noise from upstairs. I blew out a long breath, my hand gripping the mouse. I was in.

Hacking doesn't feel that different to robbing a bank. Not that I've ever robbed a bank. But I guess the feeling is pretty much the same. Like, you get to a certain point and there's no going back. You've walked through the door and turning around feels harder than carrying on. Even if you are almost paralysed with fear.

I skimmed the cursor over the menu then clicked on *Scheduled Videos*. There was one due to go live in a few hours: *We're Eva's Parents, Get us Out of Here!* On the thumbnail, Mum and Dad were in army camouflage gear and the two captions said, *Sweet Tween to Terror Teen* and *Eva Goes Rogue!!!* And suddenly, I remembered why I was doing this in the first place.

I selected the box next to the video and clicked *delete*. A warning popped up saying, *Deleting is permanent and cannot be undone*. I glanced at the framed photo next to the computer, only just visible in the light of the screen. Me, Mum, Dad and Farmor standing on the Øresund bridge in Copenhagen last summer. It had been a really good day. Farmor never let them film anything when she was there. They always listened to her, why did they never listen to me?

It took me a minute to delete that first video. Mainly because I had to click a button saying *DELETE FOREVER* and it felt kind of scary. But then I saw the other videos they were about to share:

Eva Gets Cross!

Eva's Epic Eye-Rolling Compilation!

Eva Talking to Miss Fizzy!! So Cute!!

And suddenly deleting as many *All About Eva* videos as I could seemed like the best idea I'd ever had.

Then I remembered Carys's instructions. I had to memorize the password for the channel. I opened the security settings and clicked the box that said *Show password*. It was the same as their computer login, but a mixture of capitals and lowercase and the "o" of "tambourine" was a zero. I'd never be able to memorize that. I looked around for my phone to take a picture, but I must have left it upstairs. I grabbed a pencil from the pot by the keyboard, scribbled the password on a sticky note, and stuffed it in my dressing-gown pocket. Without thinking, I doodled clouds on the sticky-note pad while I waited for the *Top Videos* page to load. I deleted *My Little Girl is a Woman!!* and *Happy Vegetarian Day!* I was about to click on their *Playlists* section, when I heard a ringing coming from upstairs. I stopped dead. It was my phone. I must have forgotten to switch off the alarm.

My heart froze with terror. I quickly closed the browser and hit *sleep*. Then I ran up the stairs two at a time, as silently as I could. I grabbed my phone from under my pillow and hit *stop* as I dived beneath the duvet. I lay there for a minute or so not moving a muscle, my heart beating in my ears like gunfire. I got up, carefully closed my bedroom door and got back into bed.

I don't know why exactly – maybe the adrenaline, maybe pure relief – but tears started falling down my face. I felt completely terrified. Not because of what I'd done, but how close I'd come to getting caught. I pushed my legs under the covers and lay my head on the pillow. And it took me ages to get to sleep.

I didn't realize it then, because I felt like I was recovering from a heart attack. But I'd left the dumbest piece of evidence ever, right next to their computer.

16

JUST ACT NORMAL

I felt sick with worry the next morning, and I was sure Mum or Dad would notice. Like, maybe the *delete* icon I'd clicked so many times was visible on my eyeballs, or tattooed on my skin. But secrets feel like that to begin with – when they're fresh and new you worry everyone can see them. But I guess you must get used to how they feel. Because they become a lot easier to live with. After a while, you barely even notice them at all.

Farmor said this thing to me a couple of summers ago, when I was climbing the giant beech tree in her garden. She'd told me not to climb it when Dad was out, because she couldn't get me down if I got stuck. But I didn't exactly listen. I climbed to the highest branch I could reach, almost at the top. It was an amazing view: I could see all the way past the harbour right out to sea. Which was good, because I had to stay there for ages until my parents got back from this play they'd gone to see in Copenhagen and Dad had to get me down. It was the most embarrassing moment of my life. But that was before the avocado costume. And the period video.

Farmor had watched me climb the tree, shaking her head and said, in the gentle Danish voice I hear whenever I think about her, "Don't sail out farther than you can row back."

While Mum filmed me and Dad making granola that morning only a few hours after I'd hacked their channel, Farmor's words crept back to me like a song. Or a warning. Her advice, sailing all the way across the North Sea and into my head. But I never paid enough attention to what Farmor said.

As we sat at the table, I quietly chewed a spoonful of granola and noticed Dad staring at me.

"Well?" he said. I blinked a few times and tried to swallow, but my mouth suddenly felt really dry. "Aren't you going to say something?"

My heart raced. "About what?"

"The granola! What do you think of the new 'morning brain booster' recipe?"

I sank back into my chair with relief. "Oh right. It's fine."

"Wow, hold back on the compliments, Eva," Dad said. "I might get a swollen head!"

"You mean, *big head*, Dad." Then I remembered this Danish expression I'd learned at Languages Club last year. It means "Everything is fine" but the literal translation is "There are no owls in the bog". Like I said, Danish is kind of weird.

I said it and Dad laughed so much he accidentally sprayed bits of granola onto the tablecloth. He patted my shoulder and replied, "Great one! Great one!" in Danish. And for a few seconds, I forgot about the cold slab of guilt that had been sitting in my stomach ever since I woke up.

Just then, Mum's voice called from the office, "Eva! Have you been in here?"

My skin went cold. I couldn't chew the massive spoonful of granola in my mouth because my jaw was stuck together with fear. Mum came out, holding out the sticky note I doodled on last night. Quick thinking is not my speciality, so maybe Dad's new brain-boosting granola recipe actually worked, because after only a few seconds of brain freeze, I said, "Oh yeah, I needed a pencil for art; I was just testing it out."

"Okay, well, please don't touch anything in there, sweetie. Our notes are all over the place." She went back in and I could finally breathe. Then she walked out again and my heart stopped. "And, sweetie, don't speak with your mouth full."

I was upstairs brushing my teeth, when I heard it.

"LARS!" Mum shouted. "Can you come in here a second? Something's happened!"

I froze. A gloopy blob of toothpaste made its way down my chin. Why didn't I close the bathroom door?

"What is it?" Dad shouted from the bedroom.

I stared at their bedroom door handle, paralysed, waiting for it to move.

Just act normal, I told myself. *Just act totally normal. And definitely don't stand frozen in the middle of the bathroom looking like a criminal!*

The bedroom door opened and I quickly closed the bathroom door. I stood still listening, my heart whacking the inside of my chest like a sledgehammer. I heard Dad's footsteps on the stairs.

"The scheduled video is missing!" Mum said. "Did you delete it or something?"

"I haven't touched it," Dad said. Then he must have closed the door, because I couldn't make out the rest of what they were saying.

I went to my room and sat on my bed for a minute, hearing Carys's words in my head telling me to *just act normal.* But I couldn't actually remember what acting normal was like. My brain felt trapped and tangled up, like a kite stuck in a tree that kept catching the wind. But somewhere under that fear, there was a tiny feeling of achievement. I stopped at the top of the stairs as the office door opened.

Dad was saying, "Yes, I know, Jen, but what else can we do? I know you *think* you uploaded it, but maybe it didn't save properly. It can't have disappeared. It's saved on the hard drive. Just upload it again. I'll get you a coffee."

Wait, it was *saved on the hard drive*? They were going to *just upload it again*? I'd practically risked my life deleting their videos and it was all for nothing! I went downstairs and put my shoes on, still listening. It sounded like they hadn't noticed the others I'd deleted. Not yet anyway. I hoped Mum dropped her coffee on the computer when she realized.

My phone beeped and I almost jumped out of my skin. It was a message from Hallie.

Walk to school just us?

I'd arranged to meet Carys at the end of Lavender Lane so I could tell her how it went. We couldn't message about it because of the footprint thing. But this was Hallie.

I replied: Yeah definitely.

I sent Carys a message saying my German homework went okay and I'd see her at school. *German homework*

154

was our code word for hacking. We were only supposed to use it in emergencies. Although, thinking about it, my parents would probably find me messaging anyone about German homework highly suspicious.

"Hey," Spud said as I practically bumped into him on the doorstep. "I signed us up to partner in the science homework."

"Okay," I said. "What science homework?"

"Don't you check the homework app at all?"

"What homework app?" I was only half-joking.

Spud smiled. "I'm going to say two words, and you tell me the first thing that comes into your mind."

"Okay, go."

"Ferromagnetic fluid."

"Spud, the idea of that game is you say words people have actually heard of."

"It's a liquid that is attracted to magnetic poles." I looked at him blankly. "So, what do you think? For our science project!"

"I think you'd be better working with Rami."

"I already tried to sign up with Rami, but Mr Jacobs said we have to partner boy-girl. You're basically the only girl in our class who talks to me."

"Okay," I said. "But maybe we should do something simple."

"It's not that complicated!" Spud grinned. "I'll show you the experiment on YouTube. It's epic."

When he mentioned YouTube, I felt a bite of guilt in my stomach, like a stitch. "Maybe later," I said and watched him cross the road to join the rest of Nerdophobia.

Hallie was waiting at the corner. Her hair was tied in Dutch-style braids, plaited halfway down so her curls were loose around her neck. I tried to read the expression on her face.

"Your hair looks amazing."

"Thanks. My auntie came over and did it for me. I'm thinking of wearing it like this for the finals."

It was awkward for a minute as we both thought about the empty seat at her last competition.

As we got closer to school, she said, "Gabi is pretty upset about what you said, you know. I've heard some bad stuff about Carys. And not just from Gabi."

"Carys wants to forget about what happened at St Aug's. A fresh start, you know," I said. Only it sounded like the biggest lie ever. I turned my eyes away from Hallie and looked at the railings. "We could all hang around together."

"It's just…" Hallie said, "I'm on the student council, don't forget. If she ends up getting us into trouble, I could lose my place. I mean, Carys did get *excluded*." She said "excluded" like it was a crime. "Becca Matthews thinks we should avoid her."

"Hallie," I said, "the student council can't tell you who to be friends with."

"I know, but Gabi thinks it's better if we don't hang around with her too. There's loads of other people in our class she can be friends with."

"But I *want* to be friends with Carys."

"More than you want to be friends with me?"

"But, Hallie…" I imagined telling her about how Carys was helping me. About secretly deleting *All About Eva* videos at two a.m. I knew how she'd react. She'd probably take me straight back home to confess. I could never tell her. But I could feel the secret in the air between us, like a glass wall.

Maybe she could feel it too, because she said, "Okay, well, guess I'll see you later," and jogged up the road to where Gabi was waiting before I had the chance to say anything else.

That morning, Mr Jacobs made us sit with our science project partners, so I sat next to Spud and Carys moved next to Rami. Every time I tried to concentrate on writing our hypothesis, I thought about what I'd done last night. I had to press my lips together to stop myself from blurting it out. I hadn't really kept a secret from Spud before. The more I thought about it, the more I realized *All About Eva* meant I'd never actually kept a secret from anyone before. My whole life was like a free-to-download movie. Only now, it had a few deleted scenes.

Mr Jacobs started handing out the scores from our physics test last week. Spud said, "YESSSS!" when he got his back. I peered at his score. *97%.* I glanced at the paper on my desk. It said *38%*, circled in red pen. Nothing good is ever circled in red pen. Not by Mr Jacobs, anyway.

"Not a great result, even for you, Eva," Mr Jacobs said, raising his bushy eyebrows. "Clearly you didn't revise."

I could feel people's eyes on me. Alfie was sniggering at the end of the row. "I was kind of busy filming, sir," I said. "I'm really sorry, but my parents think there is more to life than physics."

Mr Jacobs raised his eyebrows again. "Is that so?"

I swallowed. "I obviously disagree." I smiled weakly, and stuffed my test paper into the back of my science book as he went to the next table. I hoped he wouldn't call my parents. The last thing I needed right now was a YouTube video about me failing science.

"Okay," Spud said. "I've already written the list of stuff

you need to ask your parents to order online. Tell them to get the largest quantity they can get delivered by Friday." He handed me a piece of paper from his pocket. It felt kind of warm.

"What is half this stuff?" I asked. "And why can't your parents order it?"

"Because they're not getting me any more science materials after that sheep's lung, remember."

I screwed up my face. "Oh yeah."

"What happened with the sheep's lung?" asked Lucas, who was sitting next to Gabi. I avoided eye contact. Annoyingly so did she.

"It exploded," I said. "In his kitchen." I shuddered at the memory.

"Awesome!" Lucas said, laughing.

"You exploded a sheep's lung?" Gabi said. "That's so gross."

"I was investigating the respiratory system," Spud explained. "The explosion was a minor calculation error." He turned back to me. "I still owe Chip a new bike pump."

"Your brother's called Chip?" Gabi's face went into a sneer. "Is everyone in your family named after potatoes?"

"No. Chip means 'chip off the old block', because he looked so much like our dad when he was born."

"So why did they call you Spud?" Gabi asked.

"They didn't." Spud grinned. "They called me Euan." He went back to explaining how to make ferromagnetic fluid, which was a lot better than listening to Gabi. She had been mean about Spud ever since the beginning of Year Seven. Maybe because he was in Nerdophobia. Or because he brought a live frog to school that time.

It was raining at lunchtime, so Carys and I went to our form room. Miss Wilson said we could sit in there as long as we were drawing. We chose a table right at the back and Miss Wilson had her headphones in, so it felt safe to talk.

"It's good they didn't suspect you," Carys said, trying to sketch the raven skull that was on a nearby shelf. "Don't be surprised if they ask you about it though. I mean, *act* surprised obviously. But deny all knowledge."

"But they've uploaded the videos again. Look." I tapped on my phone and scrolled down their YouTube homepage. "*Eva's Epic Eye-Rolling Compilation* is literally online already."

Miss Wilson was humming along to her music and scraping paint onto a canvas with some kind of metal tool. I passed Carys an AirPod and tapped *play*. A song started playing that said, *I hate you so much right now*. At least that was weirdly accurate. The video sliced between clips of me

160

rolling my eyes. Some of them were from years ago. 14.8k likes. I rolled my eyes, then hoped Carys hadn't seen.

"Okay," she said quietly. "So what if we don't delete stuff next time? What if we do something else?"

"But what else can we do?"

She smiled and bit the end of her pencil. "I think I have an idea."

That afternoon in English, Miss West was going on about Shakespeare as usual. I concentrated really hard on keeping my eyes open. She kept calling the sixteenth century "the golden age of humanity!" But she'd literally told us last lesson that people only had a bath once a year and used clumps of hay instead of toilet roll. I put my hand over my mouth to cover a yawn, and thought about what Carys had suggested at lunchtime. Instead of *deleting* content, we could upload some of our own. I felt a twitch of excitement in my stomach.

"Eva!" Miss West said sharply. "Are you paying attention?"

"Yes, miss." I sat up straight and chewed my cheeks so I didn't yawn again.

"Then perhaps you can tell me how many sonnets Shakespeare wrote in his lifetime?"

Miss West always picks on people who aren't paying attention to answer her questions. I really did not see the point. Last year she caught me doodling and made me read out loud. She tutted when I pronounced the word *sorbet* wrong. I scanned the board for any information, but there was nothing about sonnets on there. I glanced over at Spud. He held one finger up at me.

"Er, one?" I said.

A few people laughed and Spud banged his head against his desk.

Miss West sighed. "William Shakespeare wrote *one hundred and fifty-four* sonnets, young lady! I can guarantee *he* didn't spend his English lessons daydreaming! Learning doesn't happen by magic, you know." Which, if you ask me, is one of the worst things about the education system.

I spent the rest of the lesson trying really hard to look interested. Which was not easy. Miss West must have read us every single one of those sonnets.

By the time I got home, I was exhausted and my jaw ached from stifling yawns. As I opened the front door, I told myself to act normal, but my hands were trembling slightly. I saw them before I'd even stepped inside. Both of them sitting at the kitchen table. Waiting for me, like an ambush.

17

GUILT TRIP

I stood in the doorway for a second, my mind see-sawing between immediate confession and total denial. There were mugs of hot chocolate on the table, and what looked like a brand new iPad. Dad's hands were resting on the table. Mum's phone was face down. They weren't even filming? This was so weird.

"Sit down, Eva," Dad said.

"Is everything okay?" I said, remembering what Carys had said earlier. *They're ruling me out*, I told myself. *They don't know anything*. But already I could feel the blood draining from my face. "You both look…serious."

"Oh, don't worry, sweetie," Mum said, wafting her hand like she was swatting away a fly. "We've just had a hard day. Technical glitches. We don't know what happened, something I did wrong probably. But it's all fixed now." She smiled. "You didn't go on the computer this morning, sweetie, did you? I mean, for school or something?"

I shook my head. "No, I'm not allowed to use that computer."

Dad smiled. Probably because I'd given a correct answer for once in my life.

I sat down at the table next to Mum. "So, what's up?" I tried to sound casual. But when I leaned back I realized I still had my rucksack on. I pretended I'd done it deliberately.

"We thought we needed a family triangle," Mum said, gently pulling my hair from behind my ear. That's what they call family meetings. Dad used to say we were three points in a triangle – him, Mum and me – and without each other we'd fall over. But our family didn't feel like a triangle to me any more. Not now there were so many people watching. It felt more like one of those 3D shapes Mr Gregory showed us once in maths. The one that Spud said blew his mind and went on about the whole summer. Some kind of truncated rhombus. Mr Gregory showed us a video of it rotating. That's what our family was like. Being stuck inside a million-sided shape with faces on each side, all staring in.

Mum shifted around on her seat. "We've had a few comments from the For-Evas—"

Dad caught me rolling my eyes. "Just hear Jen out, okay."

"They've been saying you don't seem like yourself lately. And because of these technical issues this morning, we ended up watching old videos and, you know what? They're right. You used to make up dance routines, we'd bake together. Disney Princess karaoke every Friday, do you remember?"

I smiled at the memories, even though I didn't mean to. "That was years ago," I said. "Do you think dressing up as Disney Princesses and singing 'Let it Go' live on YouTube would actually improve my life right now?"

"I'm up for it." Dad grinned. "We're just saying, it seems like you're not having so much fun on the channel." He picked up one of the hot chocolates and put it in front of me. The marshmallows had melted, and there was a layer of chocolate-marshmallowy goo that was literally the nicest taste in the world. But I didn't touch it.

"You know I'm not having fun," I said. "I don't even want to be on the channel."

"Okay," Dad said. "We also got an email from your science teacher." I looked out the window. Mr Jacobs was such a snake. "Thirty-eight per cent, Eva. It's lower than your last test score!"

"Well, maybe Hope Park Academy isn't very good then. Because it seems like I'm actually getting less intelligent by going there."

Mum tried not to laugh, then moved her hand over her mouth so Dad didn't see.

"Mr Jacobs said you told him you couldn't revise for the test because of filming. Is that really what you said?"

I swallowed. "I might have given him that impression. Accidentally."

"But you said you revised with Hallie," Mum said. "At the Crêpe Cabin."

Dad looked concerned. His forehead was all wrinkled. He put his hand over mine and squeezed. If he thought the channel was why I'd failed science, this could be my chance to convince him to close it down.

"I mean, I probably would be doing a lot better in school if it wasn't for the channel. I'd definitely have passed that physics test, for a start." I fixed my eyes on the tablecloth. I was kind of telling the truth. "Maybe we should close down the channel after all. I mean, you said Year Eight is important. And Mr Jacobs seems pretty clever. If he thinks it's bad for me then…"

Mum snorted. "That's not what Mr Jacobs said, Eva. He's never even watched the channel!"

"Yeah, Eva," Dad said. "That's not really what we

meant. We can't stop the channel – it's our job! We just need to get the balance right. So we're getting a schedule worked out so you can do your homework as soon as you get back from school. No leaving it all until Sunday night! We'll fit filming around the new schedule." Dad drummed his fingers on the table. "We're getting hundreds of new subscribers every day. So, it's really important that we stay on-brand. Our subscribers need to see fresh content. But, obviously, we don't want you to fail at school."

"And we got you this." Mum pushed the iPad box towards me. "Lars wanted to wait until your grades improve, but I managed to convince him otherwise." She smiled, like we were sharing a secret. "We know you've been wanting a new one for a while. And this way, you might actually enjoy doing your homework! It's rose gold, just like you wanted. The screen is ultra-low reflectivity – it's so versatile! You can shoot, edit and share videos, all on this one device! It's got a magic keyboard, and is actually faster than most laptops. It will even make physics homework fun! And, because we know you're good at art...*ta dah*!" She pulled a brand-new Apple Pencil from under the table. "It attaches magnetically to the side of the iPad, it has pixel-perfect precision and it's super easy to use. Perfect for all of your creative projects! And look, we had it engraved." She held it up and I could see *Eva*

Andersen in gold letters down the side. "Dream it up. Jot it down!"

I did wonder why Mum was talking like that. Like someone out of an advert. But I was kind of distracted. A new iPad with an Apple Pencil was the one thing I'd have wished for if a genie popped out of my hot chocolate. I looked at the gifts, then at Mum. And it took every milligram of willpower I had to say, "I don't accept bribes."

Mum looked at me for a second, then laughed, "Oh, Eva! I actually thought you were being serious then! It's a peace offering, silly. And a thank you, for being our star. You make us so proud." She stood up and hugged me as I opened the box. "We love you so much, Eva," she said into my hair.

It was a pretty good speech. I mean, it was definitely better than her performance in *Justice Force*. I actually felt bad about deleting their videos. Until Dad went over to the bookcase and I heard it.

Beep-beep.

I was so stupid for thinking they hadn't been filming this. They hadn't even hidden the camera. It was right there on the shelf, pointing at us the whole time. It was on before I even walked through the door. This was just another scene to be edited and uploaded and liked and shared and commented on later. This wasn't a family triangle. This didn't even feel like a proper family, not with strangers invited.

That's why I didn't feel bad about any of the stuff I did next.

18

SHARK ATTACK

The next day I was allowed to go to Carys's house after school, but only because I told my parents how good she is at languages. And only if I showed them my German homework when I got back. They wanted to make a special *We Made Half a Million Subscribers!* vlog ready for when the channel hit 0.5 million. (That was the way Spud told me to put it – 0.5 million. He said the zero would make me feel better about it psychologically. I wasn't so sure.) Anyway, with Dad's new schedule, homework had to come first. Mum was already annoyed about it. And about the unplugging day on Sunday. Miss Wilson had sent an email to all of our parents telling them about it. She invited parents to take part too, apparently. Mum was panicking in case we got our 0.5 millionth subscriber that day and we missed the big moment. It made me smile just to think about that happening.

Carys lived at the bottom of Lavender Lane, a dead-end surrounded by fir trees, a few streets away from mine. You couldn't even see her house from the road. We walked up this really long gravel drive then Carys said, "Home sweet home!" and pointed to a gigantic house. It had a name and everything. Raven Manor. It was almost completely covered in ivy, all the way up to the roof.

"Woah!" I said, gazing up at it. "All this is your house?" I really wished I'd polished my shoes.

"You don't need to be impressed," Carys said. She poked her finger into a crack in one of the pillars and a little cloud of dust escaped. "It's literally falling apart." She laughed and pushed open the door. It creaked and barking echoed up the hallway.

I quickly stepped behind her. "Would now be a good time to tell you I'm more of a cat person?" I said as a dog the size of a small horse lumbered towards us.

"Don't worry, he's perfectly friendly!" Carys said, rubbing the dog's ears. "You're a teddy bear, aren't you, Bernie?" I carefully stroked Bernie's head. "See?" Carys said, just as a blob of dog drool hit my shoes. We both laughed, Carys maybe slightly more than me. "He is kind of gross too, sorry!"

Our laughter drifted down the hallway. Carys shouted, "I'm home!" but I didn't hear anyone answer. She trailed her fingers over the keys of a dusty-looking piano and stopped at the bottom of a giant staircase. It spiralled upwards, like the giant nautilus shell Farmor kept on her windowsill.

"My mum would die to film in your house," I said without thinking. Then I felt like an idiot, because the main reason I was there was to plan our next hack. "I mean, your house is amazing."

"Thanks."

We went up *two* flights of stairs to her bedroom. "The other one leads to this really old turret," Carys said. "But there's an owl nesting in there." I really wanted to ask to see but I didn't.

Carys's bedroom had huge posters stuck to the walls with Sellotape. I was not allowed to do that in my room. Posters had to go in a frame, and Mum had this special tool to check they were straight. I never got to pick them. Mum curated every room in our house like it was an art gallery, including my bedroom. There was an old film poster above Carys's bed with a woman smoking a cigarette. Mum would literally faint if I put something like that in my room. It would be about as "on-brand" as graffitiing the coffee table. I looked at the photo stuck to the edge of the dressing table mirror. Carys and three other girls, squashing their faces together.

"My friends," Carys said. "I mean, my *old* friends. They've dropped me now."

"They stopped being friends with you?" I asked. "But you look so close here."

Carys looked over. "I guess they were worried about being associated with me or something. Sabrina still messages me sometimes, but no one else." She pointed to the dark-haired girl next to her in the photo, then walked over to a chest of drawers by the windows. I didn't know what to say, so I sat on an oversized cushion and watched Carys root around in the bottom drawer.

"So, this stuff we're going to upload," I said eventually. "It's not anything too bad, right? I mean, obviously I want the channel to lose subscribers. If they hit 0.5 million, they'll probably make *Eva Andersen's Period: The Movie*."

Carys laughed and carried on rummaging about in the drawer.

"It's just, I know it's got to be something bad for their brand, but I don't want to like…offend anyone." I felt totally awkward.

"Don't worry, I get it," Carys said, pulling out a laptop and charger. "They've just had a bunch of new subscribers, right? So, if we upload something weird, those subscribers

173

will think the channel is super lame, and unsubscribe. They might lose some of their regular subscribers too." She opened her laptop. "And their sponsors might get a little nervous if they think their page has been hijacked. We don't have to do anything mean to have an impact."

I swallowed the giant lump that had formed in my throat. "And what if my parents trace it back to us?"

Carys wiped the laptop screen with her sleeve. "They won't find anything because we're using their password which, let's face it, isn't exactly hard to guess. They might as well use the name of your cat!" I made a mental note to change my social media passwords from Ilove_MissFizzy. "You already said they think the deleted videos were a technical hitch." Carys looked at me. "Hey, if you've changed your mind, we don't have to do it."

"No, I need to do it. There's no other way to stop them." It was true, but I still felt like I was sitting at the top of the death slide at the park. "It's just, I don't want us to get in trouble."

"Don't worry," Carys said. "Look –" she held up a giant USB stick – "this is a VPN which uses an encrypted layered connection to a proxy server." I looked at her blankly. "Basically, I'm surfing as a ghost." Like that made me feel any better.

Don't ask me why I picked shark videos. I was clicking

on random stuff on YouTube and there was this one of a diver in a metal cage. Two great white sharks were ramming it with their noses. It seemed like an appropriate metaphor for my life. We were watching it for the second time when Carys's bedroom door opened and her dad poked his head round the door. Carys paused the video at such lightning speed that I wondered if she did ju-jitsu.

"Hello, darling!" he said. He looked a lot older than my dad. And he was wearing a tie. My dad never wore a tie, even when he went out for dinner. I don't think he even owned one. "Hello! You must be Eva. Carys tells me you've made her feel very welcome at school."

"Dad, we're busy with our homework right now!" Carys said, without looking up.

Carys's dad looked at the laptop, concerned.

Carys sighed. "It's fine, Dad. It's German homework. I'm helping Eva with verbs. Come and have a look if you want."

My heart stopped.

"No, it's fine!" her dad said. "You two carry on."

Then her mum appeared at the door. She looked exactly like Carys, but much older and with tidier hair.

"Hello! Hello! Lovely to meet you! I'm Caroline!"

I said hi then Carys said, "Can you go, Mum? We're really busy with homework."

"Okay, sorry!" she said. "Didn't mean to disturb you. Just saying hello! Dinner will be about six, okay? Will Eva be staying for dinner?"

Carys said, "Yes." Then her mum shut the door and just...went away. It was like visiting another planet. There's no way my parents would have believed I was doing homework. But Carys's parents didn't even want to see evidence. After everything that happened at St Aug's. She didn't even get told off for not saying please. I felt kind of dizzy with the freedom of it. Like at Spud's house where you're allowed as many fizzy drinks as you want.

After we'd finished editing the shark video, we agreed to wait a few days before uploading it. We didn't want my parents to get suspicious. So, we lay on cushions listening to music and doing German homework for our cover story. We'd almost finished before I felt brave enough to ask Carys more about the hacking she did at St Aug's.

"Most of it's been taken down," she said. "I had to hand over all my logins to the head teacher. But there is still some stuff online if you want to see?"

"Hmm, let me think," I said. "Definitely!"

"Okay, but you have to understand that this isn't the original. That got taken down. Someone reposted it with weird music. And the bat emojis are nothing to do with me."

"Just play it!" I said, laughing.

She clicked the touchpad. This creepy music started playing and a cartoon vampire popped up. "That's my head teacher's real face. And that's my PE teacher." The head teacher figure bit the teacher's neck and blood spurted everywhere. I could not stop laughing. Carys grinned. "See why they excluded me now?"

"Yeah, kind of."

"My parents have only just let me back on the Wi-Fi. And only for schoolwork."

Just then, a gong sounded.

"Dinner's ready," Carys said, rolling her eyes.

"You have a gong to signal dinner?"

"No, we have a gong and my dad finds it funny to use it when I have friends over. Not that that's happened for a while. Hey, I'll ask my parents about you sleeping over on Friday if you want. We can upload the shark video then, maybe?"

I smiled, bubbles of excitement fizzing in my stomach. "They won't know what's bit them."

19

FERROMAGNETIC FLUID

I ended up getting back late from Carys's. Mum was annoyed because she wanted us to film the 0.5 million subscribers video. Luckily, she and Dad couldn't agree about where to film it, which props to use, or which subscribers to personally thank. So, I showed Dad my homework, then lay on the sofa looking at my phone. As they were deciding which sponsors to namecheck, I asked if I could sleep over at Carys's on Friday.

Mum said, "We'll see, honey."

Dad said, "If you're cooperating." Cooperating was code for "look like you're having fun while we're filming". I sighed and scrolled through the comments on the "family triangle" video.

So spoiled!!!

Ungrateful brat. (Only "brat" wasn't the exact
word they used.)

Your honesty is such a breath of fresh air! You guys
are awesome!

Love this trio!!!!!

Sorry, guys, love you but Eva is getting worse
mannered every day.

I felt quite proud of that last one.

As I headed up to bed, Mum said, "Oh, we'll definitely be doing your day of unplugging on Sunday."

I looked at Dad for an explanation. "Someone commented on the school Facebook group that the Andersens wouldn't be taking part." Mum held a cushion above his head, ready to bash him with it. Dad laughed and tried to duck. "Jen rage-replied saying of course we would! So now we have to."

"I did not rage-reply, Lars!" she said, laughing and bashing him with the cushion on every syllable. Which obviously meant she did. "Anyway, we've got a sponsor for the day, so it's all worked out perfectly."

"You got a sponsor for my form's day of unplugging?" I said.

"Yep! We're handing over the channel to this new mindfulness app called Tranquil Eyes for the day. Should be nice! And they're giving us a special discount code you can share with your class." Dad showed me the Tranquil Eyes website on his phone. Their slogan was *KICK STRESS AND NEGATIVE THINKING OUT!* which sounded stressful to me. Anyway, I couldn't say anything about it because I was cooperating.

The next morning, while I was having breakfast, Dad was busy in the office. Mum went upstairs to have a shower and left her laptop open on the kitchen table. I could see a folder right there on her desktop with the newspaper's name on it. I genuinely only meant to have a quick look – I'd heard Dad reading the draft article aloud anyway, so it wasn't technically snooping. But when I opened the file, it must have been a different version. The final version. Because it was worse.

What to do when your miracle baby turns into an eye-rolling, headphone-wearing, grade-dropping, app-obsessed teen.

Grade-dropping? They'd written about my physics test? A cold feeling washed over me, like plunging into the North Sea. My eyes scanned the rest of the page.

Our darling Eva now has the attention span of a two-

year-old…physically incapable of putting her clothes in the laundry basket…eyes rolling so high they could ricochet off the ceiling…and of course, her new favourite word, "boring"…

I slammed the laptop closed, grabbed my school bag and headed out without saying goodbye. Apart from the grade-dropping, which was technically true, the whole thing was made-up! But worse than that – it was mean. Anger surged through my veins like electricity.

In English, Miss West was going on about Elizabethan times. She said being angry was called having an excess of yellow bile. According to her, they'd put leeches on your skin to suck it out. That day, I felt so angry I'd need a whole tank of them.

After school, me and Spud were doing our science experiment. He messaged saying:

Wear a boiler suit.

Like I had one of those in my wardrobe. I walked through his gate and down the little alleyway by the side of his house. He was wearing a navy boiler suit, an army helmet and holding what looked like a police riot shield.

"Spud, I thought you said this experiment wasn't dangerous!" I said, putting the box of equipment down on the grass. "Where did you even get that?"

"Chip made it." He put the shield down and opened the box. "Did you bring the camera?" I pulled it out of my rucksack. "Good, because I've decided our initial hypothesis wasn't ambitious enough." He shook a giant jar of iron filings and grinned. "Go big or go home, right?"

"You are at home."

He handed me some gardening gloves and a pair of safety goggles. "Trust me, Eva. Ours is going to be the best experiment Hope Park has ever seen."

"That makes me feel extremely worried for my safety," I said. But deep down I hoped he was right. Getting a good grade for this project would prove my parents' stupid article wrong. I watched Spud drag a super-strength magnet onto the grass then roll a barrel of something out of his garage. It had a hazard sign on it, like the one on the science technicians' cupboard. This experiment would be completely awesome. Or it would actually kill us. And possibly our entire street.

An hour later, pretty much all of the grass in Spud's back garden had turned black. We had an amazing video, but we were both completely covered in ferrofluid. Spud had forgotten about the idea of "going big" and instead was now worrying about whether he'd be able to bleach ferrofluid off the grass. My face ached from laughing.

I pulled off my gloves and took a selfie of us looking like we'd been inked by a giant squid. I uploaded it to my Instagram with the hashtags #scienceprojectgoals #isurvivedaspudexperiment.

Immediately a comment flashed up from Jenna saying, AMAZING!!!

I smiled, inspecting a patch of my hair at the front that had turned black. Maybe Spud would lend me his bleach.

"Don't tell me physics isn't fun, Eva!" Spud shouted as I walked home.

I had to admit he had a point. Although he probably wouldn't be alive very long after his parents saw the garden. As I walked through the door, Mum picked up the camera and pointed it at me.

"Oh my goodness, Eva!" she said, laughing. "Want to explain to everyone what you've been doing?"

I really wanted to say no, and go straight to my room. But something made me change my mind. Maybe it was the words *eye-rolling, headphone-wearing, grade-dropping, app-obsessed teen*. I looked right into the lens and explained how ferromagnetic fluid is a liquid that becomes strongly magnetized in the presence of a magnetic field, and the hypothesis we'd just proved with our experiment. Word perfect.

"Wow! Sounds great, sweetie!" Mum said, beaming.

I shrugged. "Not bad for a grade-dropping, app-obsessed teen, I guess."

Mum stared at me; her finger tapped the button to stop recording. "You read the article," she said softly, and put the camera down. "I'm sorry, Eva. The newspaper wanted a light-hearted take on parenting. I was going to show it to you. It's obviously not what we really think."

I picked at a piece of ferrofluid in my nail so I didn't have to look at her.

"Sweetie, I'm sorry. The column is just a fun read for parents. It's not based on the truth!" She kissed the small part of my face that wasn't covered in black gunk. "You're so wonderful that we have to make up all the bad stuff! See? But, oh my goodness! We cannot film the half a million subs video with you looking like that!" Her bracelets jangled as she started the camera again. "No offence, sweetie. But you kind of stink! This scientist needs to...take a bath. You know I have the most beauuuuutiful bath bombs from Living Real..."

I looked straight into the lens, thinking, *Should I tell her what I really think about her stupid article and her stupid channel and her stupid beauuuuutiful bath bombs?*

Mum said how proud she was about the effort I'd put into my science project. And I guess she found the tiny gap in my heart that still didn't want to disappoint her.

Because I just said, "Thanks," and let her film us dropping rose petal bombs into my bath.

Later, I was on the sofa, squashed between Mum and Dad, listening to them say, "Oh my God!" and "HALF A MILLION SUBSCRIBERS!!" about 0.5 million times. They let off confetti bombs, thanked their sponsors and the For-Evas and announced their "EPIC GIVEAWAY!!"

By the time Dad said, "That's a wrap!" my ears were ringing. I tried my best to look happy and excited. To sound like I wasn't remembering lines from the script they'd written. But I couldn't help thinking about the stuff Dad had said before we started filming. About "rapid growth" and "channel collaborations" and "publicity explosion". If all that stuff happened, and they started making all this extra money, there was no chance they'd ever stop. If I didn't do anything, they'd be filming me for the rest of my life. That's why I needed the shark video to work. And put an end to this entire thing.

20

SABOTAGE

To celebrate making the fake 0.5 million subscriber video, we went to Inner Peas, this vegan restaurant in town.

The waiter said, "You're tall!" to my dad as soon as we walked in.

Everyone (except me) laughed when he said, "No, I'm Lars!"

When we got our food Mum dropped a bombshell. "Your dad and I thought it might be nice if Carys comes to ours tomorrow night instead of you staying there."

"What?" I said, trying to stop my aubergine burger from sliding out of my bun. "Why?"

"We haven't met her yet, sweetie. And we feel a little uncomfortable about you staying over before we've got to know her. We thought it would be nice for her to sleep over with us instead. If her parents are okay with it."

"Fine," I said, typing out a message to Carys. My parents put my whole life on the internet for strangers to see, but they wouldn't let me stay over at a friend's house a few streets away.

"Oh, and get her to ask them if it's okay to film while she's here," Mum said, breaking a potato wedge in half.

"No!" I shouted, forgetting where we were. The people on the next table looked over at me. But I didn't care. The thought of Carys seeing my parents in filming mode was so embarrassing I actually shuddered. "I mean, you can't film Carys. She won't like it."

Dad wiped his hands and said, "Can't hurt to ask, Eva." He picked up the camera and switched into his jokey filming voice. "So, we've just found out about a fitness vlogger who makes these amazing workout videos. We thought it would be fun to try one out this weekend." People in the restaurant were looking over at us. Why did Dad have to bring the big camera?

"It's 1980s themed," Mum explained, "which ties in perfectly with the diary extracts I read to you all the other day."

So that was it, I realized. That was the reason they wanted Carys to stay at ours. For this stupid workout thing. I squashed a potato wedge into my plate with my fork and sighed.

"And it won't be long now!" Dad said, grinning. "We're at *four hundred and seventy-two thousand* subscribers! And boy, do we have something special planned for when we hit half a million."

"We have the most incredible video to show you all soon," Mum said. "Our family journey: from zero to half a million subs! Starting with the day we found out Eva existed! We are so excited!" She leaned over and gently squashed my nose with her finger. "What do you think, sweetie? Excited?"

I dropped my fork so it clattered. "I need the toilet."

Four hundred and seventy-two thousand subscribers already? I thought as I walked down the steps to the toilets. They could hit 0.5 million any day now! Maybe even this weekend. Then they'd roll out the over-the-top publicity they had planned, and dig out all the old videos. And my life would get half-a-million times worse. I waited in a cubicle until a woman had finished washing her hands, then I called Carys.

"You know the *German homework* that we were planning on doing tomorrow?" I said. "Think we could get it done tonight?"

"You mean the one about the *ocean*?"

"Yeah," I said. "It's kind of urgent for tonight. What do you think?"

Carys went quiet for a moment. I heard the sound of her laptop booting up. "I'm on it."

I stayed up late that night refreshing the *All About Eva* page, waiting for the video to appear. We didn't want my parents seeing it until tomorrow – that way it should at least get some views and shares before they realized and took it down. But I must have fallen asleep, because the next morning I woke up with my phone stuck to my face and Mum screaming.

I bolted upright and peeled my phone off my cheek. I tapped in the *All About Eva* page. There it was. *New Channel Trailer!!!* The thumbnail was a great white shark with me in its jaws. I put my headphones on and tapped *play*. It looked even better than when we made it on Wednesday. Carys had added music and graphics, and there was a new bit where a tiger shark severed someone's leg. It was definitely not "on-brand". In fact, it was like a horror movie.

I messaged Carys: Homework's perfect.

Carys had scheduled the post for two a.m. like we'd agreed. She'd also set a new password on their account, so my parents couldn't even log in to delete it. So far it had: 58k views, 1.5k thumbs up, 9k thumbs down, 238 comments. I scrolled down.

QueenSass: I don't understand the link
to parenting.

TryHarderO: Are the Andersens okay???

XxxLisaMitchxxX: this is terrible

KerLeyFries: SICK

YurtGroupy: Not your content!!!!

GaryDude: this is why I only swim in pools.

I bit the insides of my cheeks as I went downstairs to stop myself from laughing.

"I don't understand!" Mum cried. "Who would even make something like this?"

Dad was in the office speaking to Ash, their IT person, on speakerphone. "There must be some kind of security breach," Dad said. "I cannot understand how someone can get unrestricted access to upload new content. Can you get in?"

"Sorry you're hearing all this, sweetheart," Mum said, pulling at the knots in my hair as she scraped it into a ponytail. I automatically shrugged her off. "It's a nightmare."

"What's happened?" I asked. My face ached as I tried to look serious and innocent at the same time. "Is it your Instagram?"

"No," Mum said, putting her phone on the table. "It's…you know what? Don't even look. It's so horrible. Get yourself some breakfast, okay?" She kissed me on the head and walked back to the office.

"Let me know if I can help!" I called after her. I was becoming a bit of an expert at deception. I was kind of proud of myself.

Mum's phone beeped and a message flashed up from Uncle Gareth:

Had a rebrand? 🤮 🤮 🤮

I laughed then quickly turned it into a cough as Mum turned round. It's exhausting being a hacker. You have to be on guard the whole time.

"Hey, sweetie. We're going to be a little while sorting this out," Mum said. "You okay making your own lunch today?"

"Yeah," I called back.

Dad's face poked out from the office door. "And don't forget your Danish books for Languages Club."

I was halfway down the drive, talking to Spud, when Mum came out. "Hey, your Danish books." I must have left them on the table.

"Thanks." I didn't say anything else in case it sounded suspicious.

"I won't tell Dad you forgot, okay." She winked and

191

kissed me on the forehead. "Love you."

And that was the moment. If I was going to stop messing with their channel, that was it. Right then, as I felt Mum's kiss through my fringe. Her eyes were kind of blotchy, so she must have been crying. And I suddenly felt bad about what I'd done. But it's weird how easy it is to ignore bad feelings like that. I knew Mum cared about me. Just not enough to stop the channel. Her being upset now was nothing compared to the humiliation I'd had for years.

So I hugged her, said, "Love you too," and ignored the weird feeling in my heart when I couldn't quite meet her eyes. And whatever my heart was trying to tell me, the thing I could feel it shouting at me from inside my chest, got missed.

21

LET'S GET PHYSICAL

That day, my parents filmed a special vlog explaining what happened with the shark video. A technical glitch, was the story they were going with. They uploaded the wrong video. Dad had made the shark one as a prank on Mum. But after school, Mum told me her real theory about it.

"Family vlogging is competitive, Eva. I'm telling you, that woman has it in for us."

"So," I said, "your prime suspect for uploading a shark attack video is a vlogger called LittleMummaBear?"

Dad didn't look convinced. "It was probably some bored teenager on the other side of the planet! Cyber attacks are how they get their kicks these days! "

I went upstairs and deliberately took ages changing

out of my uniform. Then I waited by the front door for Carys, trying my best not to look like I was the kind of teenager who got any kicks from cyber attacks.

"Hi, Carys!" Mum said as I opened the door. "Come in, make yourself at home!"

"Thanks," Carys said, taking off her coat. Her hair had been blown about by the wind. Mum was probably itching to straighten it out. But she smoothed down mine instead.

We went into the snug to watch TV and Miss Fizzy curled up in between us. My stomach had a weird plunging feeling. Like just before you have to go onstage. I didn't feel guilty exactly. My parents had posted videos of me looking like an idiot my whole life, so I didn't feel that bad for getting my own back. But I was worried I might accidentally give something away. When secrets can't come out of your mouth, they kind of stay just under your skin. Mine wasn't visible to anyone, but it felt itchier than chickenpox to me.

Mum stuck her head round the door. "Want to come and help with dinner, you two? Dad's making *indbagte gulerødder.*"

"It's baked carrots," I said to Carys. "Only slightly less disgusting than it sounds."

"Hey!" Mum said, gently chucking a cushion at me. "It's delicious! It's an old family recipe. It was the first meal your dad ever cooked for me."

"And you still married him?" I said.

"Well, it's a good job I did, right?" Mum took out her phone and held it in front of her face. My heart sank as she started talking into it. "So, Eva has just asked me about the first meal Lars ever cooked for me!" Carys nudged me, but I was too busy dying of embarrassment to look at her. "It was actually really romantic." She sat on the arm of the sofa so I knew this would probably take ages. "As you know, we met at university in Copenhagen. We were both students back then and Lars still lived with his mum, which was super cute…"

I tried to signal to her to stop. But she waved at me the same way she shoos Miss Fizzy away from the plant pots. We couldn't leave the room without walking past the camera. We were trapped. Like hostages. There was nothing to do except wait for her to finish. And pray the floor would open up and swallow me.

"Eva's squirming in the background," Mum said, laughing. "If Lars hadn't been such a good cook maybe I wouldn't have married him. And what then, hey?"

"You would never have got *All About Eva*?" I said.

"Ha!" Mum said. "Got *you*, you mean, silly."

"Same difference," I said, but she acted like she didn't hear me. They'd edit it out later.

"I mean, it's a good job Lars can cook, because he certainly can't dance, right, Eva?" Mum laughed as if I was agreeing with her. She started telling everyone about their wedding dance, when Dad trampled on one of her feet and then the other one. I'd only heard that story ten thousand times.

Mum put her phone down, trying to hide how annoyed she was with me because Carys was there. "Okay!" she said, smiling. "Now you're definitely on kitchen duty."

Carys chopped the salad while I stirred a black-bean sauce that reminded me of ferromagnetic fluid. I watched thick bubbles rise and burst as I strained my ears to hear what Dad was saying on the phone. It was definitely something about the shark video. I don't know how long I'd been listening, but when Mum nudged me to stir the sauce, I jumped.

"All sorted?" Mum asked, as Dad put the phone down. He leaned down and kissed her on the lips, right in front of me and Carys.

"Gross," I muttered, then Dad picked me up and spun me round like he used to do when I was little. That's the thing about having a dad who's 198 cm – you're always little. "Dad! Put me down!" I said, trying to wriggle out of his arms as he repeated, "*Gross? Gross?*" Carys was doubled over laughing. I was so glad he didn't pick her up as well.

"So?" Mum asked again when he finally put me down.

"It's all sorted," Dad said. "We are safe from sharks! Time to celebrate." He took a beer out of the fridge, topped up Mum's wine, then handed me and Carys a bottle of Coke each.

"But what about all the subscribers we lost?" Mum said. "I don't think that's something to celebrate, honey." My ears pricked up when I heard this. Like Miss Fizzy's do when she hears the cupboard where we keep cat treats opening. I exchanged a look with Carys, my heart practically leaping across the kitchen.

Dad told her not to worry, that they'd soon come back. "Or we'll get some new ones." He threw a peanut in the air and caught it in his mouth. "Our newspaper column goes live tomorrow, remember. Ash has secured the channel. We're doing the workout video in the morning. We've got nothing to worry about!" He planted a kiss on Mum's head as I gently clinked my Coke bottle against Carys's. We didn't need to log in this time to cause trouble. We locked eyes and smiled. *That's what you think.*

That night, Carys lay on the pull-out bed that's usually hidden underneath mine. We were supposed to be asleep. I reached up and switched on all my fairy lights. The ceiling lit up with stars, only slightly wonkier. And some in the shape of pineapples.

"Your room's epic!" Carys said, looking up at the ceiling.

"Thanks," I said. "My mum did it."

Carys leaned on her elbows and looked up at me. "So, the plan is to do the workout video tomorrow, then *afterwards* say I can't be on the channel?"

"Yeah," I replied. "Then they've wasted all the time filming it, and they won't even be able to use it. It's foolproof! Although my mum's head may explode."

Carys giggled. We were both silent for a while then she whispered, "Do you feel bad about what we're doing?"

I thought for a second, then whispered back, "No. Why, do you?"

"No," she said, and both of us laughed so hard we had to put pillows over our faces.

The next morning, Mum came in to wake us up. She had her hair in a side ponytail and a fluorescent green sweatband round her head.

"Ready to do the workout video, girls? I have leg warmers!"

I groaned. "Can't you and Dad do it on your own?"

"Oh, come on!" Mum said. "It'll be fun!"

Carys yawned and stretched. "I'll do it. I don't mind."

"That's the spirit, Carys!" Mum said. "Did you call your

parents? Are they okay about you being on the channel?"

Carys nodded, then glanced at me. Suddenly music started and Dad appeared wearing a purple leotard over his cycling shorts and a fake moustache. He gave Mum a kiss on the cheek and started moonwalking.

"Come on, you two! Get into the groove!" He wiggled and sang, "My hips don't lie, ladies!" and we all burst out laughing.

"Okay, fine!" I said, chucking a pillow at him. "Just please stop doing that!"

Half an hour later, Dad had pulled the projector screen down in the living room, moved the sofas and put four yoga mats on the floor. I pulled at the green shiny catsuit Mum had made me wear. I looked like an alien. Carys was in yellow cycling shorts, a pink leotard, sunglasses and matching leg warmers. We'd both refused the sweatbands.

Dad stretched his arms and they almost collided with the ceiling. "OKAY, LET'S DO THIS!" he said and pressed the remote. Andrea, the workout woman, appeared on the screen. She was wearing a leotard and the same purple leg warmers as Mum.

"Welcome to my workout channel!" she said. "I'm Andrea and today it's 1980s workouts! Before we start, those of you who know me, know I am completely obsessed with doing my nails." Andrea waved her fingernails at the camera. "So, here's a little word about my sponsor…"

Dad did warm-up lunges as Andrea revealed that the secret to feeling "truly confident and proud of who we are" was using Super Freak gel polish. At this point in my life I was willing to give it a go.

When the workout finally started, Dad must have done a hundred different warm-up lunges. Me and Carys were already in hysterics. We were standing behind my parents, so we had no choice but to witness them do the move Andrea called "buns of steel". That kind of stuff should be illegal.

"Oh my God, that was so funny!" Carys said afterwards, taking a massive swig of water. I opened the patio doors and we went into the garden for some cold air. I was still out of breath. "Your parents are actually really cool." I looked at her. "I mean it! Mine are so boring and normal. They would never do anything like that."

"I dream about my parents being normal," I said. Carys followed me to the swing seat and we both sat down. "I mean, you don't actually want people at school to see us wearing this stuff?"

Carys looked down at our outfits. "No, definitely not. So, if I get my mum to call yours and say she doesn't want me on the channel, your parents can't post the video?"

"Yeah," I said, sipping my water. "They need permission. Hallie's mum thinks the channel is psychologically damaging, so she never let Hallie be on camera. Any time she came over, Mum and Dad couldn't film." I pulled up my leg warmers, then changed my mind and pushed them back down. "Anyway, it got really awkward. Then Hallie stopped coming over."

"Is that why you're not good friends with Hallie any more?"

I gently pushed my feet against the ground so the seat started swinging. "Kind of," I said. "Then Gabi happened."

"What happened with Gabi?"

I shrugged. "I hate her guts."

We both laughed as Dad walked through the patio doors.

"Hey, girls, you want your pancakes out here?" He brought over a tray of chocolate pancakes, strawberry smoothies and watermelon triangles. Mum brought out the Bluetooth speaker and my new iPad so we could listen to music.

"Download something new if you like," she said. And after that it was hard to convince Carys that my parents were genuinely ruining my life.

"I don't know, Eva," Carys said, taking a bite of chocolatey pancake. "I thought your parents would be, like, mean or something."

"They're okay when I'm cooperating," I said. "Call your mum now and get her to say they can't put the video up, you'll see what they're really like." I heard some rustling coming from the bushes. "Hey, Spud," I called.

"I smelled pancakes," he said, emerging from the hedge. "Hi, Carys."

Carys waved, then got up, holding her phone to her ear. "I'll be back in a bit."

"Want my dad to make you a pancake?" I asked Spud, even though he'd already started eating mine.

"I wanted to ask you something," Spud said. "But it's kind of personal."

"Is this about the Roundhead haircut again? Because honestly, if you are even considering that…"

"No, not that." He fiddled with the edge of his phone cover. "If you were a girl, would you like getting a poem?"

"What do you mean, *if* I was a girl?"

He laughed. "Sorry, I meant, like…a girl from school. I mean, not you. It's not for you."

"What's not for me?" I quickly grabbed the phone out of his hand. It was open on the notes page.

"Roses are red,
Violets are blue,
Ferromagnetic fluid is magnetic,

Paramagnetic metals are too…"

"Eva!" Spud snatched his phone before I could read the rest.

"Is that supposed to be our experiment write-up? Because honestly, I can't see Mr Jacobs appreciating poetry."

"No, not for that," Spud said. "You know like Miss West said, how people used to write poems in the sixteenth century?"

"Yeah. She also said they used to wipe their bums with hay. Wait a minute. It's Valentine's Day in a couple of weeks." Spud's cheeks turned red. "Oh my God, Spud. Who's it for?" He wouldn't meet my eye. "Spud, you're not seriously planning on sending this to someone at school, are you?" He smiled awkwardly. "Is the whole thing science-related? Because, no offence, but I think it's just you and Nerdophobia who are into that stuff." Spud squinted up at the sky. Then I felt bad. "Sorry, I'm just trying to look out for you. If you send that poem to someone at school, they'll share it with our entire year. Everyone will make fun of you from now until eternity."

"Not everyone cares about that stuff, Eva."

"Okay, well, whoever it's for, make sure she knows what ferromagnetic fluid is. Otherwise she might not get it. And the 'roses are red' thing? Kind of dumb." Spud winced, like I'd just given him a dead arm. "Sorry," I said. "It's sweet. But I know what people at school are like." Spud's face looked kind of sad. "But, I dunno. If she's into science then she'll probably really like it."

"Okay, well, it turns out she's not that into science. Or poetry. So I'm deleting it. I've got to go," Spud said, running towards the hedge. "Thanks for the pancake!"

Before I could respond he'd jumped head first back through the bushes.

"Did Spud just jump through that bush?" Carys said, sitting back down.

"Yeah," I said, watching the patch of bushes he'd disappeared through. "He does that. Did you speak to your mum?"

"Yep," Carys said. "She did actually freak out about the idea of me being online after all the St Aug's stuff. Anyway, she's calling your mum right now." My eyes shot to hers. "Don't worry – I made her promise not to mention that. I just hope your parents don't hate me."

"They won't! But anyway," I pointed to my catsuit, "what choice did we have?"

After my parents had spoken to Carys's mum, the atmosphere in the house changed. Carys packed her stuff in my room and we could hear Mum downstairs saying, "It just seems like such a waste now!" and "We'll have to do the whole thing over!" It was kind of majorly awkward.

"I'm really sorry," Carys said, as we walked downstairs. "I should have asked my mum first. I didn't realize she'd be so strict about it."

Mum blinked a few times. Weird how some people can make blinking look angry. "Oh, don't worry, sweetheart. We just thought you'd already asked your parents."

"Sorry," Carys said, biting her lip.

"It's fine," Mum said, getting up from the sofa and giving Carys a hug. "We understand. We'll just…redo it! You don't mind putting your leg warmers back on, do you, Eva?"

"Actually, my legs are kind of aching," I said. "I've pulled a muscle or something. Also, I have my science experiment stuff to write up for Monday."

Mum smiled, but I could tell she was already regretting the homework schedule. I didn't care. How she felt was nothing compared to how bad I'd feel if thousands of people, including half my school, saw me in a bright green catsuit doing the booty roll.

But I was stupid. I thought something like Carys's mum not wanting them to upload the video might actually stop them.

22

UNPLUGGED

The next day was Sunday, and the day of unplugging. Only I'd already forgotten and accidentally went on TikTok while I was getting dressed.

"Eva!" Dad called from downstairs. "Don't forget we're riding to Bourton Hill today."

I groaned. Dad's idea of a perfect day involved a way-too-long bike ride, and unfortunately it wasn't technically below freezing this morning so there was no way of getting out of it. I clicked on Google Maps to find out how far it was to Bourton Hill. Eleven miles! I pulled on another pair of leggings.

"Unplugged day today, remember, sweetie," Mum said, appearing at the door.

"Whoops," I said, closing Google Maps and trying to

figure out how to switch off my phone.

I eyed the bright pink cycling helmet Mum was wearing. "Is that new? Why have you got it on already?"

"Check it out!" Mum said and turned to the side.

"Is that a...horn?"

"Yes!" Mum squealed. "Isn't it cute? It's called the Unicorn."

"Well, don't impale anyone."

"Ha! Well, I hope you don't either!" She held up a fluffy helmet with a gigantic horn on each side. "Yours is called the Highland Cow!"

"Please tell me you are joking."

"Think yourself lucky," she said. "Dad's wearing the Beast!"

"Oh my God," I said as she handed the helmet to me. "I'm supposed to wear this for eleven miles?"

"Twenty-two!" Mum said. "We have to cycle back, remember."

As I was getting my bike out, I was so relieved it was our unplugged day. At least no one would see me looking like this. At that exact moment, Spud appeared at the bottom of the drive.

"Woah!" he said.

"Say anything and I will kill you."

"It looks like you actually could!" he said. "What's

it supposed to be? A minotaur?"

I sighed. "A highland cow."

"Well, just to warn you, Chip's got his BB gun out."

"Ah, Spud!" Mum said, pushing her bike out of the garage. "Perfect timing. Take a photo for our Instagram, will you?"

I glared at Spud and shook my head.

"I'm afraid I can't, Mrs Andersen."

"Oh, come on. Just a quick one once we're on our bikes." Mum held out her phone.

"I'm afraid that would constitute an infringement of the rules of the 8W Official Day of Unplugging."

I mouthed "Thank you" then said to Mum, "We're doing this for our special assembly! Spud takes these things kind of seriously."

She sighed. "I don't know why I ever agreed to this."

"Right!" Dad said, jogging down the front steps. His cycle helmet was grey with a massive red mohawk.

Spud's eyes lit up. "Woah, Mr Andersen! You look epic! Could I borrow that off you one day? It would go down a storm at Games Club."

Dad smiled. "I'm sure it would, Spud. So, are we ready to roll?"

After six miles of cycling over massive hills, my hands were freezing and my thighs were burning. Mum had complained about the Instagrammable landscape shots she kept missing. I'd have to somehow do my history homework without the internet when we got back. Mrs Peters said we could look up the English Civil War "in a book". Like anyone has books about that at home.

"Lars, can we stop for a minute? Look at that view!" Mum said, gazing out towards the hills. "One selfie won't do any harm."

"Come on, Jen," Dad said, wiping the sweat from his top lip. "We agreed to unplug today." And for a few seconds, I actually thought Dad cared about my assembly. "That's the whole concept of the Tranquil Eyes takeover. If you post any pictures it's obvious we weren't screen-free."

"Okay, you're right," Mum said. "But I'm not missing the opportunity to photograph you in that helmet." I turned away and heard the click of her phone. "Eva, smile!" I turned round and did the fakest smile I could. "Beautiful!" I'm not sure if she was being sarcastic.

By the time we got to Bourton Hill it had started raining. Which my dad seemed delighted about. "Ah, this is so invigorating!" he said, pulling off his Beast helmet and tilting his face towards the sky.

"Invigorating?" I said. "I literally can't feel my fingers. Where's whatever it is we're supposed to be looking at anyway?" I looked around for a monument or building. Or any sign of human life.

"What do you mean, *where is it*?" Dad said. "This *is* it! We're here! Beautiful countryside, nothing for miles around. Peace! This is being truly unplugged."

I took a seat on the nearest rock. "Okay, but what are we supposed to do?"

Half an hour later, we were squashed inside a pop-up tent playing *Bezzerwizzer*, this Danish board game which Dad likes because he always wins. It was so cold I was forced to wear Dad's spare cagoule.

All the way home, he went on about how wonderful it was to "get back to nature". He only stopped after me and Mum had to pee behind a hedge, and she threatened to call an Uber if he said anything else. But I guess, apart from the wild peeing, and getting soaked by the rain and the dumb cycle helment, it felt pretty nice not worrying about it all going online.

On Monday morning, Miss Wilson made us write our reports about what we'd done yesterday. Only I knew half our class didn't even take part properly, because I'd checked Instagram and Snapchat before I went to bed. I tried to think of something to write that didn't involve a cattle-themed cycle helmet, *Bezzerwizzer* or wild wees. *We went on a bike ride*, I wrote, then chewed the end of my pen. What was I supposed to say about being unplugged? My entire life was still online, even when I wasn't.

"And Eva?" Miss Wilson said as she collected in everyone's reports. "Did you enjoy the digital detox?"

"My parents forced me to go on a bike ride in the rain."

Miss Wilson smiled. "A bike ride in the rain sounds invigorating to me!" Which was literally what my dad said. "I'm sure I'll enjoy reading your report." She would probably feel differently when she actually read it. "I thought you could take centre stage for this assembly, Eva. Talk about your experiences a little. It will add an extra dimension to our assembly."

"Oh," I said, glancing at Hallie. "I thought the form captain was supposed to lead assemblies."

Miss Wilson flicked through the bunch of papers she'd collected. "They do normally, but I'm sure Hallie doesn't mind sharing the limelight considering the topic, do you, Hallie?"

"Sure," Hallie said, but I could tell she was disappointed. She knew an assembly was exactly the type of thing I would probably mess up. "I can help you write the introduction if you want. I mean, I kind of already wrote

211

something last night."

"Thanks," I said.

"Yes, thank you, Hallie," Miss Wilson said. "That's settled then. I'll have a look through your reports, and we'll have a practice on Friday lunchtime."

"Oh," I said. "I have Languages Club on Friday."

"Me too," said Rami. "Madame Chapelle doesn't let us skip it."

Miss Wilson sighed. "Well, that's the only time the hall's free. We'll just have to practise without you. But I'm counting on you to learn your lines off by heart!"

I'm not sure if I mentioned this already, but Miss Wilson could be kind of unreasonable.

The next day, she handed my report back to me with one comment on it: *Too short – tell me what you learned! Something to hold the audience's attention!* So, that night, I googled *digital detox* and wrote down a bunch of stuff about feeling calmer, physically healthier and getting to sleep earlier. I didn't notice any of those things actually happening to me on Sunday, but I realized ages ago that life is a lot easier when you just tell people what they want to hear.

After I'd finished, I went downstairs to show Dad.

I heard one of the songs we did the workout video to coming from the office. I mean, "Super Freak" is a pretty distinctive song. Plus, if you've seen your parents doing butt clenches, it's not something you're ever likely to forget. I took a pear from the fruit bowl and wandered over to the office door. It was only open a fraction, so I couldn't see the computer screen very well.

"Yeah, that bit. Cut it there," Mum said, and Dad clicked the mouse a few times. What were they doing? Carys's mum had said they couldn't upload the workout video. I moved a bit closer, trying not to drip pear juice on the floorboards. And there we were on the screen, mid-squat. One of my leg warmers had fallen down and my face was glistening with sweat. I tried to push the door open a tiny bit more, but I overbalanced and it swung all the way open.

Mum turned around. "Oh, hey, sweetie. You okay?"

I tried to look casual, which isn't easy when you've been caught spying. "I've finished my homework," I said, "for the assembly."

"Great!" Mum said. "Such a shame we can't come and watch." She pulled my hair out from behind my ears. "But I'm glad Miss Wilson finally listened to my advice! I told her she ought to make more of you in these things."

Great, I thought. So it was Mum's fault I had to do it.

"Want to see the 80s workout video? It turned out *so* good!" She nudged Dad. "Play that running man bit again. Oh my God, Eva! You are going to die when you see this."

"I already got to see it live, remember. Anyway, I thought Carys's mum didn't want her on the channel."

"Oh, don't worry about that," Mum said. "We've sorted it."

"Super Freak" started playing and there we were doing synchronized butt clenches. They'd put an emoji over Carys's face.

"You're going to post it like that?" I said.

"I know," Mum said. "It's not ideal."

"I meant with me. In that catsuit! It's so embarrassing!"

"Not this again, Eva," Mum said. "It's *supposed* to be embarrassing! It's funny."

"I'll add some stickers," Dad said. "It will look good, Eva. Don't worry so much."

I stood watching them for a while in silence. Because what was the point in even trying to get them to listen? The edges of my pear had gone brown, so I dropped it in the bin on my way back upstairs. Anyway, I didn't feel hungry. Knowing a video of me wearing a skintight shiny catsuit was about to be posted to the entire world kind of ruined my appetite.

I got ready for bed and lay under my duvet looking up at the fairy lights for a while, trying to think what I could do. Deleting their content had done literally nothing. Posting that shark video had only lost them a few thousand followers. And they were still posting embarrassing stuff. I'd been trapped inside *All About Eva* my whole life. And no one could hear me shouting for help. So, I really didn't have much choice. I had to do something big to make them stop.

And things got a lot worse after that.

23

WAR

The next morning Spud jogged into my house singing "Super Freak" with his tie around his head.

"See?" Mum said. "Spud thinks it's funny!"

I gave her a look. "Spud thought it was funny to bring a frog to school in his lunchbox."

Spud laughed. "Now that was funny! What you got for lunch?" He did an exaggerated squat to try to reach my lunch bag. I swung it at his head, but he ducked. "First rule of ju-jitsu, Eva. Always be prepared for attack."

As we walked up the hill, I swiped my phone to check how many people had viewed the workout video. "Over eighteen thousand already." I groaned.

"Don't worry about it!" Spud said.

"You wouldn't be laughing if it was a video of you

wearing a shiny catsuit." Spud grinned. "Actually, forget I said that." I sighed. "I wish it was half-term already. Then I'd be at Farmor's and could pretend none of this was happening."

"Mum said I can maybe get some hydrofluoric acid at half-term," Spud said. "To replicate Mr Jacobs's light bulb experiment, but on a much larger scale! It can corrode human flesh down to the bone."

"It's reassuring to know I'll be in a different country," I said. "If you could drop the *All About Eva* channel in that acid stuff too, that would be great."

Hallie had said she'd help me write the assembly introduction. So, for the first time, me, Hallie, Gabi and Carys all sat together in the canteen at lunch. It wasn't that awkward, mainly because Gabi never stopped talking.

"...then I do a tuck jump half turn, then split leap and finish on a front walkover." She held up her arms like she'd just completed an Olympic gold medal routine, narrowly missing hitting a Year Seven in the face.

"Sounds great," I said, trying my best not to sound sarcastic because Hallie was listening.

"Shame you don't do gymnastics any more, Eva," Gabi said. "Especially considering your workout skills." Then she sang, "Super Freak! Super Freak!" I smiled at her for less than half a second.

"So, the competition's on Saturday?" Carys said, who was a lot better at being nice to Gabi than I was.

"Yep," Gabi said. "Hallie's routine is amazing!"

"Thanks," Hallie said. "But I still need to perfect my back handspring. I'm not landing it properly."

Gabi started gushing about how good Hallie's landings were, so I pushed my phone across the table to change the subject.

"What do you think of this intro? I'm not even sure what Miss Wilson expects me to say."

"It's good," Hallie said, scrolling through my notes. "Only, you could try opening with something more dramatic?" I smiled as she started typing onto my phone. "And make sure you say that last bit without sounding sarcastic." We smiled at each other, and for a minute things felt like they used to.

After we'd finished eating, Hallie asked if we wanted to watch her gymnastics routine, so we sat on the floor at the edge of the sports hall while she got changed. Gabi turned to Carys and said, "So, is it true you hacked St Aug's website?" She just blurted it out like that. No warning or anything.

Carys smiled. "Don't believe everything you hear about me, okay?"

Gabi shrugged and that would have been the end of it if I hadn't said something stupid.

"It's none of your business anyway, Gabi," I said, picking at a dried bit of mud on my shoe.

"It is my business if Carys is hanging around with *my* friend," Gabi said, ignoring Carys and pointing her dead eyes straight at me.

"I'm not your friend," I said, dusting off my hands.

"I know," Gabi sneered. "I meant Hallie."

"Well, thanks, Gabi," Carys said, standing up. "It's so nice getting to know you."

Just then, Hallie's routine music started. "Priceless" by Melanie Fiona. I smiled. We'd listened to so many tracks last summer as she'd tried to find the right song for her routine. "It's got to be an artist with Guyanese roots like me," she'd said. "But nobody in my dad's record collection, and the beat needs to be like… " And she'd drummed her hands on her knees. When "Priceless" played, she'd squeezed my shoulders and said, "This is the one!" We'd listened to it on repeat and practised cartwheels and handstands in her garden all afternoon. Her dad had brought us fiery ginger beers and Hallie laughed when the spice tingled my nose and made me sneeze non-stop.

We watched as Hallie ended her routine with a back handspring and stretched her arms up to finish. Our applause echoed around the sports hall. Hallie did an over-exaggerated curtsy, then ran over to us.

"So, what do you think?" she asked. "Good enough to finish top three?"

"Definitely," I said, as Gabi jumped up.

"Can we ask Mrs Marshall if she'll get the vault out? I wouldn't mind doing some practice actually." I could tell Gabi was lying to get Hallie on her own.

"Okay," Hallie said, reading the awkwardness on our faces.

"Your routine is so good, Hals," I said.

"Yeah," Carys said. "It's amazing."

"Thanks," Hallie said, then Gabi mouthed something to her. "Well, see you later, okay." And they jogged over to Mrs Marshall, who was collecting up the mats. I stood for a moment watching them, but they didn't look back over, so I followed Carys outside.

Hallie didn't speak to me much the rest of that week. She said she was busy practising for the competition, but she'd posted a video of her and Gabi at the Creep Cabin. They were sharing a double chocolate crêpe and laughing over this dumb dance move Gabi kept doing. They hadn't even invited me. Jealousy snagged at my heart. I didn't want to see any more, but videos kept popping up of them having "the best time". And with each one I felt worse.

Eventually, I clicked on their profiles and tapped *mute*. I'd unmute them later. But at least for now, I wouldn't have to look.

On Friday lunchtime, I headed to Languages Club with Rami. Some Year Elevens walked past us in the corridor. "Clench those buns!" one of them shouted. Another called out, "Streeeeeeeeeetch!" so loud it echoed all the way down the corridor. As we got to the classroom I heard, "Tell your mum I think she's hot!"

Rami looked at me. "You okay?"

"Yeah, no big deal," I said and pushed the door open.

"Exactly, who cares!" Rami said. "It's not like we haven't seen you do millions of embarrassing things before."

And suddenly, I felt like I was about to explode. I turned around and shouted down the corridor, "MY MUM IS FORTY-SEVEN YEARS OLD!"

I took a deep breath. Shouting at them like that actually made me feel a lot better. Until I realized the whole of Languages Club was staring at me.

That night, I waited until I was certain my parents were asleep, then I crept downstairs. I pushed a chair up against the office door – I'd watched enough episodes of *Justice Force* to know it's better to be overly cautious. I tapped the mouse and watched the computer screen light up, then softly typed in the password. The screen froze for a second, and my heart stopped. Did they change this password too? But then the desktop appeared and I could breathe again. I clicked on *Security* and found their new channel password. I noted it down and silently logged on to *All About Eva*. This time, I knew exactly what I wanted to do. This time, I wanted it to hurt.

Once I'd started deleting videos, I couldn't stop. I started with the ones from years ago, before we even moved to this house. My first words. My first steps. My first haircut. Everything Mum meant by the "enormous bank of amazing memories that we get to keep and share" that she'd talked about on TV. Well, by the time I'd finished, it wouldn't be so enormous.

The Andersens go to Disneyland!!!
Eva's first time in Denmark!!!
Trip to A&E 😣 😣 😣
Christmas shopping!!!
Did Eva just say Mummy??!!

All deleted. They didn't even feel like memories to me. It was like on Star Fox, this video game I used to play with Spud where you have to shoot down your enemies. You just keep pressing *fire* until you run out of ammo. I don't know how many of the old videos I watched on mute that

222

night. Or exactly when I started crying. But after a while the screen looked all blurry. And the desk had tear splashes on it.

24

SUPER FREAK

The next morning, I heard, "Lars! Something's happened again!" A pool of dread collected in my stomach. They barely noticed me eating my cereal at the kitchen table. They were in the office listening to Ash, their IT consultant, who was on loudspeaker.

It reminded me of this time Mum and Dad were having an important meeting with Ash downstairs. I was only nine, so I wasn't invited. I wasn't even allowed in the snug to watch TV. The entire house stank of coffee because they'd had the machine on for ages. They said they'd only be an hour, but they'd been almost two and I was starving. I peered through the bannisters, wondering if I could get a snack without them noticing.

"To be honest with you, I think your content's okay,"

I had heard Ash say. "It's just…how can I put this?" He tapped his password into his phone quicker than I'd ever seen anyone do it. "The problem is, you need a new angle. You see, Eva's nine now, right? She's reached that age where she's just not cute any more."

It was like being whacked in the face with an oar. I didn't feel so hungry after that. I went back to my room, lay on my bed and listened to the muffled voices discussing new angles for the channel. And the whole time tears were falling silently down my face. They sank into the pillow, along with the realization that I was the reason they'd been losing subscribers. People didn't like me any more.

Sitting in the kitchen, I stirred my cereal then heard Dad say, "You mean, someone's guessed our password?" I dropped my spoon and it clattered into my bowl.

"Eva?" Mum said, opening the office door. "Morning, sweetie. We're having a bit of a crisis with the channel." She took a deep breath, then burst into tears. I didn't know what to do. I mean, I'd seen her crying before, loads of times. But not when it had definitely been my fault.

"Are you okay?" It was probably the dumbest thing to say in that situation, but it was the only thing I could think of.

"Ash thinks someone's hacking our channel," she said.

"They've deleted videos from when you were a baby! I mean, who would do that? To a *baby*?"

I swallowed, my heart beating ten times faster than normal. I hoped Mum wouldn't notice.

She pulled a tissue out of her pocket and blew her nose. "Lars is seeing if we have the files backed up. But still, it will take days, maybe weeks to get everything back the way it was. Ash says the hard drives could have failed by now. These things don't store very well apparently. So, we might have lost all your baby videos." She sniffed and caught a tear running down her cheek in the tissue.

It felt a lot better at the time, when I was actually deleting the videos. But now, seeing Mum upset, my heart felt kind of grey. "Oh," I said and I could feel bits of granola stuck in my throat, like guilt.

Spud insisted on listening to my assembly introduction as we walked up the hill on Monday. I was supposed to learn it off by heart over the weekend, but let's just say that never happened.

"You think Miss Wilson will let me use my notes?"

"Er, those ones?" Spud looked at the creased bits of paper in my hands. "That would be a negative."

My heart sank. "I can't do it without my notes! And

there's no time to write it out again before assembly starts."

"Here," Spud said, tugging the notes out of my hands. "If I run all the way, I'll have time to type and print them out before the assembly."

"Thank you, Spud!" I called after him as he raced up the hill. "You're AMAZING!" And all of Nerdophobia turned round and stared at me.

As I got to school, I noticed Hallie's mum in the car park.

"That's weird," I said. "What's Hallie's mum doing here?"

Carys looked over. "Maybe Hallie forgot her PE kit or something."

"Hallie? Forget something?" I said. "No way."

Miss Wilson had told us to go straight to the assembly hall, and by the time we got there most of our class had already arrived. The rows of chairs facing the stage seemed to go on for miles.

"Eva!" Miss Wilson said as she saw me come in. "Thank goodness! We don't have much time. You'll be standing here at the front." She beckoned me onto the stage. I took a deep breath and walked up the stairs to the spot she was pointing to. I watched the door at the side of the hall, willing Spud to come through it. But it was Gabi. She held the door open for Hallie, who was on crutches. She had a blue cast on her ankle.

"Oh my God," I said, forgetting about staying on the spot Miss Wilson had marked. I ran down the steps and looked at the cast on her ankle. "What happened?"

Hallie gave me a look like she was about to cry, but also like she wanted to push me over with her crutches. "You didn't see my post? About the competition?"

"I-I…" I said. But she didn't let me finish.

"Didn't think so. Come on, Gabi."

"Some friend you are," Gabi whispered and barged past me. She helped Hallie into a seat facing the audience, and I felt like the worst person ever. How could I have forgotten about her competition? How could I have missed her post? I felt all the warmth drain out of my body. *I'd forgotten to unmute them.* Then the bell went and people started pouring in.

"Here!" Spud said, handing me a neat stack of paper. "Took ages to log on!"

"Thanks." I looked over at Hallie. A group of girls from our class surrounded her. She'd been training for the competition for months. Now she was hurt and I had no idea what had happened. This horrible feeling swept into my stomach, like cold soup. Gabi was right. I was a bad friend. The worst.

"Don't mention it," Spud said, walking off. And it was only then I realized he'd still been standing there.

Miss Wilson called me to get back onstage. I took my place in the centre, wishing for this whole thing to be over so I could speak to Hallie. And say a proper thank you to Spud.

"Good morning, everybody!" said Mr Andrews, the principal. He only came out of his office on special occasions, like assemblies and the Christmas carol concert. "It is my absolute pleasure to introduce 8W for their form assembly, which is all about their special day of hugging!" A wave of laughter went around the hall and I felt my stomach drop through the stage.

Miss Wilson loud-whispered something from the front row like it was a pantomime.

"Sorry!" Mr Andrews said. "Misunderstanding!" He grinned at us and clapped his hands together. "Their special day of *unplugging*. That is a relief! Thank you, Miss Wilson. Take it away, 8W!"

My mouth felt dry, like I'd just swallowed a mouthful of sand.

"Good morning," I said into the microphone. The first note Spud had given me said *MAY THE FORCE BE WITH YOU!* and was surrounded by smiling emojis. I laughed, then looked up at the million faces staring at me.

I straightened my face. "Did you know, young people today spend less time outside than prisoners? So, on the thirty-first of January my classmates and I decided to do our own digital detox for twenty-four hours. We were all really excited about taking part." *Techically a lie*, I thought. But then I stopped. I could hear humming coming from the audience. Miss Wilson gestured for me to carry on. I swallowed. "So, from sun-up to sun-down, we put our phones down and switched off our computers and…" I looked up at the sea of faces in front of me. The humming was getting louder. "And, um, instead of screen time, we spent the day in…um, FaceTime. I mean, real time." The notes were shaking in my hands. Because I recognized the tune they were humming. It was "Super Freak". The song from the workout video. I could feel every single pair of eyes on me. Not just the ones in the assembly hall, but every pair of eyes that had seen that video. And all the others. Millions and millions of eyes, all staring directly at me. They felt heavy. Like I might collapse under their weight.

Miss Wilson and the other teachers on the front row were looking round, trying to figure out where the sound was coming from. But it was coming from everywhere. Then I heard Hallie's voice. It somehow sailed over all the humming.

"Keep going, Eva."

I cleared my throat and said, "We hope you enjoy hearing what we found out." Then I stepped backwards, into the shadow of the stage curtain.

Lucas started saying his bit about visiting a reservoir. I could still hear the humming faintly, only maybe it was just in my head. When the assembly was over everyone clapped and I heard the humming again as Mr Andrews dismissed everyone.

"Well done, everyone!" Miss Wilson said, and she clasped my hands. "Oh, you're trembling, Eva! Bless you. I didn't think you'd get so nervous."

"You did amazingly!" Carys said. "Guess you heard the song?"

I nodded. "Didn't everyone?"

"Forget them," Carys said, linking my arm. "They're just jealous of our butt clenches."

I tried to laugh, but my insides were churning, like they were getting dredged. "Hallie hurt her ankle at the finals," I said. "I totally forgot it was this weekend."

"Maybe you should talk to her." Carys nodded towards Hallie, who was waiting by the hall doors. Gabi was standing beside her holding her bag. "I'll see you in class."

I smiled at Hallie. She looked back at me, but she didn't smile.

"Hey," I said. "Thanks for helping me in there."

"No problem," she said. "The humming was mean."

"So, what happened?" I said, looking at her cast. Gabi's name was written in purple felt-tip.

"I messed up landing my backflip," Hallie said. "But you'd already know that if you'd asked how it went."

"I'm sorry." I knew those words weren't enough. But I couldn't think of any better ones.

She looked at me, her brown eyes shining with tears. "You didn't even say good luck."

I really wanted to give her a hug, but it was like the invisible wall between us was thicker than ever. "I'm really sorry, Hals. It's just there's been this thing happening with the channel and…"

"Right," Hallie said. "Well, next time I break my ankle, I'll be sure to comment on *All About Eva*. That way you might actually notice."

And there was nothing I could say. She was right. It was her biggest competition and I didn't even wish her good luck. I didn't even remember.

I sat in maths that morning listening to Mr Gregory talking about vectors, whatever they are, while Alfie hummed "Super Freak" at the back of my head. I thought about the channel, about what I'd done. About all the people who watched me every single day. The people who had seen me grow up. Who talked about me like they knew me. But they didn't know me at all. I'd known Hallie since Year Four. I knew she loved spicy food, and hated the sight of blood. That she couldn't go cross-eyed properly no matter how many times she tried. How she sometimes sang without realizing. I knew practically everything about her. But I didn't even notice her break her ankle.

And there was this one thought I couldn't shake out of my brain. Okay, I hadn't exactly been a great friend. But this never would have happened if it wasn't for the stupid channel!

And call it a coincidence or whatever. But that night, Carys sent me a link. It was this vlogging family called *The Grant-Laceys*. They're an American family with eight million subscribers. I'd seen a few of their videos. Their eldest daughter was a bit older than me. I remembered watching a video where her parents went berserk after she bleached her hair. Mum kind of idolized them. She got annoyed at Dad once when he called them "dysfunctional". Just as I started watching, a message from Carys popped up:

Look at her T-shirt.

I watched closer. The mum was talking to the camera. But she was wearing a button-up shirt, not a T-shirt. Then I saw the daughter standing in the background. I couldn't make out what her T-shirt said at first. But she straightened it out, and then I saw it in big black letters: *STOP FILMING ME.*

And that's when I realized. I'd been trying to take control of the channel from the wrong side of the screen.

25

CLEAR-OUT

It was a few days later, the last week of term, and Mum and Dad were still glued to their computers. They'd put up a special vlog about the hacking. And instead of losing subscribers, they were gaining them. They watched the subscribers counter like hawks, ready to film my live reaction. The celebration video we'd already filmed wasn't enough apparently. They needed something live too, so they had the cameras going 24-7. I didn't really see how they could film it live. What if, at the crucial moment when the counter turned to 500,000, I was at school? Or on the toilet? But Mum rolled her eyes whenever I brought it up.

*   *   *

On Thursday, Miss West had given us a load of Shakespeare quotes to memorize for homework, and I felt like doing it about as much as I felt like sticking my head into the fermenting experiment Spud had in his garage. So, I put my new plan into action. I took the pictures off the walls first. Then the pink canopy that cascaded over my bed. I pulled down all the fairy lights I could reach and the giant bow on my wall. I collected up all the plants and ornaments, everything from my parents' dumb sponsors, and dumped it in a pile outside my door. It was almost reaching the other side of the landing by the time Mum came upstairs.

"What's all this!" she asked as I peeled heart-shaped stickers off the wall.

"I'm redecorating."

"Is that what you call it?" She chuckled in a way that told me she was filming. "Eva seems to be having a spontaneous spring clean! I hope you're going to put all this stuff back when you've finished!"

"Nope," I said, matter-of-factly. "It's all your stuff, so you can have it back."

"Eva!" she said, stepping over the pile into my room. "You've emptied the whole room out! It looks like a prison cell in here."

"It suits my life then."

"Did you hear that?" Mum said, turning the camera on herself. "My darling daughter, everybody!"

I stood on a stool to take down the wall stickers by my wardrobe. "It's so dusty up here!" I said loudly. "Like properly disgusting."

I heard the *beep-beep* of the camera switching off.

"Eva!" Mum said. "I don't know what's gotten into you! Lars and I have a lot to deal with at the moment, with all this hacking stuff. I'm sorry if you're not getting enough attention."

I peeled off a wall sticker and let it flutter down to the carpet. "Like I haven't had enough attention to last me ten lifetimes."

Mum sighed. "You're not serious about changing your room, are you? Because I really don't think we have the time right now."

I wiped my dusty hands down my leggings. "I want to do it myself, anyway."

"Okay, well, if you are serious, I've got some lovely things still boxed up in the garage. But I wish you'd picked a better time, sweetie. We'll need to do an unboxing video and a before-and-after. Honestly, I don't think I have the energy for it this week. We already have the Valentine's Special scheduled and then we're off to Farmor's next week."

"That's okay," I said. "I actually like my room plain. It's called minimalism. Miss Wilson told us about it."

"You can't be serious, Eva," Mum said. "How are we supposed to film in here with it looking like this? What would people think? It really does look like a prison cell."

"I don't care," I said.

She looked at me for a few seconds. "Okay, sweetie, I can see you're not in the mood for talking." She waited for me to contradict her. But I didn't. So she kissed me on the head and walked out.

Later, Dad called, "Prisoner Andersen! Dinner's ready!" So I deliberately didn't go downstairs for ages.

That night, I looked up at the blank ceiling where the fairy lights used to be. It was dark in my room without them. I guess it *was* kind of prison cell-ish without all of my stuff. I mean, *their* stuff. But it felt like a blank page too. Like I'd turned over a new page in my sketchbook and I could draw whatever I wanted.

On Friday, I went to Carys's straight after school. I was supposed to be at home in case the 0.5 million subscribers thing happened, but I'd begged Mum and Dad so many times they agreed just to get some peace and quiet.

We were taking silly photos in Carys's room when she

peered at herself in the camera and pulled at her fringe.

"Needs cutting," she said. She rummaged around in a drawer for a while then pulled out a black case and took out some scissors. "These are strictly for professionals."

"You're not going to do it yourself, are you?" I watched her take off her glasses and carefully comb out her fringe.

"I always cut it myself," she said. "Well, my fringe anyway."

"Your parents let you cut your own hair?"

"Yeah, course," she said. "It's my hair."

I fished in my pocket for a bobble. "I wish I could have my hair short," I said, moving closer to watch. "I hate it long."

"So, get it cut." Carys snipped at her fringe in the mirror. Tiny bits of jet-black hair scattered onto her nose. "It would suit you short."

"Yeah, like my mum would let me." I pulled my hair back to see how it looked short. "Think I'd look older with shorter hair?"

Carys snipped at the edges of her fringe, then picked her phone up off the floor. She flicked through it for a minute then handed it to me. "Something like that would really suit you."

I studied the picture of Emma Watson on her phone. "Oh my God, that is seriously short. I meant like…" I searched through hairstyle pictures for a while, then held up one of a girl with wavy hair just above her shoulders. "Like that," I said.

"Oh, yeah, nice!" Carys said, studying the photo. "I could probably do that."

"You could cut my hair like that?"

Carys shrugged. "Yeah, my auntie's a hairdresser at this super expensive place in London. I watched her cut my cousin's hair at Christmas. She let me do the back. With her help, obviously." She took back her phone and flicked through her photos. "Look. That's her before. And that's after."

"Wow," I said. "And you think you could do mine like that?"

"Sure. I mean, my auntie showed me and she's really good. She let me have these scissors. We'd have to go in the bathroom though as hair gets stuck in the carpet."

"Oh," I said. "I'm supposed to do this ad for a hair mask thing for long hair next week before we go to Farmor's. It's in the schedule."

Carys grinned. "Sounds like the perfect time to me."

Just then, the gong sounded and her dad called up the stairs, "Girls! Dinner is served! And would you like to try my elderflower and mint sparkle?"

We looked at each other and burst out laughing. I can't

really explain what we found so funny. Maybe just the randomness of her dad. But for that moment, actually, for the whole of that night, I felt like I could be myself. The Eva I actually wanted to be. The Eva I would actually be already if there were no strangers watching.

After dinner, I sat in Carys's bathroom with butterflies in my stomach.

"You sure about this, Eva?" she said. "Because it's not like I can stick it back on if you don't like it."

"Yep," I said. "I've wanted it short for ages. Just do it." I closed my eyes and listened for the first snip.

After a few minutes, Carys nudged me. She was holding up my ponytail. It looked weird, not attached to my head. I felt my hair at the back. "Oh my God." I shook out my hair and looked at my reflection in the mirror.

"It already looks amazing!" Carys said. "But I'll cut those bits at the front so they're more level." I sat back down and felt Carys's hands on my shoulders. "Everyone is going to love it."

When Carys had finished, I looked at myself in the mirror. I looked so different. I twisted a short strand around in my fingers. "You really think it looks nice? Like, better?"

"One million per cent," Carys said, beaming at me in the mirror. "Oh, come with me!" I followed her back into her bedroom where she rummaged around in a box by her wardrobe. "Here it is!" She held up an old-fashioned camera, stuck out her tongue and the flash went off. It made a whirring noise, then a photo slid out of the front. "Test photo," Carys said, and waved it around for a few seconds. "Okay, your turn. Smile!" I looked into the camera, tilted my face to the side and did a half-serious pose. "Amazing," Carys said, handing me the photo.

I watched as my face slowly came into view. "I really love it," I said. "Thank you."

"I love it too," Carys said. "But don't tell your parents that it was my idea to cut it, okay? I don't fancy getting on the wrong side of your mum. Not after those air punches she was throwing during that workout."

I smiled and carefully dropped the photo in my pocket. "You know she'll probably faint or something."

Carys laughed. "Maybe we should call the ambulance now."

I grinned, picked up the ponytail and folded it into the pocket of my bag. Then I headed downstairs, stepping over Bernie, who was snoring in the hallway.

"Hope she likes it!" Carys said as I left.

"You might be hearing from their lawyer!" I called back. And I could hear Carys laughing as I closed the door.

26

EMERGENCY

The excitement I'd felt at Carys's house turned into nerves as I walked home. *It's only hair,* I repeated to myself. *And it's my hair.* But that message didn't exactly make it to my heart, which was beating so fast I wondered if I really should call an ambulance.

"Hey, sweetie," Mum called cheerfully as I opened the door. Then the colour completely drained from her face. "OH MY GOD! EVA!" She screamed and jumped up from the sofa, knocking over a glass of wine on the coffee table.

"Jen!" Dad said as he caught the glass with weirdly good ju-jitsu skills. Then he saw my hair and said, "Ah," and nothing else.

"What on earth have you done?" Mum said, pulling

the strands of hair around my face. "Where did you get this cut?"

"I did it myself," I said, like cutting your own hair was something normal people did all the time.

"But…why? I mean, it's so short! Why would you do this, Eva?"

"I've had a haircut, Mum, not a facial tattoo," I said.

"Lars, will you please say something."

Dad stood up. "Well, it's a little dramatic. But actually, it suits you."

Mum stared at him open-mouthed. "Are you serious? I can't believe you've done this without even speaking to me, Eva!" She spun me round to look at the back. "There's no way you cut this yourself. Did Carys do it?"

"Only because I asked her to." I stared at my shoes. "I take it you don't like it."

"Jen," Dad said, putting his arm round Mum's shoulder. "It is only hair. *Eva's* hair, right? It looks more like mine now!" I hoped he wasn't serious. "I'll get you another wine."

Mum wiped her hands over her face and looked at me. "Right. It is your hair. But I'm texting Sasha right now to see if she'll do an emergency appointment for tomorrow."

"Jen!" Dad called from the kitchen. "Since when is the hairdresser's an emergency service?"

Mum put her hands on her hips. "Lars, we all know

your hair defies gravity, so I don't expect you to understand. I suppose you forgot about that hair mask ad next week?" she said to me. I twisted my mouth into an apologetic smile. "Well, Lars, it looks like you're doing the hair mask with me instead now Eva's cut hers off!" I picked up my school bag and headed upstairs, then Mum said, "Oh, and I'm calling Caroline before it gets too late." I stopped mid-step.

"Who's Caroline?" Dad asked.

Mum tutted. "Carys's mum. Don't you remember anyone?"

"What are you calling Carys's mum for?" he said.

"Are you joking?" she said. "Her daughter's just done an Edward Scissorhands on our daughter!"

"Mum, please!" I shouted. "It's not Carys's fault! It was my idea."

"Shh, it's ringing."

I crept to the top stair, pulled out my phone and quickly messaged Carys:

My mum's calling yours about the haircut!!!

😖 sorry. I said it was my idea.

Carys replied: 😂 It's okay. You're still alive yay!!

I typed: She's taking me to the hairdresser's tomorrow. Don't take it personally.

Carys: For extensions???! 😂

I typed back: Hope not. Anyway, Dad likes it 👍

Carys: What's your mum saying? Did she say
we can't hang out?

I listened for a moment.

"Yes, I know," Mum was saying. "I'm sure they were having fun. I'm sure Carys was trying to do a good job. But obviously she isn't a hairdresser. With the channel and everything, we just prefer to get these sort of things done professionally...yes, I know what they can be like... yes..."

I replied: Think it's okay. She's mainly annoyed
it happened off camera.

Carys: It looks amazing! Hope hairdresser
doesn't mess it up 😊

Mum laughed down the phone, so maybe it wouldn't be too awkward next time I saw Carys's mum. I went into my room and closed the door. There was a cardboard box on my bed that Mum or Dad must have put there. I probably wasn't supposed to open it until they were filming. I looked inside. I pulled out a framed picture that said "Be YOU-tiful" in gold swirly letters. I dropped it back in the box and closed the lid. It was just a load of stuff to put my room back the same as it was before.

I sat on my bed and took out the photo Carys had

taken of me. I put it on my desk, took a picture of it and uploaded it to my Instagram. It took about three seconds to get the first comment. I scrolled down for a few minutes liking and replying to comments from people at school: Eva!!!! You look AMAZE 🔥 and 🔥🔥🔥 love your hair and ♥ hair looks so good!!!

I was replying to the third comment from Jenna when Mum called up the stairs. "Eva! Sasha can fit you in at seven-thirty."

"In the morning?" I called back.

"Yes!" Mum said. "She's fully booked tomorrow so she's opening early as a favour to me."

Great, I thought. *That means we'll definitely be filming it.*

"And wear that new top I put on your wardrobe door, okay?"

I sighed. Why couldn't I ever wear what I wanted? Carys was allowed to bite her nails and wear that little stake in her ear. I wasn't even allowed to choose my own T-shirt. I held up the top hanging on the wardrobe. It actually didn't look too bad. Then I turned it round. There was a picture of a cartoon pea wearing trainers and in massive letters it said: *I GOTTA PEA!*

27

FIRST RULE OF JU-JITSU

The next morning, I had to wear the *I GOTTA PEA!* T-shirt to the hairdresser's. There was "no choice about it" unless I wanted to be banned from Carys's house for the rest of my life. I thought about writing over it with my Sharpies, but I'd had to get up really early and Mum was rushing me.

"Oh, it looks fabulous short, Eva!" Sasha said, putting her hands through my hair. I felt her long nails gently scratch my scalp. "Oh, yeah, I can tidy this up, no probs. Shall we get started?"

I'd decided not to speak at all during the haircut. But it was hard to stick to because Sasha is so nice. I stared up at the ceiling as Mum filmed me getting my hair washed.

"How shocked was I about you cutting your hair,

Eva?" Mum said. "Tell everyone how shocked I was! I seriously had no clue she was going to do this! I don't think Eva can hear me because of the water," Mum said, and laughed like she didn't mind. She did though.

As Sasha snipped around the back of my hair, Mum pointed the camera at the mirror.

"It was so funny!" she said. "She comes home with all her hair cut off and I completely freak out!" She told everyone about what happened last night, leaving out the bit about knocking her wine over and calling Carys's mum. I could have corrected her, but what was the point? They'd only edit it out.

Later that day, they posted *Eva Cuts All her Hair Off!!!!!* with scream emojis on the thumbnail. I scrolled straight down to read the comments.

hilarious!!!! 😂

can't believe you did that, Eva!!!

So pretty with short hair! Love it.

can you do more challenge videos?

I was on the hundredth comment or something, when there was one from somebody called TheThinker. It said:

Eva's face 4.45 and 5.20. She don't wanna
be there, Mom.

It had nine thumbs up, and sixteen thumbs down. I tapped on the replies.

Haha. Yes. That was funny.

I noticed too. Shouldn't film if she don't want to.

Child exploitation.

NO! She always does that. She's A TEEN! Great family.

Yes. Making the kid cut her hair for ad revenue.

THAT KID IS FAKE.

I dropped my phone when Mum knocked on the door.

"Hey," she said. "Want to come down and do an unboxing? I've got some gorgeous things for your new room."

"Not really," I said.

"Are you sick? Your cheeks look a bit red." Mum came in and put her hand on my forehead. "Your temperature's okay. You know what, it might be your period coming."

I took a deep breath. "I just don't feel like it right now."

"Want me to bring you up a hot squash? We can always do the unboxing tomorrow. Watch a film instead, just us two?"

I actually did want to do that. It would be nice to curl up next to Mum and watch a movie. But I knew she didn't mean just us two. She meant all of their subscribers too. She was probably planning an *EVA'S SECOND PERIOD!!!* vlog and I didn't exactly feel like hanging around for it.

"No, I'm going over to Spud's. He said something about watching a film with this new projector he's made." It was only a half lie. Spud did say something about making a film projector.

Mum smiled. "Okay. But whatever you do, don't let Spud touch your hair."

Like I'd ever be that stupid.

I walked down Spud's drive and the security light came on. I noticed the side gate was open. I hadn't gone into Spud's bedroom the back way for years. There's this old oak tree in their garden, and one of the branches goes right up to Spud's bedroom window. We always used to climb down it out of his room when we were younger. I looked up and saw his light on.

I messaged: I'm coming round. Then I put my leg up on the first branch. It was harder than I remembered to get a grip. I pushed my other leg off the ground and swung it up over the branch. *Okay*, I thought, looking at the branches above me forming a kind of archway. *This doesn't seem that hard.*

I'd been stuck in the tree for about five minutes before I called for help. I'd tried to get onto the branch under Spud's window, but I don't know, his dad must have pruned it or something. There was nowhere to get a foothold, and I wasn't strong enough to slide myself all the way along. I tried to get back down, but climbing backwards down a tree is harder than it sounds. I couldn't get my phone out of my pocket, because that would mean letting go of the branch I was gripping onto. So, basically, I had no choice.

"SPUD!" I yelled as loudly as I could. "Spud!"

The curtains opened at the next window and Spud's brother Chip appeared. He squashed his face against the glass so his nose was flattened. I hadn't seen him for ages. He looked like he'd grown a metre since starting college. Chest hairs were poking out of the top of his T-shirt. My cheeks went hot with embarrassment.

"Eva?" His breath steamed up the window around his mouth. "Are you in the tree?"

"Can you get Spud, please?" I shouted.

He pushed his bedroom window open. "Are you spying on Spud?"

"No! I'm coming round to watch a film!"

Chip looked at me suspiciously. "We do have a front door."

"Yes, I know. Look, my hands are slipping. Just get Spud to help me, will you?"

He stood there for a minute. "Would it help if I threw you a rope?"

I sighed. "Not really!"

Chip disappeared and a few seconds later Spud peered out of his bedroom window. "Eva? Have you got short hair?"

"Spud!" I shouted. "Please, just help me get down."

"Should I get your dad?"

"Yeah," I said. "Because what I really need right now is a clip of me stuck up a tree on YouTube."

Spud leaned further out of the window, checking the distance. My palms felt sweaty against the branch. I was about to tell Spud to hurry up, when I heard Chip say, "I could probably get that old chainsaw working."

"Spud!" I shouted. "Don't let Chip anywhere near this tree. Spud?" And that's when I realized they'd both gone.

The next thing I heard was something being dragged across the grass.

"It's okay!" Spud called from below. "You can jump!"

"Are you actually crazy?" I said, trying to see what was down there.

"Come on! The trampoline's right here."

I repositioned myself so I could see. "You can't be serious. I'll break my legs!"

"It's fine!" Spud shouted. "I've done a rough calculation. You'll only bounce a couple of metres, I promise. I would catch you, but I think from that distance, there's a significant chance you'd crush me to death."

Chip stood next to Spud with his arms folded. "Ten quid says she breaks a bone."

Something glinted in the moonlight. "You'd better not be filming this!"

"Course not!" Spud said. "It's my army helmet. Catch!" Spud threw the helmet up to me and caught it again when I didn't grab it.

"Eva, you need to catch it!" Chip shouted.

Spud threw it again, but I didn't dare let go of the branch.

"I'm not wearing that stupid helmet, Spud." I peered beneath me. I could see the vague outline of a trampoline. "Are you sure this is safe?"

"Trust him!" Chip shouted. "He's going to be a doctor one day."

I took a deep breath and slowly lowered myself down until my legs were dangling in the air.

Then Spud said, "An academic doctor. Not a medical one. Just to be clear."

Chip laughed and shouted, "Disclaimer!"

But it was too late to climb back up. I took one last look down, held my breath and let go.

Twenty minutes later, I was sitting in Spud's bedroom with a bag of frozen peas on my head. I'd bashed it on the branch as I'd bounced back up. Just like Spud said I would. He looked at me and laughed for the hundredth time.

"Okay, I should have worn the helmet," I said. "Is it really noticeable?" I asked, feeling the golf-ball-sized lump on my forehead.

Spud peered at my head. "It looks like an egg," he said. "Why were you climbing the tree anyway? You haven't done that for years."

"Yeah, and now I know why," I said. "It's a deathtrap. You should chop it down."

Spud laughed, then he looked serious all of a sudden. "Hey, I want to run some ideas by you," he said, pulling a bit of paper out of his pocket. It looked like a list. "I've been thinking about a new name and I wanted to test some out on you."

"A new name? Are you getting another guinea pig?"

"No, a name for me. Instead of Spud."

"What's wrong with Spud?"

"It lacks maturity." I gave him a look. "I just think being named after a potato isn't doing me any favours socially."

"Says who?" Like I even needed to ask. "You mean what Gabi said."

Spud shrugged. "I'd been thinking about changing it anyway. So, what do you think about Fossil?"

"*Fossil?* You can't be serious."

Spud sighed.

"Sorry," I said. "It's just you've always been Spud. I'm finding it hard to imagine you being called something else. Especially Fossil. Please tell me the rest. I won't laugh, I promise." I clamped my lips together.

"Volt?" he said and a laugh came snorting out through my nose. "Okay, that's it. I'm not telling you any more."

"I'm sorry!" I said. "But you're saying names that sound like…wrestlers."

He picked up a plastic puzzle from his desk and started playing. It was one of those where you have to get the tiny silver balls in the holes.

We sat in silence for a while. Well, not exactly silence. The anime film we'd been watching was still playing, but it was in Japanese and neither of us was looking at the subtitles. I could hear the bubbles popping in my lemonade.

"I'm sorry," I said, putting the list on his desk. "I do get it. But, you know, being Spud of Nerdophobia is actually pretty good. You can just…be yourself. Like, make weird stuff in your garage and come up with Minecraft theories and no one's judging you the whole time. You're like, free. Or whatever. I cut my hair and a million people have an opinion about it."

Spud smiled. "Don't read the comments," he said, in an accent that I think was supposed to be my dad's.

"Yeah, don't read the comments," I repeated and tried to smile. "Anyway, if you are serious about a new nickname, surely you haven't forgotten about this?" I tapped a website into my phone and held it up.

"The name generator!" Spud laughed. The last time we went on the name generator we created nicknames for our entire primary school class. Mr Eliot's came up as CaptainLegsPopper and I laughed so much I couldn't breathe.

We typed Spud's name into the name generator and it came up as SnivelWeepie. We both laughed so much that his mum came up to check we were okay.

"Thanks for the frozen peas," I said later, as I pushed the door open to go. "And for saving my life, obviously."

"Any time," Spud said.

"I don't think you should change your name, by the way. You're pretty okay the way you are."

Spud smiled. "Thanks." Then as I went downstairs he called after me. "Hey, you know what I realized when you were stuck up the tree? Your ju-jitsu skills are lame."

And I was laughing too much to say anything back.

On the way home I realized I was grateful for *All About Eva* for one thing. That we got to move next door to Spud.

Even though he was the kind of friend to accidentally explode a sheep's lung in your face, he was also the kind of friend to know when you needed a crash helmet. Maybe he was the kind of friend I should have been listening to all along.

28

SECRET WEAPON

When I got home that night, the living room had a gigantic banner across it saying *HALF A MILLION SUBSCRIBERS!!!* And I felt like someone had chucked a hand grenade into my stomach.

"You hit half a million?" I said to Dad, who was arranging gold helium balloon numbers.

"Ah, Eva, there you are," Dad said, moving a gold balloon zero further away from the wall. "No, we're still a few thousand away. Grab those confetti cannons on the side, will you?"

"So, what's this for?"

"Jen and I decided that the video we made before didn't really hit the mark, you know?"

I picked up the confetti cannons Dad had pointed at.

"So, we have to do it again?"

"Yes, take two! Hopefully this time we'll get it. Also, you changed your hair, so…"

"Eva, you're back. I was just about to text you," Mum said, unwrapping a string of gold bunting. "Oh my God. What's happened to your head?"

I felt the lump on my forehead. "I jumped out of a tree. It's fine. It only hurts if I press it." Suddenly, one of the confetti cannons exploded in my face.

"Eva!" Mum screamed.

"Whoops," I said, pulling bits of gold confetti off my eyelashes. "Those things are lethal."

Mum dropped the bunting on the table and inspected my forehead under the light. "Oh, this looks really bad, Eva! What were you doing in a tree?"

"It wasn't deliberate."

"Well, we can't film it now, can we?" she said over my head to Dad. "Not with this massive lump on her head. Oh, Eva, you do pick your timing!"

"Hmm," Dad said, coming over to have a look. "Is it such a big deal?" Mum glared at him. "Okay, could you cover it up?"

"I could wear Dad's balaclava," I said, but I don't think they heard me.

"I've got some make-up, but you'd still see the lump."

Mum let out a sigh. "We'll have to wait a couple of days. And pray it goes down before we leave for Farmor's on Wednesday! No more climbing trees, okay? At least not before we hit half a million. I thought you'd grown out of that by now." She gently kissed the lump on my forehead. I wondered if getting minor head injuries would be a good way of getting out of filming in future.

Farmor called me that night on FaceTime so she could see my new hair. She said she loved it as I held up my phone so she could see it from the back.

Then she said, *"Dit indre er endnu smukkere end dit ydre."* Which means, "Your insides are even more beautiful than your outsides." She must have forgotten I could see her, because she held the phone up to her ear. But I didn't care. I listened to her talk about the new cakes in the cafe by the waterfront, and the noisy fishing boats in the harbour and a new art collection in the museum she thought I'd like. Her words collected like fallen leaves around me and made my room seem less empty.

Mum and Dad were pretty much snogging when I put my cereal bowl in the dishwasher on Sunday morning. There was a gigantic bunch of red roses on the table and a card with a picture of two triangles of cheese holding hands. It said *We Brie-long Together*.

"Can't you wait until I'm not in the room?" I said.

"Oh, lighten up, Eva!" Dad said. "It's Valentine's Day!"

"Really? I hadn't noticed," I said, holding up a heart-shaped piece of toast.

Mum laughed as she fiddled with the camera. "Oh, Eva, put those on!" she said holding a fluffy red headband with two glittery hearts attached on springs. As I backed away, my head almost smacked into a beam.

"Watch your head!" Mum shouted.

Just then, Miss Fizzy padded in wearing a vest covered in pink hearts.

"Oh God," I said, picking her up. "They got you too, huh?"

I noticed a card on the kitchen worktop that said *We're Gouda Together*. I wondered if they got matching cheese-themed cards deliberately.

"Have some strawberries!" Dad said, handing me a bowl.

"I'm not that hungry." I pulled off Miss Fizzy's jumper and she immediatey scarpered under the table. *Good idea*, I thought.

Just then, I heard Spud's signature knock on the door. He walked in holding a tiny plant.

"I managed to propagate my Venus flytrap," he said proudly. "I thought you'd like it for your new room."

262

"Thanks, Spud!" I said, examining the plant. "Baby Venus flytraps are actually pretty cute."

"Awww, look, Lars!" Mum said, pulling Dad's arms around her. "Spud's plants have had a baby and he's given it to Eva for Valentine's Day!"

Spud's face went bright red. "Is it Valentine's Day today?" He laughed awkwardly. "I didn't realize. I just felt bad about Eva's head injury." He grabbed a handful of strawberries. "And Venus flytraps don't have babies, Mrs Andersen, they're called offsets. They reproduce asexually, you see, erm…"

I guess he got the hint to stop talking because my dad was kind of glaring at him, and me and Mum couldn't stop laughing.

That night, as I flicked through Instagram, I felt nervous about my short hair all over again. I clicked on Hallie's new profile picture. Her braids were in a big bun on the top of her head, and she was pulling her jumper up so half her face was hidden. Then I saw she was online. I was about to message her when a message from her popped up.

I really like your hair, she said.

Thanks, I replied.

Hallie: Your mum finally let you cut it short 😊

I replied: Kind of 😊 I'm so sorry about your competition. I should have been there.

Hallie: It's okay. Doctor reckons it will mend fine in a few weeks.

I tapped to like her message then uploaded a photo of my new baby Venus flytrap. Jenna immediately liked it. I thought about commenting on one of Gabi's pictures, to show Hallie I was making an effort to be nice. I clicked on a video of Gabi doing a front flip in Hallie's garden. But I couldn't help wishing she'd fall face first into the compost heap. I clicked back onto Hallie's profile picture and liked that instead. Hallie put a love heart on the picture of me and Spud doing our ferrofluid experiment. I put one back, and it felt like part of my heart had clicked back into place.

It was the Monday of half-term, and I was at Carys's house helping her play Arcadia Colony, this world-building game. I was half watching the screen while I flicked through the *All About Eva* channel on my phone. I tapped a new vlog called *Eva's Room Clear-Out!*

"What's Mum doing in my room?"

Carys looked up. "She's filming in your room?"

I nodded and tapped *play*. After the usual adverts, Mum

was saying, *"So, as you can see, we've cleared everything out! It's literally like a prison cell in here!"* The camera spins round absorbing my entire bedroom. *"I'll show you her wardrobe space!"* She opened my wardrobe doors and started pulling out all the things hiding my sketchbooks. My skin went cold. *"We're going to get some larger storage. Eva's got so many clothes, right? So, I'm thinking a really dark blue on that back wall, and maybe some kind of 3D arty thing."* She picks up one of my sketchbooks and opens it. I can barely even watch. *"Look at this beautiful picture of a butterfly that Eva's drawn, isn't this amazing? I just LOVE it!"* Mum films the page of my sketchbook with the butterfly doodle I'd drawn ages ago. Angry tears burned the back of my eyes. It was like the entire world seeing my diary. *"I'm thinking we could get this butterfly made up really big, in gold, and put it over there. And, we definitely need a lighting solution. We'd really love to hear your suggestions for Eva's room. Pop them in the comments below and if we end up using your idea, we'll send you one of our gorgeous goodie bags. Don't forget to subscribe!"*

I covered my face and felt Carys put her arm around me.

"I like your mum, Eva. But that's seriously not okay."

I angrily bashed a message to Mum:

Don't film in my room without me there.

"I've got to do something, Carys," I said. "All that stuff I deleted, it's not made any difference! And cutting my hair just gave them even more content. Look – the *EVA CUTS ALL HER HAIR OFF!!!!* video has had three hundred thousand views. They're just not getting the message."

Carys thought for a moment, twisting the stake in her earlobe. "Okay, so we've got to get a message out there to your parents, and all their subscribers. We've got to show them that you don't want to be on the channel. I'm pretty sure not many people would subscribe to *All About Eva* if they knew how much you hated it. But that message can't come from *you* directly, because obviously then you'd get into trouble. So…" She picked up her laptop.

"So?" I said.

She smiled at me mysteriously. "It's time to implement Plan B."

"Plan B?" I said. "What's Plan B?"

"Maybe I have a secret weapon."

"Come on, Eva, please," Dad said later, as he passed me the bribery muffins he'd made while I was at Carys's house. They had extra sugar syrup and fresh strawberries and icing sprinkles. I took two. I'm not saying he wasn't good at bribery. "Just a short clip saying how close we are to half a million. Then you can do whatever you want. All you have to do is look excited."

I took a massive bite of muffin and pointed to my mouth like there was no way I could say anything.

"It's a lovely thing for our subscribers," Mum said. "To say thank you. And it's a celebration for us. We've almost hit half a million subscribers! Lars, can you remember how excited we got over a hundred!"

Dad kissed Mum's cheek. "I remember how excited you got over one!" They smiled at each other and I looked away in case they started snogging or something. "Feels good, right?" Dad said. "We've made a lot of people happy over the years. Why don't we do the video, then take a drive out to Redcliffe Woods. It won't be dark for a couple of hours."

"That sounds perfect," Mum said. "We could film a Family Special."

I shook my head. "No, thanks."

Mum looked at me. "Okay…how about we make it just us three? No cameras."

Dad raised his eyebrows. "Sounds good to me. Eva?"

Maybe it was the sugar rush from the muffins. Or maybe it was impossible to implement Plan B without giving my parents a final chance. I smiled and said, "Okay."

* * *

It wasn't exactly warm that evening, but the sun was setting and the sky looked like it was on fire. Dad shook out a picnic blanket and Mum was looking in her rucksack for something. I wiped some leaves off a tree stump and sat down. I'd said to myself in the car on the way over that if they could do this one trip just us three, then I wouldn't upload the new video I'd just made with Carys. Putting it like that, it sounds like a test. Maybe I *was* testing them. Seeing if they could do one normal family thing. Just for us, not their subscribers. I guess I was clinging onto a tiny bit of hope, like the scrappy bits of paper left in the margin after you've torn pages out. If they could spend time with me right now, just us, without sharing it, then there was a chance that things could change.

I closed my eyes and listened to the leaves rustling above me, daydreaming. Maybe they could start vlogging only once a week. Like, slowly share less and less about me. And we could have certain days, like now, when they didn't do any filming at all. I wouldn't even mind if they kept that stupid newspaper column. It was basically fiction anyway – Mum had even admitted that. And it's not like anyone at school read newspapers. I felt a beam of sunlight cross my face and then I heard it. A sound that made my skin crawl. *Click.* I opened my eyes. Mum was a few metres away in the shadows, pointing her phone at me.

"I thought you said no cameras," I said, jumping down from the tree stump.

"Oh, it's just for Instagram, sweetie. No caption." She blew me a kiss then looked back down at her phone.

So if you want to know why I did it, that's the reason. Because no matter how much you want there to be a better way – a nicer way – to do the stuff you have to do, a way nobody gets hurt…sometimes that way just doesn't exist.

I reached in my pocket for my phone and messaged Carys.

Okay, Plan B tonight.

29

PLAN B

Carys had told me that nothing would happen instantaneously. It might take a while, she'd said, maybe even weeks, for our new video to get noticed. So, I didn't expect everything to happen so fast. I'd found all the clips we needed on the *All About Eva* channel. I chose the music too – this old 1980s song by Kim Wilde. Mum had mentioned her in the diary she'd vlogged about a while ago. The title was my idea too:

> Does ALL ABOUT EVA want her vlogger parents
> to stop filming her?

We wrote the subtitles together. But Carys came up with the "exploitation" stuff. She's way better at English than me. She made it sound exactly like stuff an adult would say. There was no way anyone would suspect me and Carys. We even used a fake name to set up the YouTube channel we posted it on.

I knew that if my parents saw our video, they wouldn't close the channel down immediately or anything. They'd told me enough times that our "financial security" rested on *All About Eva* being successful. And as much as I hated the channel, I didn't want my real life to collapse around me. But I hoped it would make them stop and think. Stop them invading my privacy all the time. Make them finally listen to me. I knew my parents would see the video eventually. I mean, it was kind of a drastic way to get their attention, but I honestly didn't think it would get so out of control. I thought it would take ages for anyone to even watch it.

So, the next morning, when I looked at the number of views, I went cold. *Eight thousand?* Last night it had only had nine.

"You okay?" Dad asked, poking his head round my bedroom door. "You look like you've seen a ghost."

"Just playing a game," I said, my hands frozen on my screen.

"Well, hurry up and get dressed. We're leaving for the airport in an hour."

271

I nodded and he closed the door. I stared at my phone. How did it jump from nine views to eight thousand over night?

I messaged Carys:

Did you post the video anywhere else?

I saw the message bubbles come up, then they disappeared. A few seconds later, she called me.

"Don't leave a trail, remember," she said as soon as I answered.

"Oh, yeah, sorry," I said. "It's just that the video has had loads more views since last night and…" I let my voice trail off.

"I tagged a few people," Carys whispered. "A few *significant* people. It's up to ten thousand now. Told you this was my secret weapon." I heard Carys's mum in the background. "I've got to go. Don't message me about it, okay. It's all going to plan. Loads of people are going to see it. Don't worry. We'll speak about it properly when you get back from Denmark."

I hung up and scrolled down to the comments.

literally wanna cry that poor kid

I'm embarrassed for her

The whole family makes me feel ill 😔

Awful

Feel so sorry for eva

FREE EVA!!!!

I put my phone down and headed into the bathroom. *It's fine*, I told myself in the shower. *It's good so many people are seeing it. I want people to see it.* So why did I feel like my heart was getting sucked down the plughole?

Back in my room, I scrolled through the rest of the comments. I had to make sure no one had tagged my parents' account. Yesterday, my parents seeing the video had seemed like a brilliant idea. Like it would fix my entire life. But now, all I could think about was how complicated it made everything. What if my parents somehow figured out I was behind it? I looked at the views counter. 15k. 16k. 17k. It was happening.

Just then I heard my mum's voice. "Eva! Have you finished packing, sweetie?" She peered round the door. "Sorry to hurry you, but we need to leave soon-ish." She stepped into my room. She was wearing pink and white stripy leggings, a jumper that had a rainbow knitted on the front and a giant yellow bow in her hair. It looked like she'd painted freckles on her face too. I stared at her, waiting for some kind of explanation. "It's my travelling outfit! I got you one too." She held up the exact same outfit she was wearing. "Now, before you say anything…"

"Please, no."

Mum laughed. "It's a little bright, I know, but…"

"Mum! That outfit is *exactly* the same as yours!"

"I know! Isn't it the cutest thing? Pretty and Proud sent it specially!"

I sank onto my bed and put a pillow over my face.

"Eva!" Mum said, laughing. "Come on, you don't have to wear it for long, I promise. Just a few pictures at the airport. Take something to change into in your hand luggage if you're that uncomfortable." She lifted up the pillow I was hiding under. "Pretty and Proud are donating ten per cent of profits to educating girls in disadvantaged communities this month."

I groaned. "Fine." I took the outfit from her hands. "But only because it's for charity. And I'm getting changed before we get on the plane."

"Thank you, sweetie," Mum said, planting a kiss on my head. "You are an angel. But we do need some onboard pictures, so change when we get to Copenhagen, okay."

I groaned again and stuffed a pair of leggings into my rucksack. By then, any doubts I'd had about the video had vanished. Actually, I couldn't wait to see her face.

"Looking great, Eva!" Dad said as I came downstairs. He was wearing a giant yellow bow in his hair too. "What? I didn't want to feel left out!"

I wondered if my life could get any worse. Then Mum

handed me a key to take round to Spud's, so he could feed Miss Fizzy while we were away.

"Couldn't you have reminded me to do this before I put the outfit on?"

"Make sure his mum looks after the key, okay!" Mum shouted, ignoring me.

Spud burst out laughing as soon as he opened the door.

"Don't say anything," I said, chucking him the key. "And don't forget to give Miss Fizzy her treats."

"Have a good trip!" Spud called as I walked back down the drive. "If the aeroplane's engines fail, at least you can use that bow as a propeller."

We'd been in the car for about twenty minutes when my phone beeped. Carys had sent me a screenshot of my parents' Instagram page. Dad had posted a photo of me and Mum in our matching outfits, with his head just poking into the shot.

Carys had written: It's a form of child abuse.

I snorted.

"What's so funny?" Mum asked, twisting round.

"Nothing," I said. "Carys sent me a funny picture."

"You two are thick as thieves," she said, checking her

make-up in the passenger mirror. "You're not planning any other major image transformations I should be aware of, are you?"

I smiled at her in the mirror. "Nope." It wasn't technically a lie. Posting a video about them on YouTube wasn't a "major image transformation". I tapped my phone to check the views. It was almost up to twenty-five thousand. I put my phone down and watched the traffic out of the window. Dad turned on the stereo and they both started singing along. It wasn't until I took my lip balm out of my bag that I noticed my hands were shaking.

Once we'd checked in our cases, we went to the airport coffee shop. I sat next to Mum as Dad went to get hot chocolates.

"Everyone's staring at us," I said, fidgeting with my jumper. "It's so embarrassing."

"What, sweetie?" Mum said, taking her phone out.

I felt a sprinkle of nerves in my stomach as I watched her unlock it. "Everyone's staring at us."

"Oh, don't be silly!" She squashed up closer to me and took a picture while the people on the next table stared at us. "They're just jealous of our bows," she whispered. A few of the freckles on her nose had smudged but I didn't say anything.

People in the queue were staring at Dad's giant hair bow.

I glanced over to the bookshop opposite. "I'm going to look in there," I said. Mum barely looked up. I pulled the bow out of my hair, and dumped it on the table.

I wandered into the bookshop and picked up the first book that caught my eye. *Ghost Lair*. I was reading the blurb on the back when I heard it.

"Eva? Eva Andersen? It is you, isn't it? I recognize your picture!"

I looked up to see a complete stranger gawping at me. It had happened before a few times, but not for ages, and never when I was on my own.

"Hi," I said, and nothing else. My brain always went blank in these situations.

"I just saw the picture of you and Jen at the airport and I couldn't believe it!" she said. "We're on our way to Berlin, aren't we!" A girl a couple of years younger than me stared out from just behind her.

I stood there, silently blinking, unable to think what to say.

"You're off to your grandma's!" she said. Her skin was shiny and she had rosy patches on her cheeks. She was maybe about forty. Or fifty. It was hard to tell. "I've been watching you since you were this high!" She put her hand out by her knee. "Your parents are hilarious! I love them! Where are they? Think they'd mind if I said hello?"

I glanced over to Mum and Dad drinking their hot chocolates. Dad's long legs were stretched all the way out, so they practically went under the next table. I hated it when he did that.

"It's so lovely to meet you!" the lady said. "Do you mind?"

"Um…" I started, but she was kind of squeezing my arm. Her phone took my picture a few times before I had a chance to say no.

"Jen and Lars!" She waved at them. "I can't believe this!"

I stood at the edge of the bookshop and watched Mum's face light up as the lady and her daughter went over. I paid for the book, but stayed in the shop, watching the woman speaking to my parents. She was clutching her phone in her hand and taking photos with them. They'd probably be online in a minute. At least she wouldn't be on our plane. I didn't think Berlin was in Denmark. But like Mr Khatri put in my Year Seven report, geography isn't necessarily one of my natural strengths.

Me and Mum were still dressed like identical twins when we boarded the plane. Dad offered to put everyone's luggage in the overhead rack like he usually did.

"No problem," he was saying, "I'm up here anyway!" Thankfully he'd removed the giant bow by then.

I stuck my head in *Ghost Lair* and wrapped a blanket around me. I was way too hot, but at least you couldn't see my outfit. My phone beeped in my pocket.

"You'd better turn that off, honey," Mum said.

It was a message from Hallie. I smiled. Maybe she'd remembered I was going to Farmor's. Only when I read it my heart stopped.

Not sure if you know about this already, but I
just got sent it. You're on it at 6.50. Just wanted
to check if you'd seen it? Hope you're ok.
Really sorry x

I angled my phone away from Mum, who was busy reading the flight menu, and clicked on the link Hallie had sent. Only it was taking a million years to load.

"Hey, off your phone now, Eva," Mum said. "We're taking off soon."

"Just a second." I heard the beep of the seat-belt sign just as the page came up. It wasn't my parents' channel. Or the channel me and Carys had made. It was a video called *Meet the Family Vloggers Turning their Kids into Profit*. My stomach flipped over.

"Off," Mum said, nudging my elbow. "Or flight mode. Ooh, what's your book about?"

279

I glanced underneath the video. 264k views. I closed the app and switched my phone to airplane mode, my heart thumping. Mum took my book off my lap and read the back cover so loudly half the plane could probably hear. Then she started talking about this ghost TV show she'd auditioned for when she was younger. She kissed the side of my head and handed me a packet of chewing gum.

"So your ears don't hurt, sweetheart."

Dad was chatting to someone across the aisle in Danish. I tried to focus on what he was saying, to distract myself from the thoughts racing through my head: *Turning their kids into profit? Is that what they think my parents are doing? Was whoever made that video one of the significant people Carys tagged?*

The words Mum had said to me about *Good Morning* kept circling around in my head: *Dealing with the media is like juggling fire. Say one wrong word and that's it, total disaster.*

As the plane took off, and I felt Mum squeeze my hand like she always did, I couldn't shake this one thought out of my mind: *What if this makes everybody hate them?*

30

FARMOR

When the plane touched down in Copenhagen, I felt sick. I didn't dare switch my phone back on while I was with my parents. But I couldn't stop wondering what the video said about me. Any time my parents looked at their phones my heart stopped. I was still dressed as Mum's mini-me as we waited by the luggage carousel. As soon as Dad grabbed our suitcases, I walked over to the toilets to get changed. Mum huffed the whole time we were queuing because she wanted to get a photo of us in our outfits outside the airport.

"I don't see why it's such a big deal, Eva," Mum said through the toilet door as I pulled on my leggings. "It's not like you know anyone in Copenhagen!"

"Farmor," I said, pulling off the rainbow jumper.

"Farmor would think it was cute," Mum said, like she genuinely believed that. "I should have got an outfit for her too, then we could all be matching!"

"I hope you are joking." I put on my yellow hoodie then felt kind of annoyed when I opened the cubicle door and realized I still matched her slightly. Dad hadn't put his hair bow back on, so at least that was something.

I didn't feel like talking, and the bus ride to Dragør was short enough for my parents not to notice. I couldn't even check my phone because Mum sat right next to me and I knew I'd probably have a million notifications. I peered over at her screen. She was replying to people's comments on Instagram with smiley faces and love hearts. I tried to relax. But my heart was hammering inside my chest, and I was sure that my parents would notice.

It was dark when we arrived at Farmor's cottage, but the outside light was on. Farmor was sitting on the little wooden bench outside, waiting for us. When she spotted me she held out her arms and I ran into them like I was a little girl. I didn't hug my parents like that any more, but I guess I'd never grown out of hugging Farmor that way. She smelled of the sea. Her silver hair was tied in a plaited bun at the back of her head, like it always was, and a few wispy bits had escaped and tickled my face in the breeze.

"Hello, my darling girl," Farmor said, planting kisses

on my face until it tickled. "It's so good to see you, *lille majroe*!" It means "little turnip". It's what I looked like to Farmor when I was born, apparently, and it kind of stuck. It's one of those nicknames that I'd hate if it came from anyone else, but with Farmor it felt like home. "Come in, come in!" she said, kissing and hugging Mum and Dad. She held my hand as she led us down the cobbled path to her front door and into her yellow cottage.

Farmor's house always made me feel like I was little again. There are vines and flowers painted on the outside walls, and the thatched roof has a criss-cross pattern you'd only notice if you paid attention to that stuff. There's a thatched mushroom right at the top near the chimney. It felt like an enchanted cottage from a fairytale when I was younger, and it still gave me that kind of feeling now.

The doors are kind of low, so Dad had to duck his head. Farmor's tiny, even shorter than me, so I always imagined my grandfather as a giant. I never got to meet him, so that idea of him as a giant has always been stuck in my head. Dad used to tell me that he had to leave home when he was ten years old because he was so tall he couldn't fit through the door any more. I know now that's not true, but I did believe him for ages.

"Ah, it's so peaceful here, Mathilde!" Mum said, looking out at the little lights dotted along the harbour.

"Yes," Farmor said. "But yesterday the wind was blowing half a pelican! I couldn't even ride my bike." I smiled, and sipped the cup of *kartoffel* soup she handed me. Her weird expressions always made me smile. Google Translate can't help you with half the stuff my *farmor* says.

"I still can't get a signal here!" Mum said, holding up her phone.

"Me neither," Dad said. "It's one of the many benefits Dragør has to offer!"

Mum smiled, the way she does when she doesn't find something funny. "Want to walk down the road with me later then, so I can check my messages before bed? I usually get a signal by the waterfront."

I noticed Farmor give Dad a look, meaning she didn't approve. She never let them film anything in her house, which was one of the reasons I loved coming here so much. It always felt like a completely different world.

"Why don't you give yourself a night off, Jen?" Dad said, bending down to kiss her head. "We can get up early tomorrow. It's the holidays. You've already posted the clothing thing."

Mum's face broke into a smile. "You're right," she said, and chucked her phone into her bag. "Goodness knows we could do with a break!"

After supper, the butterflies in my stomach began to settle. Probably because I knew Mum and Dad couldn't see the video tonight. And maybe because I was full of potato soup and *æbleskiver*.

"Right, my darling," Farmor said, cupping my face in her hands, "you'd better get to bed! You don't want to go cucumber!"

The next morning I overslept, which I never normally did at Farmor's because the church bells chime every hour. But I couldn't sleep for ages last night, thinking about what was on that video Hallie sent me. I checked my phone, but I still had no signal and Farmor didn't have Wi-Fi. She didn't even have a TV. It was like going back in time. I brushed my teeth, pulled on my jeans and a jumper and went down the creaky wooden stairs.

"Good morning!" Dad said in Danish. "Sleeping Beauty awakes!"

I yawned, trying to think of the right phrase. "Why have you got your coat on?" I asked eventually.

"We're all going into Copenhagen," he said. "Want a quick bowl of *havregrød*?" *Havregrød* is basically warm oats. If Dad made it, it definitely wouldn't have enough sugar in. I screwed up my nose.

"Let's take buns," Farmor said, filling a paper bag with freshly baked buns from a bowl on the side. "We can get something proper in Copenhagen."

"Put on your coat," Dad added. "We'll have to catch Jen up."

I waited for my brain to translate what they'd said. Speaking Danish with Dad and Farmor was harder than the advanced level on *Hej Danmark!*

"Okay," I said, which I think is the same in Danish.

We caught up with Mum, who was standing by the bus stop. She was staring at her phone so hard she barely even noticed us arrive.

"What's happened?" Dad said, reading the expression on her face at the same time as I did. I shoved my hands into my pockets so no one would see them shaking.

"You'd better take a look at this," Mum said, handing her phone to Dad.

The church bells rang and made me jump. Farmor rubbed my back. I kept my eyes on my dad's face. His forehead wrinkled up, like it did when he was concentrating on something. A bus appeared at the end of the road.

"Shall we get this one?" Farmor said. "It's a little cold to wait for the next one."

But my parents didn't reply. They were both staring at Mum's phone.

A man's voice was saying, "*Okay, so now let's talk about privacy. And I think this is a separate issue from the fake, scripted, set-up kind of content that some family vloggers are posting. Today I'm going to talk about some of the family vloggers who are actually pretty popular but who are exploiting their children for money.*"

The way he said it sounded bad. Like, really bad. I didn't want to look at my parents, so I stood there trying not to feel worried. But it was impossible because the bus came and went and we didn't get on it. And the man's voice kept coming out of Mum's phone.

"*There are kids out there, right now, who have their entire childhoods online. And maybe some are okay with that, but I'm going to show you some kids who make it so clear they are not okay with it. I've already talked about the Hadley family and the cruel pranks they play on their twins. But let's take a look at some clips of the Andersen family. The parents are Lars and Jen and they're established family vloggers. They have about half a million subscribers and vlog usually two or three times a week about their only daughter, Eva. You might have caught the vlog they made about her starting her period. Yep, you heard me right – these people vlogged about their daughter's period!*"

I gasped. Only by accident it came out really loud.

Dad looked at me. "Eva, I don't think you should

watch this."

Mum nodded. "You shouldn't see this, Eva." Her eyes were watery and I could tell any minute she was going to cry.

"It's okay. I want to." But actually, I felt like I was falling into the sea. "Who is it?"

"Someone called Brooklyn Evans," Dad said. "And he doesn't seem to like us very much. Look at his other videos: *Family Vloggers Should Not Exist. The Worst Families on YouTube.* He's made a stack of them!"

I swallowed. Brooklyn Evans sounded like the kind of significant person Carys might have tagged in our video. I felt Farmor's arm around my shoulders. She said something in Danish to my dad, but I didn't understand what it was.

"Yes. Sorry," Dad said. "We have to deal with this right now, thanks, Mor."

"And I've got a voicemail from the newspaper," Mum said.

"Let's go for a little walk along the docks, just me and you," Farmor said. "We can go into Copenhagen another time." And she led me away.

I knew Farmor was trying to protect me. But what would she think if she knew I had caused all this in the first place?

31

A STORK IS NOT ALWAYS A STORK

The sea looked calm, but the wispy bits of Farmor's hair were blowing all over the place. Boats bobbed against their docks and coloured sails rippled in the breeze. I'd been here like a million times. But everything felt different that day. It's weird how having a secret can change the way things appear. Even Farmor's eyes, which always got watery in the wind, seemed to look at me differently.

"Your parents are having some problems with the website," Farmor said, sitting on a bench facing the sea. She sounded out of breath. Maybe we'd walked faster than I realized.

"I guess so," I said, keeping my eyes on the ocean.

"And what about you, my *lille majroe*?" She pulled me closer. "What are you having trouble with?" She gave a nudge, and I felt her warm breath on my cheek.

"Nothing." I brushed my hair out of my eyes.

She tutted. "Oh, you don't want to tell your old *farmor*, hey?" She smiled. Her wrinkles spread all the way from her eyes to her hairline. "All right. So, tell me – what mischief have you and Spud been getting up to?"

I laughed, and told her about our ferrofluid experiment. I felt my racing heart go kind of back to normal. Farmor still spoke to me the way she did when I was about six. But that felt okay. Nicer than okay.

Farmor has this thing she says when she feels really cosy: *Jeg har det som blommen i et æg*. It literally means "I feel like an egg yolk". It sounds weird, but it means you feel happy and safe and like you have everything you need. I didn't realize it at the time, but being cuddled up next to Farmor on that bench looking out to sea, was the last time I would feel like that for a while.

When we got back to Farmor's house, Mum and Dad weren't there, and a cold feeling made its way over my skin. I really had to watch the rest of the Brooklyn Evans video.

"Would you pull a chair out for me, darling?" Farmor said, out of breath. She had her hand on her forehead like she was dizzy. I pulled a wooden chair out from the kitchen table and guided her into it.

"Are you okay, Farmor?" I asked and she fanned her hand at me, which was her way of saying not to fuss.

"Yes, yes!" she said. "Just need a moment to get my breath back. Pop the kettle on, *lille majroe.*"

We had a cup of tea and ate squares of Farmor's home-made *drømmekage*, which translates as "dream cake". I mean, it is pretty good. And way nicer than her home-made dandelion root tea, which I pretended to like but tasted like mud.

"So, everything going well at school?" Farmor asked, putting another slice of *drømmekage* on my plate.

"Kind of," I said. "My grades aren't exactly…you know."

Farmor smiled and her cheeks dimpled on both sides. "Grades isn't what I meant. I mean the juicy stuff!" She laughed. "The stuff you don't tell your parents."

I smiled. The last thing on earth I'd tell Farmor about was the hacking. She probably didn't even know what hacking was. I definitely didn't know the Danish word for it.

"Not much to tell," I said. But her eyes pushed me to say more, so I told her about Hallie and me not hanging out so much.

"Ah, well," Farmor said. "You know what they say, a stork is not always a stork."

Like I had any idea what that was supposed to mean.

Mum and Dad got back a couple of hours later. I was helping Farmor plant seeds in her garden, and suddenly I heard Dad calling us. I froze. I still had no idea what the video said about them. And it was impossible not to look guilty.

"*Hej,*" Dad said, "what are you up to out here?"

"Eva's helping me plant some cucumbers."

"Ah, pickling again, huh?" Dad's face looked more relaxed and he smiled at me when I glanced up from the soil.

"Everything okay with your channel?" Farmor asked.

"Nothing to worry about," he said. Only when Mum came into the garden, they exchanged a look that told me that wasn't true.

Later that night, after Farmor had gone to bed, I heard Mum and Dad sit at the little table on the patio just outside the kitchen door. My bedroom window was open, so I sat under it, hardly breathing, trying to listen to what they said. I made out, "damage limitation" and "brand" and "press on our side". Then the church bells started chiming, and they must have gone back inside.

The next morning, I heard the little latch go on the door of my bedroom.

"Morning, sweetie!" Mum said as I sat up. I'd already

been awake for a while, but I couldn't face going downstairs. The way Mum and Dad had been acting told me whatever was on the video was really bad. And the whole reason Brooklyn Evans was targeting my parents, was because of me. "Want to take a walk into town, or down to the sea or something? Would be great to get some fresh air, and have a chat, just me and you."

I took a deep breath, examining Mum's face for clues about whether or not she suspected something. "Sure!" I said, which came out way too enthusiastic. Inside, my heart felt like lead.

Mum's phone beeped non-stop when we got to the waterfront. She replied to messages while I sat with my legs dangling over the stone wall, watching boats bob in the harbour. I found myself looking for flat stones to skim, even though I hadn't done that for years. My phone vibrated. Three messages from Carys. I pushed it back in my coat pocket.

"So, sweetie," Mum said, sitting down next to me. "Listen, this probably isn't going to be very nice to see, but I'd rather you watched it with me than on your own or with someone at school." She took my hand, and with the other she unlocked her phone. "I just want to say, he's not meaning anything bad about you, okay? It's about your dad and me."

"Okay," I said.

I watched her type *Brooklyn Evans* into the search bar, and the video came up. Already I felt a lump in my throat.

Mum squeezed my hand. "It's okay, sweetie. It's us he's getting at."

"*Yep, you heard me right – they vlogged about their daughter's period,*" Brooklyn Evans said and a photo of me came up on the screen. I was holding my head in my hands. It was from an old video because there was a streak of pink in my hair that I'd had done last summer holidays.

"*This poor girl, right?*" he said. "*I mean, can you imagine? I've had a video brought to my attention. It's made by RottenFang and I have permission to show you guys.*"

My blood went cold. RottenFang was the name me and Carys had used for our account. We got it from the name generator. I could feel my heart beating in my throat and the hand Mum was holding felt sweaty. "*It's a compilation showing all the times Eva Andersen has clearly felt uncomfortable with the filming, and in some cases actually asked her parents to stop. And guess what? They carry on! In fact, they make it a funny part of the vlog. I'm going to play a little section of it. If you want to see the rest click on the link in the description.*"

I watched as the 1980s song I'd chosen began playing.

294

And there it was: the video that me and Carys had made. Eye rolls, sighs, closing doors, covering my face, crying. The subtitles we'd written saying "exploitation" and "child cruelty" and "Free Eva!" By the time the video ended, I felt sick. I didn't dare open my mouth in case whatever I said sounded guilty. I dropped a few pebbles into the water and waited for Mum to say something.

"Apparently this Brooklyn Evans guy targets family vloggers," she said. "That's literally the point of his channel." She tapped on another video. "Look, in this one he says all family vloggers are evil." She sighed. "Anyway, the newspaper's been in touch. They're going to run a piece on it when we're back home."

"An article?" I said, feeling dizzy even though I was sitting down.

"Yes," Mum said, tapping her screen again. "This one's had a million views! We'll have to film a response. I mean, we're not cruel, are we?"

My hands were trembling. And my voice didn't come out very loud in the wind. But I knew this was my chance to say it. I took a deep breath. "It feels a bit cruel sometimes, I guess." I watched a yacht crossing the water, not wanting to look at Mum's face.

"It feels cruel?" Mum put her hand on my arm. "It honestly feels like we're cruel to you? *Cruel?*"

I wished she would stop repeating that word. "Kind of," I said. "Sometimes. Not deliberately."

"Like when?" Mum asked, her voice only just above a whisper.

I felt sick, like I'd swallowed too much seawater. "Well, the period stuff, obviously. And the filming in my room, in my wardrobe. I know you don't see it, but sometimes it feels like you care about the channel more than me."

"Oh, sweetheart," Mum said, and she pulled me into a hug. I could hear her phone still pinging in her hand. "I'm so sorry it feels like that. I'll do better. Your dad and I, we'll do better." She stroked my hair and for a second I felt like telling her everything. About how the video Brooklyn Evans had played was made by me and Carys in her bedroom. How I'd had no choice because she and Dad never listened. How I'd had to do it. Because there was no other way.

"I do get the privacy thing, Eva. I do understand. I still see you as my little girl." She sniffed. "But I need to remember you're getting older. You're becoming your own person." She stared at her phone for a minute. "Fancy hitting the ice cream parlour? It's only a little way along the harbour. It's getting cold out here."

"Sure," I said.

Mum hugged me and I breathed in the sea air, and

listened to the waves and I thought, *It's worked! Things are going to change. It's going to be better.*

Then, as I started walking towards the ice cream shop, Mum said, "This way, sweetie. We'll have to go back to Farmor's and get changed first. Sorry, sweetheart, but we still have to do the Pretty and Proud posts, remember."

And I suddenly wanted to plunge head first into the freezing waters of the Baltic Sea.

32

HELP

The next day, Mum and Dad took a bike ride round one of the neighbouring islands. Farmor said she wouldn't make it all the way round, so I volunteered to stay at the cottage with her. I was planting some beetroot seeds when I heard her spade drop onto the cobbled path. I stood up and went over to her.

"Are you okay, Farmor?" She was out of breath and her cheeks had gone red. "Shall I get you some water?" I said, because I didn't know what else to do.

Farmor nodded and closed her eyes. She staggered to the metal bench by the shed, sat down, and took deep breaths. I quickly went inside and filled up a glass of water, then held it out to her. But she didn't take it. Her forehead was covered in beads of sweat, even though it wasn't very warm. She took big gulps of air. I wondered how bad it was if an old person couldn't breathe very well.

"Are you okay, Farmor?" I said again. She still had her eyes closed. I wished Dad was there. "Should I get someone, Farmor?" I said, trying not to cry. "I don't know what to do!" My mind flooded with useless Danish phrases. Why couldn't I think of the word for "help"?

Farmor reached out for my hand. Hers was hot and trembling. Then her other arm dropped down over the side of the bench and her body slumped over and the glass of water smashed all over the path.

I don't really know what happened after that. Only that I didn't get help quick enough.

My eyes were swollen with crying by the time Mum and Dad got to the hospital. Astrid and Stefan, Farmor's neighbours, had been sitting with me for what seemed like hours. They stood up when Mum ran down the corridor towards us. I couldn't stand up because my legs felt like they were made of concrete. Mum wrapped her arms around me and sobbed into my neck. I thought I'd run out of tears by then, but loads more slid down my face onto Mum's cagoule.

"Oh, sweetheart, you poor thing. I'm so sorry."

Dad's eyes were red and there was half a packet of tissues stuffed into his cycling shorts. His legs were splattered with mud. He kneeled down and wrapped his arms around both of us.

"It's my fault," I said, in between sobs. "I didn't know what to do."

"No, no, Eva," Dad said. "The doctor said she'd had a bad heart for a long time. She didn't tell us. I think…she was waiting for us so she could say goodbye." I squeezed him as tight as I could. "I wish I'd been there," he said. "How could I not have noticed she was ill?" And for the first time in my life I heard my dad swear in Danish.

A doctor came through the double doors and spoke to them. Dad said how he wished he'd known she had a bad heart. The doctor said a load of stuff I didn't understand. I stared at the speckled tiles on the floor, thinking about how this morning I could hug Farmor and hear her voice and plant seeds in her garden. Now I could never hug her again and those seeds I planted would grow and she'd never get to see them. And I knew that my heart would never go completely back to normal.

Farmor's house felt grey and echoey when we got back. Mum couldn't find any normal teabags so she made us dandelion root tea, which reminded me so much of Farmor I couldn't drink it. But I couldn't let go of my cup either. My heart felt weird. Like the world wasn't the way it was supposed to be. Even the cottage itself seemed sad. It was like someone had opened a window and let all the happiness out.

The next day, I sat on the sofa with an untouched morning bun in front of me, while Mum and Dad wrote a list of things they needed to do. My face felt numb from crying and there was this sort of haze around me, like a bubble that wouldn't burst. Nothing felt real. Like part of me had been rubbed out.

"So, I guess I should see if my cousins want to fly over for the funeral," Dad said. The word "funeral" hit me like a stone. I put my hand over my eyes and I felt Dad's arm around me. "It's all right. It's all right. She's with your *farfar* now." And I was suddenly reminded of Christmas, when Farmor had talked about seeing my grandfather again. "When I die, I'll be with your grandfather. It's been a long time, you know. We have catching up to do!" she'd said. I felt a tear slide down my cheek as I wondered if she'd known she was sick then. Dad stroked my head and said, "You'll always be her *lille majroe.*" It was like he'd pressed a bruise. Thousands of tears poured out of my heart. I'd never hear her call me that again.

Upstairs, I pulled my sketchbook and pencils out of my case and curled up in the blanket that still smelled of Farmor. I drew a big dandelion clock in the middle of the page, with some of the seeds sailing away. I sketched waves and sailboats and gulls and a porpoise. The thatched mushroom on her roof. A little turnip. Everything that reminded me of her. Everything I loved about her. After I'd finished, the page was splotched with tears. But my heart felt a little bit lighter.

I heard the latch on the bedroom door go, and Mum said gently, "Hey, sweetie, Lars made some soup." She carried a tray of soup and bread over to the desk by the window. "He's looking through Farmor's old recipe books." She looked over at my sketchbook and for once, I didn't hide it away. "Oh my goodness, Eva! This is so beautiful." She cupped my face in one hand. "We're all going to miss Farmor so much."

Later, I went for a walk down to the sea on my own. Mum and Dad were talking to someone from a funeral place, and said they'd meet me once they'd finished. I sat with my legs over the wall, dropping pebbles into the water, waiting for my phone to pick up a signal. It beeped. Then it didn't stop. Messages from Spud, Carys, Jenna. Even Gabi. And a voicemail from Hallie. All saying they were sorry about Farmor. How did they know she had died? Then a horrible feeling crept over my skin. The *All About Eva* Instagram. Mum wouldn't have done that, would she? I tapped on my app and there it was. The drawing I did about Farmor. I'd left it on the desk. Mum must have taken a photo of it while I was downstairs. The caption said: *Yesterday we lost Eva's beloved grandmother. She meant the world to us.*

I wanted to scream. Everything I felt about Farmor, all my memories of her, stolen out of my heart and shared with the entire world. My whole body trembled with anger. And I couldn't really think straight after that.

33

GOODBYE

"How could you?" I shouted at Mum as she and Dad came into view. I stood up from the edge of the water. "That picture was for Farmor! Not you! You didn't even ask me if you could share it! After everything I've been telling you!"

I heard the click of Mum's heels on the pavement as she ran towards me. "Eva, I'm so sorry. Calm down, sweetie. I didn't think. Our followers are like family and—"

"No, Mum. Farmor was family. She would have *hated* you putting it on there!"

"Hey, Eva, come here." But even Dad's gentle voice couldn't calm me down. It was like my heart had been gouged out.

I glared at Mum. "Everything Brooklyn Evans said

about you in that video is true! You are *cruel*!" I spat the words out then ran towards Farmor's cottage. I knew Mum wouldn't be able to keep up in her heels, but I heard Dad walking a little way behind me. Anger tore through me like a tornado. I grabbed the key from under the yellow flowerpot, stormed upstairs and tore the picture into pieces.

"Eva!" Dad said, bounding up the stairs behind me. "What's happened? What is all this?"

"It was private, Dad," I said, tears streaming down my face. "All my memories of Farmor." I was crying so hard I couldn't breathe.

"Oh, Eva." Dad hugged me and I felt my tears soaking into his woolly jumper. "We'll take it down, okay. We'll take it down."

I heard the latch go and Mum say, "I'm sorry, Eva. Your picture's just so beautiful and—"

"You can have it," I said, and kicked some pieces of it towards her.

"Oh, Eva!" Mum said. "You didn't have to rip it up! I would have taken it down. But the comments were—"

"I don't care about the stupid comments!" I screamed. "Those people are not my friends." I wanted to say more, but my chest felt like it was about to break apart.

"I'm sorry," Mum said quietly. And I heard her go downstairs.

After a while, Dad said, "I'm sorry Farmor's gone," in Danish. "She would have said it's like swallowing a camel." And then I cried and laughed at the same time.

The days ran into each other after that. Dad wanted me and Mum to go home so I didn't miss any school, and fly back over for the funeral. But Mum wanted to stay with him in Dragør. They thought about asking Spud's parents if I could stay with them for a week, but Dad changed his mind when Spud FaceTimed saying he'd accidentally shot a hole in their garage door with Chip's BB gun. So, Mum emailed Miss Wilson saying I'd be back a week later, and changed our flights.

Dad asked if I wanted to do a reading at the funeral, being Farmor's only grandchild. But I felt too embarrassed about my Danish. Mum said she'd help me find a nice poem to read. But there's no way I could have read anything out loud without crying. Or making mistakes. So, Astrid, Farmor's neighbour, sat with me the day before the funeral and showed me how to make a wreath of wild flowers from Farmor's garden instead. I drew hearts on a cardboard tag and added a tiny little turnip – a *lille majroe* – in the corner.

Dad was sitting on the little bench outside the front

door, but when I went to show him, Mum said, "Leave Dad for a little while, sweetheart. He needs a bit of time thinking about his *mor* on his own." I hadn't really thought about Farmor as anyone other than my grandma before. But that day, and at the funeral, she was my dad's *mor*. Mum. And I missed her more than ever.

Mum held out her arms and I sank into them. It's hard to stay angry at someone when you need them so bad. Her eyes were filled with tears, just like mine.

"We both have to do our best to speak Danish tomorrow, and to be there for each other. But remember, you can say goodbye to Farmor in your own way too. This is beautiful," she said, picking up the wild-flower wreath I'd made. "Really special."

"Don't—" I said.

But she must have known what I meant, because she squeezed me even tighter and said, "I won't."

The next morning, the wardrobe door creaked as I lifted off the outfit Mum had helped me choose in Copenhagen the afternoon before. It was dark grey. Over the dress, Mum had hung a necklace with a pale blue oval stone. Like Farmor's eyes, like the sky. I opened the curtains and watched the sun appear behind the clouds on the horizon as gulls circled boats. The bells of the old church chimed seven times.

I wrapped Farmor's yellow crocheted blanket around me, breathed in her scent, and said, "*Farvel.*" Goodbye.

I didn't sleep on the flight home. But I pretended to so Mum and Dad would stop checking if I was okay. Mum asked the air steward for an extra blanket and I felt her tuck it around my legs. I waited to hear the click of her camera, but I didn't. So that was something.

It was late by the time we got home. The house felt cold and weird, and I didn't feel like unpacking or anything. I went straight to the back door to call Miss Fizzy. Mainly because I wanted to check she was still alive after two weeks of Spud looking after her.

"You sure you want to go to school tomorrow?" Mum said.

"Yeah, I want to go," I said, picking up Miss Fizzy and cuddling her to me. She smelled like lavender. I hoped it was from the lavender bush in our garden and not from some weird experiment Spud had done on her. Mum kissed me and said goodnight, and I carried Miss Fizzy up to my room.

I heard Dad bring the cases in from the car.

"Jen," he said, "you'd better take a look at this email from Ash. It's about the hacking."

I stood still for a minute, with the thud of my heart and Miss Fizzy's purr in my ears. And my guilt floating out into the room like an oil spill.

34

WARNING

I didn't sleep properly that night. I stayed up late looking at *All About Eva* stuff for hours. It was the first time I'd looked since Farmor died. And the whole thing had blown up way bigger than I'd imagined. Everywhere I looked there were headlines and videos and more headlines and more videos.

All About Eva: The Case Against Family Vloggers
Exposing Kids to Internet Fame Too Young
Meet the Family Vloggers Under Fire
Can YouTube Kids Consent?
Influencer Questions Safety of Kids Growing Up
on YouTube
Would You Actually Want to be Eva Andersen?

In a way, it was my dream come true in terms of bad

publicity for the channel. It was just a lot more than I'd expected. My parents wouldn't tell me how many subscribers they'd lost, but when I checked they were down by almost two hundred thousand. I should have felt pleased. Plan B had worked. Like Farmor would have said, the goat had been shaved. But sometimes, it's only when you get what you want that you realize what a massive mistake you've made.

Before I'd even finished my breakfast the next morning, Mum had read out nine emails from sponsors pulling out. Dad was talking about difficult phone calls he'd have to make. I felt kind of cut off from everything, like I was sitting at the bottom of a lake, and there was nothing I could do to swim back up.

I was staring into space when Mum nudged me and handed me my untouched orange juice.

"Eva," she said gently. "You sure you're up to going in today? I know I feel like getting back into bed."

"Jen," Dad said, "she's missed enough school already."

"It's fine," I said. "I want to see my friends." It's weird how trying to act innocent makes even the truth feel like a lie.

"Course you do, sweetie," Mum said. "We've warned Miss Wilson about all this stuff in the media, so if anyone says anything, let her know, okay."

"Sure," I said, leaving my juice and heading out the door.

"Text me at lunchtime, okay?"

"Okay!" I called as the door closed, then straight away I phoned Carys. She hadn't replied to my last three messages. It rang for ages. No answer.

I waited on the corner for Carys, with Spud stuck to my side like glue.

"I'm not leaving you on your own today," he said when I protested. We waited for a few more minutes, but Carys didn't show up. I walked into school with Spud, and a weird feeling in my stomach. Why wasn't Carys here?

"So," Spud said as we joined the line in the canteen at breaktime. "What do you think?"

"About what?"

"My whole theory behind the game."

"What game?" I said, scanning the tables to see if Carys had maybe come in late.

"Did you listen to any of what I just said?"

"Sorry, Spud," I said. "I've kind of got a lot on my mind."

"I know. Farmor was a legend," he said. "Or do you mean the *All About Eva* stuff?"

"Does everyone know about that?" I said, grabbing a biscuit.

"Not *everyone*," Spud said. "Miss Wilson told us you were coming back today and if we mention the stuff in the news, we're in big trouble."

"Great," I said.

"Anyway," Spud said, tossing a torn-off piece of croissant into his mouth, "I forgot to tell you, we aced the science experiment. And if anyone upsets you today, they're getting ju-jitsu-ed."

"Thanks, Spud," I said. And it was the first time I'd smiled in ages.

"Does he have to sit with us?" Gabi muttered as me and Spud sat down. Hallie nudged her. "I mean, hi, Spud! Blown up any sheep's lungs recently?"

Spud grinned. "It's funny you should say that, Gabi, because I did look after Eva's cat while she was away and…" I glared at him. "I better save that for another time."

After lunch, I tried phoning Carys again, but it went straight to voicemail. *Maybe she's run out of battery*, I told myself. But she had like a million chargers.

In English, Miss West made us write an essay with the title *Would we all be happier in a world without the internet?* I chewed the end of my pen, and coloured in the gaps in the title.

Miss West must have noticed I wasn't doing anything, because she said, "Just write the first thing that comes to mind, Eva. Your thoughts, that's all." And she smiled at me. It was weird. She was acting almost human.

Farmor always used to say the world was better before computers. Not that she'd know because she didn't even have one. She used Dad's laptop to type an email to her friend in New Zealand once, then said how silly it was and took out some writing paper instead.

I don't think my grandmother ever went on the internet, I wrote. *She kept her phone switched off most of the time. And she never looked stuff up on Google. So, I don't know how she knew so much. She always used to say this thing*

I stopped for a minute, trying my best to remember it. *Hvor skønt det er at ikke gøre noget,* I wrote, not totally sure if it was right. But if I used my phone to check, Miss West would confiscate it.

It means: it's beautiful to do nothing. Being at her cottage was like that. We'd play wooden board games and she'd cook recipes from her memory, and there were always pressed flowers inside her books. It was annoying sometimes, because I couldn't message my friends or find out anything that was happening. But it was nice too. Like her cottage was a completely different world. A world where you could just be yourself. And not have an audience. I guess that's what the olden days felt like. When you had one life, not two.

*   *   *

"Spud, was Carys in school last week?" I asked him on the way home.

"I think so," he said, karate-chopping a low-hanging branch. "Yes, she was in on Friday because Mr Scott made her partner me in German."

I tapped my phone to call her, but it went to voicemail again. Her profiles had disappeared too. It was like she'd vanished.

I told Spud I'd see him later and took a shortcut through the alleyway that came out at the bottom of Lavender Lane. I had to walk through a field and go over a stile, and there was a massive puddle I had to jump over. But it was quicker than going the road way. Then, just as I turned the corner, I saw it. A police car. Parked in Carys's drive. And it felt like my blood had frozen solid.

35

DON'T SAY A WORD

As soon as I saw the police car, I ran. Not towards Carys's house, away from it. I don't exactly feel proud of myself for that. I headed back up the lane as fast as I could in my school shoes, and I was completely out of breath by the time I reached my street. Only, when I got to the bottom of my drive, there was a police car outside my house too.

I froze. I guess that's how bank robbers feel when they're surrounded. My heart was thumping so fast, I wasn't even sure I could get my feet to move. But then, Mum spotted me out of the window and waved at me to come in. I couldn't tell if she looked angry or not. I slowly walked past the police car. My hand was trembling as I opened the front door.

"There you are!" Mum said. A police officer with a thick, grey moustache was sitting on the sofa. There were cups of tea and a plate of *kanelsnegl* on the coffee table, the Danish version of cinnamon swirls. Dad must have made them specially. I tried to relax a little bit. If he'd known I was responsible for the hacking, there was no way he'd have made pastries, was there? I took a deep breath and smiled at the police officer without looking him directly in the eyes.

Mum put her teacup down on the saucer. It was the tea set they usually used when Farmor was here. A flicker of pain went through my heart at the memory. "Eva, this is Sergeant Edwards," she said. "He's from the Cyber Crimes Unit."

I don't know where I expected Sergeant Edwards to be from, but not there. That sounded serious. A lot more serious than cups of tea and *kanelsnegl*.

"Hi," I said, hovering by the front door.

"He's been investigating the attacks on our channel," Dad said.

The word "attacks" rang in my head like a gunshot. There were crumbs from the *kanelsnegl* on the floorboards and Sergeant Edwards hadn't taken off his shoes.

"This is going to come as a shock, Eva," Mum said. "Sergeant Edwards has been able to trace the breaches to our channel, even though the hacker was…what's it called, Sergeant?"

"Ghosting." Sergeant Edwards said, clearing his throat. Hearing that word "ghosting" felt like being hit in the face with a hockey stick. I flinched. "Most of the time they used a VPN. But they uploaded one of the videos without it, so it wasn't too difficult to trace them." I thought back to when I uploaded the video we'd made at Carys's house. Did I forget to use the VPN? Was it me?

Sergeant Edwards leaned back against the sofa and sipped his tea. "Oh, they always make mistakes, Mr and Mrs Andersen. And when they do, we catch them."

I tried to listen to what he was saying, but it felt like the words didn't quite reach me. Like they all just drifted past.

"This isn't nice for me to say," Dad said, shifting around in his seat, "but it's someone we know. One of your friends actually, Carys Belfield."

"No!" I shouted.

"I know. We're shocked too," Mum said. "She must have accessed the computer when she stayed here that time and found our passwords. Sergeant Edwards thinks she might have even made friends with you deliberately."

"No…that's not true," I said. But no other words would come out.

"I know, it must be very difficult to hear," Sergeant Edwards said, looking at me. Possibly wondering why I was still standing by the front door. "But Miss Belfield has admitted it. She said she was working alone. No one else involved, apparently. So that's something."

It was like the entire room was collapsing around me. Carys had said she'd done it by herself? She didn't tell them it was all my idea? And why wasn't I telling them the truth? I could feel the words, right there in my throat. But I couldn't get them to come out.

"So, what happens now, Sergeant?" Dad asked. Only Sergeant Edwards had just put a whole *kanelsnegl* in his mouth so we all had to wait until he swallowed.

"We have limited options because of Carys's age," he said. "But as I was saying, her actions have contributed to your loss of business, it's damaged your brand, et cetera, so we certainly can't let her get away with it."

"Can you believe it, Eva?" Mum said, handing Sergeant Edwards another *kanelsnegl*. "That shark video, deleting your baby videos, the reel of clips making it look like you hate the channel. It was all Carys!"

"It's like I said when you first contacted me weeks ago, Mrs Andersen," Sergeant Edwards said. "It only takes one mistake for them to reveal themselves. My team is one of the best in the country."

I leaned against the wall to stop myself falling down. It felt like when I used to play chess against Farmor. I'd think I was moving to a square that was totally safe. Only I didn't spot her bishop in the corner, casting its long, diagonal shadow over my queen. The moves I thought had been clever were actually all mistakes. And it was only a matter of time before she said *skakmat*. Checkmate.

Sergeant Edwards said Carys would get a formal warning. She had to go to the police station with her parents. They'd have to sign some kind of form that wasn't a criminal record, but would stay on their special computer system.

"A prank gone too far," Sergeant Edwards said, wiping *kanelsnegl* crumbs from his moustache. There were newspapers out in front of him on the coffee table. I glimpsed a headline that said, *The Truth About All About Eva* and another one, *Meet the Andersens: The Vloggers Exploiting Their Daughter for Fame*. I'd gone so cold I couldn't feel my feet.

"Eva?" Mum got up and came over to me. "You're in shock." She rubbed my arms like she was drying me after a bath. "Lars, grab Eva a Coke or something." I felt her kiss my head. "It's all right, sweetie."

"It's crazy Carys even knows how to do this kind of thing at her age!" Dad said.

"Oh, you'd be surprised, Mr Andersen," Sergeant Edwards said. "They can teach themselves all sorts these days. But we try to stay one step ahead."

Dad handed me a can of fizzy elderflower and noticed my hands shaking as I took it. He caught my eye before I could look away. "Are you sure you're okay, Eva?" he said, putting his hands over mine. "You didn't let Carys use our computer, did you? You didn't know about any of this?"

"Of course she didn't know about any of this!" Mum said. "Eva knows how awful this has been for us. You really think she would keep quiet knowing how much damage it's done? I can't believe you're even asking her, Lars."

I felt like I was underwater, suspended in one of those giant aquariums they have at the Sea Life Centre. I could see and hear everything that was happening, but I didn't feel part of it. I was drowning in my own silence.

"I think I'd better take you upstairs," Mum said. "Sorry, Sergeant. It's a big shock for her."

"Of course," Sergeant Edwards said and he stood up. He was almost as tall as Dad. "But, Eva, if you remember anything that might be relevant to our investigation, get in touch. The stronger a picture we have of what was going on, the better. I'll leave my card in case you think of anything."

I didn't listen to the rest of what Sergeant Edwards was saying, and I was already upstairs by the time he reached the front door. There was no way I'd be contacting him. I wasn't planning on speaking to anyone ever again for the rest of my life.

When I got to my room, I realized I was still holding the can of fizzy elderflower. Mum took it off me, opened it and held it to my lips. "Take a sip," she said. "You need the sugar. I can't stop shaking myself! What a horrible shock for all of us."

I sat on my bed and closed my eyes. Mum pressed her hand on my forehead. "You do feel a bit warm. You know what," she gently put the duvet over me, "I think you're exhausted. Take a nap. I knew I shouldn't have let you go to school today."

I heard the door close, and Dad's muffled voice downstairs in the hallway. There was nothing in my room. Just bare walls, and my heart beating into the silence, reminding me what a horrible person I was.

36

SORRY

I didn't go to school the next day. Mum said I was still in shock. Which I guess was partly true. But mostly I was too ashamed to face anyone. Dad made pancakes for breakfast. And I stayed in my bedroom all day. I had millions of messages from people at school asking what had happened. Someone who lived near Carys had seen the police car, apparently.

I replied, Not too sure right now, to pretty much everyone.

I ignored Alfie's police emojis. And the thing he'd put on TikTok with the police siren sound effects. I scrolled through old messages from Carys, but I didn't dare send her anything. Partly because I thought Sergeant Edwards would be monitoring her phone. But mostly because I was a coward. How could I ever repay her for taking the blame? And what must she think of me for letting her? I wondered if Mum and Dad would let me change schools. Or maybe we could move to Denmark permanently. I'd surely be able to speak fluently eventually. Anything was better than facing everybody. Or even worse than that – telling the truth now it was way too late.

Hallie called me at lunchtime. I didn't want to answer, but I kind of had no choice.

"So, what happened?" she asked. "Is it true about Carys? Did she hack the channel? Everyone's saying she's been arrested!"

"She's not at school?"

"No," Hallie said. "Miss Wilson won't say anything about it. But everyone's saying she's been excluded. I knew there was something not right about her, Eva," she said. "I tried to warn you. Me and Gabi both did."

"It's not like that, Hallie. Honestly, it's not Carys's fault," I said.

"You don't have to defend her," Hallie said. "Not after what she's done."

I really wanted to tell Hallie the truth. But it was like my brain had sealed the truth up. So I said, "I think there's just been this giant misunderstanding." And with every word that came out of my mouth, I felt like

I was drifting further and further away.

I tried to watch a film, but I ended up scrolling through *All About Eva*. Mum and Dad had posted a new vlog saying that they were investigating some illegal activity on their channel, and they'd be back again soon.

"*We love you guys!*" they said at the end.

I scrolled down. *Comments are turned off.* I wondered if Carys had seen it. A pang of guilt went over my skin when I thought about her, like stinging nettles. I lay on my bed, looking up at the empty ceiling, for once wishing I could be the other Eva. The one who had bits of her life edited out. Then I could drag a cursor over this whole section and hit *delete*.

The next day at school, I avoided everyone, even Spud. At lunchtime, some Year Ten girls cornered me outside the art block and asked me loads of questions I couldn't answer. *Is it true Carys Belfield's been arrested? Is it true she hacked into your channel? Did she make videos about you? Is she going to prison? Did you know she's been excluded?*

I went inside and ran down the empty art corridor towards the toilets, but when I turned the corner I crashed straight into Miss Wilson.

"Eva! Slow down," she said, then she saw my face. "Oh, you poor thing, come with me."

We sat in her classroom while she sketched and handed

me tissues. I was glad no one else was there because I could not stop crying. Mainly because Miss Wilson kept telling me it wasn't my fault. I wanted to tell her the truth so badly my face itched. But I couldn't get the right words to come out.

That night, I sat at the desk in my bedroom, trying to write Carys a letter. I figured if I could post her a letter saying sorry, telling her about how I panicked with the police officer being there when I got home, then at least she would understand. I would say how I had never expected her to admit it all and take the blame. Then everything would be okay. *I'm so sorry, Carys*, I wrote. *I don't know what I'm supposed to do.*

Then the door burst open. I quickly stuffed the letter in my desk drawer.

"Spud!" I said. "You almost gave me a heart attack!"

"Have the cops showed up again yet?" he said, grinning.

"You can't just burst into my room like that any more!"

"Sorry, your mum said it was okay to come up." He sat on my bed and looked at me. I kept my eyes on the floor. "So, have you spoken to Carys?"

"Her phone's off." I couldn't even look in Spud's direction. Because that's the thing about secrets. They don't disappear. Even when you tell yourself they don't matter any more. They hang around behind your eyes, refusing to leave.

"Don't you care about what's happened to her?" Spud said. "She might get excluded!"

"Of course I care," I said. "She's my friend. I mean, she *was* my friend…" Spud moved so he was directly in my eyeline. "What?"

"Nothing," he said. "It's just, if you were thinking of owning up, you should probably do it soon. That's all."

37

CONFESSION

Every time I closed my eyes that night, I imagined Carys at the police station. Or living with her Aunt Edna on The Island With No Broadband. And, worst of all, I pictured her alone.

I told my parents I was going to Hallie's after school. I figured one more lie wouldn't make any difference. I felt terrified when I pressed the doorbell. I didn't even know if Carys would let me in. Or what her parents would say. Maybe they had moved her to Aunt Edna's already. I wondered what Carys must have told them. I didn't know anything really, apart from going there felt like the right thing to do. And also a bit like falling off the edge of a cliff.

"Eva!" Carys's mum said as she opened the door. "Oh,

darling, it's lovely to see you. But I'm not sure you should really be here, under the circumstances." She grabbed Bernie's collar just as he tried to launch himself at me. "We're all so dreadfully sorry for what Carys did."

"It's okay, Mum." Carys was standing at the bottom of the stairs. I could see the tiniest trace of a smile. "We probably need to talk."

"Well, maybe just ten minutes then." Her mum smiled and let me in.

I followed Carys into a room I hadn't been in before. It had loads of paintings on the wall. One was of a woman with long red hair, sailing down a river, her dress caught in the reeds. "You can sit down if you want," Carys said. She sat on a sofa underneath the window and I hovered awkwardly next to her.

"I tried calling you," I said. "Loads of times."

"I'm not allowed my phone right now. My parents think I'm some kind of criminal mastermind." She let out a laugh and I smiled.

"I'm so sorry," I said. "For everything. It's all my fault!"

The floorboards outside creaked and Bernie padded in. He sniffed at my shoes then plonked himself down on my feet. He was kind of squashing them, but I didn't try to move.

"What did the police say?" I asked.

"Oh, you know," Carys said. "You have the right to remain silent. Anything you say may be given in evidence." She grinned. "I'm kidding! I did have to go to the police station. They told me not to do it again. And I can't anyway, because Dad's got my laptop."

"I'm really sorry. I had no idea my parents had called the police, I promise."

"I know," she said. "The stuff I did at St Aug's didn't exactly help matters. Nor does the fact they think I intentionally made friends with you to target your parents. And they think I did it all by myself."

I looked down, wishing the carpet would swallow me up. "Is it true you've been excluded from Hope Park?"

Carys shrugged. "They're still deciding. I'm not sure I want to go back there now anyway."

"I'm sorry," I said again, feeling like the biggest idiot for not having anything better to say. "Carys, I wanted to tell the truth. I really tried. I was just so shocked with the police and everything. And Mum was saying I could never have done anything so awful. I just couldn't get any words to come out. I really wanted to tell my parents later, but you'd already said it was you and no one else so…" I couldn't finish my sentence because tears started in my eyes. "I feel so bad."

"The last few days haven't been that great for me

either." Carys studied my face for a minute. I hoped she could see how sorry I was. "Eva, the whole reason we did this was to show your parents how much you hate the channel. So, when we got caught, I figured you would tell them. But now everyone's saying I was jealous of you, and that I wanted to ruin your life. When, actually, this whole time, I've been trying to help you get it back."

I swallowed. "I know. I'm so sorry all this has happened." I watched Bernie's fur moving up and down as he breathed. "You could still tell them it was all my idea."

Carys shook her head. "I can't be the one to say that, Eva. Why would they believe me? If you really want your parents to stop the channel, this is your chance. But *you* have to tell the truth. Not me. I've admitted what I've done. And if you don't say anything, that's okay. But then, we kind of did all this for nothing. Look, my mum will probably come in here in a minute. You'd better…"

"Yeah. I'd better go." I prised my feet from underneath Bernie and just before I left, said, "How come you didn't tell the police it was me as well? I mean, it *was* all my idea."

Carys shrugged. "You're my friend."

And the words *you're my friend* seemed to echo louder and louder in my head as I walked home.

* * *

That night, I waited up until Mum and Dad had gone to bed. I didn't need to set my alarm this time because I was too nervous to fall asleep. I thought about them hearing me, and coming downstairs to see what I was doing. But, even if they did, maybe it wouldn't be such a bad thing. Like ripping off a plaster. It would be done right then and there and I wouldn't have to wait until the morning. Maybe seeing Carys had made me feel a little bit braver. Or maybe I'd realized I needed to be a better friend. To everyone.

My hands weren't shaking this time. After all the stuff I'd done – the deleting, the videos, the lying – now I was telling the truth, I didn't actually feel that scared. I know Carys would never have told. Maybe we'd have even stayed friends. In secret, obviously – my parents would never have let me see her again. The trouble was, I'd spent too long clinging to the thought that if I never told anyone about my part in all this, then it wouldn't matter. But actually, the opposite was true. Secrets matter the whole time. When they're fizzing with excitement in your stomach. And when they sit on your heart like they're crushing it. A secret always matters to someone. It's always going to find a way to get out.

The floorboards outside the office creaked. I held my breath as the door slowly opened and Miss Fizzy padded in. I sighed with relief. Maybe I *was* feeling a bit frightened actually. I turned on the camera and checked I was in the picture okay. I pressed record, and heard its familiar beep. *No going back*, I told myself. I took a deep breath and smiled.

"*Hi everyone. I'm Eva Andersen, although you probably already know that. What you don't already know, is everything I'm about to tell you. And you also don't know how sorry I am. I don't know what you'll think of me once you've heard what I have to say. But if I don't tell you the truth about myself, what you think about me can't exactly be right anyway. So here goes...*"

I said my name again and the date at the end of the recording. I wasn't sure if I was supposed to do that, but it made it seem more official-sounding. It wasn't that easy to log on to the channel, as my parents had changed their password again. But I found the new one written on a sticky note in their filing cabinet. So they definitely had no idea the person who'd been logging in this whole time was me. My heart flinched when I thought about my parents watching my video when they woke up. About everyone at school watching it. I wondered if I'd get a criminal record for lying to Sergeant Edwards. Although, right then, that felt like the least of my problems.

I clicked *create* and fiddled with the edge of the mouse

333

mat as I waited for the video to upload, trying not to think about what might happen next. When millions of people would watch: *NEW Eva Andersen's Hacking Confession*. I uploaded the thumbnail I'd made, set the video to *public*, then hovered the mouse over the *save* button. I listened to check my parents were still asleep. The house was completely silent. Apart from Miss Fizzy purring at my feet and my heart pounding against my ribcage. I clicked the mouse and watched the little dots go round in a circle as my video was published on *All About Eva*. I'd almost finished.

I pulled Sergeant Edwards's card down from the notice board and turned it over in my hands. Farmor used to say: *jeg er trådt ind i spinaten*. It means "I've made a mistake". Well, literally it means "I stepped in the spinach". I wondered what she'd say if she was here to find out what I'd done. I wondered if she'd understand. She'd probably be disappointed. But she'd still make me *kartoffel* soup and remind me that no matter what's going on in the outside world, there's another, more important world inside your heart. And that's the world you need to protect. I always felt safe with Farmor. She always knew the right thing to do. I still wasn't sure if this was right or not.

I copied the link for my video and pasted it into an email. I typed in Sergeant Edwards's email address and clicked *send*. I did the same with Carys's email, Spud, Hallie, Gabi, Jenna. And Mum and Dad. I listened out for their phones to beep, but I couldn't hear anything.

As I got into bed, a cold feeling hit me, like when you walk along the seafront in winter. But as I lay and watched the views counter creep up and up on my phone, I knew it was too late to take it back. Even if I wanted to.

THE TRUTH

I don't know what I was expecting to hear in the morning. A scream, maybe. But when I heard my bedroom door burst open, I felt scared. Mum stood in the doorway with tears rolling down her face. Dad was right behind her and ducked under the door frame to come in. My chest felt weird, like I was getting the hiccups.

"Is it true?" Mum was wringing her hands on the belt of her dressing gown.

"Well, Eva? Is this confession the truth?" Dad said, holding up his phone. "Jen thinks you might have done this out of some misplaced loyalty to Carys."

I took a deep breath and swallowed the boulder I could feel in my throat. "It's true," I said quietly. "Carys was the one protecting me. Hacking the channel was all my idea."

"But, Eva," Mum said, leaning back against my bedroom wall. "Am I really that awful?"

I'd never seen Mum look that bad, apart from when she had a migraine ages ago. It was the only time she didn't want to do any filming. I thought about the avocado stuff at school. And the sanitary pad stuck to the Cool Wall. The humming in assembly. And the picture I'd drawn for Farmor on Instagram.

"I'm sorry," I said. "I should have told you straight away that it was me. But I had said I wanted you to stop filming me. I told you a million times I hated being on the channel. And you wouldn't listen. You wouldn't stop. I didn't feel like I had any choice."

Mum walked over and sat on the bed. She had red marks around her eyes where she'd been rubbing them. Maybe she was getting another migraine. "Oh, Eva. I'm sorry," she said, "that you felt this was the only thing you could do."

Dad rubbed his hands over his face. "We won't recover from this. The papers have picked up the story already. Look, *Family Vloggers' Own Daughter Confesses to Hacking Channel*." He groaned. "My phone's ringing again."

"Switch it off, Lars." I'd literally never heard Mum say those words before. "Just switch it off. Mine too." She took her phone out of her dressing-gown pocket and handed it to him. "I don't want to speak to anyone today apart from our daughter." She took my face in her hands. "I'm sorry it's taken all this for us to listen to you, Eva. For me to see what it was like for you."

Dad sighed. "I don't think you needed to take it quite this far."

"Dad, millions of people knew I started my period!" I shouted. "It had already gone too far by then. For me anyway. I couldn't get you to understand any other way. I had to try to stop the channel myself."

"Well, you've certainly done that," Dad said, swiping his phone. "Your confession video has already got half a million views." He looked at Mum. "Should I take it down?"

"Just leave it, Lars. It will look even worse if we take it down now." Mum stroked the hair away from my eyes. "There's no way we can carry on *All About Eva* now anyway. God knows what people must think of us."

"I'm sorry," I said. "I didn't want people to hate you or anything. I didn't think it would get this reaction. I just didn't want people watching me the whole time. I wanted *my life* to be my own life. Not yours to share with everyone."

"We get it," Mum said. "I just wish we got it a long time ago."

Dad rubbed the back of his head and sighed again. It was the first time I'd seen him lost for words. Even Danish ones.

"I didn't see it," Mum said. "I'm sorry. I'm so used to sharing everything. Maybe I just didn't want to see it." She looked up at Dad. "We knew we'd have to end the channel one day, I suppose."

"Yep," he said, and reached over to hold Mum's hand. If they kissed on my bed I would literally die. "But not like this. I don't know what we're going to do, Jen. Our reputations are shredded. Our vlogging career is over."

"Will we have to move house?" I asked. Moving house didn't sound too great, but at least maybe I could go to a different school and not have to face everyone.

"I don't know, Eva," Dad said. "We'll have to figure something out. Who knows? Maybe we'll be invited on *Strictly*."

Mum laughed, but part of me wondered if she was seriously thinking about it.

They got up off the bed and Dad said, "Okay, one day at a time. First, I'll make pancakes."

"That sounds like a really good idea." Mum smiled and reached over to squeeze his hand.

"So…I'm not in trouble then?" I asked.

"Oh, you're in trouble," Dad said, but he was smiling.

"You've stepped on the spinach, all right! And you're writing letters of apology to…let me see." He counted on his fingers as he said, "Sergeant Edwards, Carys, Carys's parents, Mr Andrews, Miss Wilson. I'll let you know if I think of anyone else. And Jen and I will be coming up with a pretty brutal chores-and-homework schedule. But in the meantime, I'll make some pancakes. And listen, Farmor would be really proud of you."

"For wrecking *All About Eva*?"

"No," Dad said, almost knocking his head on the door frame. "For owning up like that. Although come to think of it, she's probably up there smiling about the channel being wrecked too. We can try to have…what was it you said in your vlog? *Et normalt liv.* For today anyway."

I smiled as they headed downstairs. I was pretty sure what he meant, but I checked on Google Translate just to be sure. *Et normalt liv.* A normal life.

I swung my legs out of the covers, rubbed my eyes and looked at my phone. I had about twenty million notifications. I replied to Hallie's: OMG EVA!!! with: I'm sorry I didn't tell you the truth. Hope you can still hang out with me?

She replied straight away: I might have to run it past the student council 😉 call me later x

Then I tapped the ones from Spud.

If you're still alive, want to have a Star Wars
marathon?
Nerdophobia said you may as well be a full
member now.
Strong ju-jitsu skills btw 😊
I smiled and replied: yeah okay x

Because weirdly, a night watching films with Spud
sounded like the best normal life thing ever. My kind of
normal life, anyway. Then, because I knew it would annoy
him, I added:

Is Star Wars the one with that hobbit thing?

IN REAL LIFE

The air felt fresh as I jumped down from the stile at the bottom of Lavender Lane. The giant puddle that was there the last time I came this way had dried up. Although there was still a patch of sludgy mud in the middle. The fir trees framing the lane still looked the way they always did. But the cherry trees were covered in blossom; the petals scattered on the wind like confetti cannons. I pressed the doorbell, and heard Bernie charging towards the door. Sunlight glinted on the windows and Carys's face peered through. I waved. And that expression that Farmor used to say came to mind about feeling like an egg yolk. I shouldn't have felt contented. Not after everything that had happened. Everything that'd been written and posted about me in the past few weeks after my confession vlog. All the apologizing I'd had to do. I mean, that was embarrassing. But standing there on Carys's doorstep feeling the last glow of April sunshine on my skin, I did kind of feel like an egg yolk. Like, the worst bit was over. And I was okay. I was putting things back together the way I wanted them to go. Trying to, anyway.

"You ready?" Carys said as she opened the door.

"Yep." I smiled and patted Bernie's head, minding out for the blobs of falling drool.

"Come on." Carys led me down the hallway, through the kitchen and up the back staircase.

Her mum called, "Hi, Eva! Me and Carys's dad will be there later, okay!"

"Thanks, Mrs Belfield."

"Call me Caroline!" she said, like she always did.

The back stairway was cold and narrow, and I held onto the bannister as we climbed. Carys turned around and put her finger on her lips.

"You have to be really quiet."

I nodded. Carys smiled as we got to the top. It smelled kind of weird, like wet hay. She carefully undid the latch of a wooden door, opened it and pointed towards the top of a tiny room.

"Up there," she whispered. "Don't get too close."

I crawled past her and crept in. Above my head was a tangle of twigs and straw. I carefully slid along the stone floor and stood on my tiptoes to peer inside. I had to slap my hand over my mouth to keep from screaming with excitement. Inside the nest were three baby barn owls. Their tiny heart-shaped faces peered back at me. The smallest one put its head on its side. They were covered in grey fluff, like they'd been dunked in cotton wool. Tucked in beside them, their mum watched me with black, beady eyes. My heart soared into the sky. It was the most amazing thing I had ever seen. In real life.

Later, on the way into town, Carys asked me, "You sure you want to do this? Give all of your stuff away?"

"Too late to change my mind now," I said. "Mum's invited half the internet. Including the For-Evas. Or Ex-For-Evas as Dad's calling them now."

Carys laughed and linked my arm. "What's this place called again?"

"The Crêpe Cabin," I replied. "You may know it as the Creep Cabin."

"And how many people from school will be there?"

"Hallie and Gabi. Jenna, Nadira, Rami. Maybe a few others." I caught a piece of blossom as it fluttered towards me. "Miss Wilson said she would come. And Spud, obviously."

"And you're selling all of your stuff?" Carys said. "Even the clothes?"

"Not everything," I said. "I'm keeping my fairy lights. And a giant llama cushion I found in one of the boxes. But we had all of this brand-new stuff. Most of it hasn't been opened. And my parents didn't even have to send it back. So, I figured, we could sell it and make some money, you know, for charity. Anyway, one of the pictures says, *Eat glitter for breakfast and shine all day!* I mean, it literally says to eat glitter. That is really bad advice."

"Eat glitter for breakfast and spend the day in A&E." Carys laughed and took her invitation out of her bag. The gold swirls I'd designed caught the sunlight. "*Brighter Future*," she said. "That's the charity?"

"Yeah," I said. "It's Mum's latest project. There are millions of girls around the world who don't get to go to school. And not in a good way. Like they really want to go but they're not allowed. And we have all this expensive stuff we don't need. So, a pop-up shop seemed like a good way of raising money for them. Dad's happy because we're repairing The Brand. They're still planning on using their platform for something. They haven't decided exactly what. I'm just glad it's not going to be me."

"I'm glad they're not going to totally forget about your brother, The Brand," Carys said, and we both laughed.

As we reached the main street in town, I could see a line of people waiting outside the Creep Cabin. I mean, the *Crêpe* Cabin. I had to remember to not call it that today.

"What are they going to do with *All About Eva*?"

"They're keeping some of the videos on there. Old ones mostly," I said. "I don't care so much about those. I mean, it's not everyone who can say their hamster's funeral has had 1.5 million views." I smiled. "But they're not making any new ones. They made that vlog about it and everything. *All About Eva's Final Vlog*. So they definitely can't go back on it."

Maybe Mum and Dad would delete the rest of *All About Eva* one day. Or turn it into something else. You can't totally erase stuff from the internet anyway. It carries on existing somewhere. Just like your memories in real life. But from now on I could live my life without millions of strangers living it with me. I'd even put one of my sketches on the Cool Wall. Miss Wilson loved it so much she photocopied it and and put it up in the art corridor. Although it was probably only a matter of time before Alfie Stevens stuck a sanitary pad on it.

"Shall we go in?" Carys said.

"I'm just waiting for Spud. He said to meet him here." Carys's eyes widened. "Is that him?"

I turned, and there was Spud walking up the road wearing an avocado costume.

"Fits like a glove!" he shouted.

A month ago, I would literally have died seeing Spud walking towards me dressed as an avocado. I'm not going to lie, it was kind of embarrassing. And I did bash him in the stomach with my bag. It's not like I'm perfect or anything. But that's the best thing about having friends who like the real me. I don't need to be perfect. I don't even know who I am exactly. I don't have everything in my life figured out. But that doesn't matter. Not now I'm the only one watching.

ACKNOWLEDGEMENTS

An enormous thank you to Luigi and Alison Bonomi at LBA Books for your support and encouragement with this book. As always, you were there when it was just an idea (and a rather scrappy synopsis!). Thank you for helping me bring it to life.

To the utterly brilliant Sarah Stewart – there are not enough Likes in all of cyberspace to reflect how amazing you are. Thank you for your expert editorial guidance, your belief in this book, your kindness, and for spotting when I'd gone an *æbleskive* too far. I also owe a gigantic thank you to Rebecca Hill. Finding your "Ha ha!"s on my manuscript is a thing of joy. Thank you, both, for your unwavering enthusiasm in my stories, and for not batting an eyelid when my character has an exploding sheep's lung in their backstory.

I'd like to say a huge thank you to Anne Finnis and Hannah Featherstone for your excellent (and kind!) editorial notes. Thank you to the phenomenal Charlotte

Forfieh for your invaluable advice and guidance on Hallie's Guyanese heritage. A million thank-you-hands emojis to Alice Moloney and Gareth Collinson for your super-strength proofreading-eyes.

I would also like to say a massive smiley-face thank you to the incredible worker-of-magic Charly Clements for your beautiful cover illustration. A billion starry-eyed-emoji thank yous to Kath Millichope for designing another Insta-perfect cover. And to Sarah Cronin for the super gorgeous inside pages.

A gazillion love-heart-eyes emoji thank yous to everybody at Usborne Publishing. The passion and dedication you give to creating children's books is mind-blowing. I'm so proud to be part of it.

A super love-heart-eyes emoji shout-out to everyone at Usborne Books at Home. Your energy, support and enthusiasm for getting books into the hands of young people is mind-blowing. I hope you love Eva's story too.

To the real DI Charles Edwards, thank you so much for helping me research cybercrime, and for answering my million questions about hacking, even before I understood it myself. I couldn't resist naming Sergeant Edwards after you; I thought it only right I gave you a Danish pastry (albeit fictional!) after all your valuable help and advice.

Writing a book during lockdown was not easy, but it was made a lot more bearable by my amazing support bubble. Mum and Dad – thank you for the discos, cocktails, food parcels, baking competitions, virtual chess matches, and everything else you did to make lockdown entertaining. But mostly, thank you for the care you take of Felix. (Let's not mention the haircut!) Thank you to my fabulous family for believing I could write another book. And for all the love and support you give me while I do it. Mainly in the form of crying-with-laughter emojis.

I also owe a very special thank you to my beautiful friend, Bettina, who I think must be responsible for at least 50% of my book sales. Thank you for your advice on all things Danish, and for your relentless support of my writing. You are truly exceptional and I can't wait to see you in person again. I owe you the biggest aubergine burger!

To the centre of my universe, Felix. Your boundless energy, creativity, imagination, silliness and love lifts my heart. You've been the best lockdown buddy I could ever wish for. I love you infinity and beyond.

And finally, to my readers. I've been blown away by your love, kindness and enthusiasm for *Being Miss Nobody* and *Jemima Small Versus the Universe*. I hope Eva's story takes a place in your heart.

ALSO BY TAMSIN WINTER

When Rosalind is bullied at her new school for not speaking, she starts a blog – Miss Nobody; a place to speak up, a place where she has a voice. But there's a problem... Is Miss Nobody becoming a bully herself?

"A wonderful book about finding one's own voice."
Ann M. Martin, author of THE BABY-SITTERS CLUB

Shortlisted for the Waterstones Children's Book Prize

Jemima Small is funny and super smart...and not happy about being made to join the school's "special" healthy lifestyle group – A.K.A Fat Club. But she knows that the biggest stars in the universe are the brightest. And maybe it's her time to shine...

"An uplifting and heartening read to help inspire body confidence in everyone." SUNDAY EXPRESS